SAVAGE ESCAPE

SAVAGE SECURITY
BOOK 1

HELA RICHARDS

To caffeine, for always being there when sleep wasn't.
To my laundry, which I promised I'd fold after writing this book,
but we both know how that ended.
And to the countless hours I spent procrastinating—this one's
for you.

CONTENT WARNING

This story contains physical and sexual assault. Please take care of yourself and avoid if this content will be disturbing.

1

CADEN

Caden had been caught and tortured a fair amount of times in her long and colorful career. Which maybe wasn't saying too much for her reputation, but there it was.

Her job was a dangerous one.

Smarter and faster were basic requirements for a Retrieval Specialist (which was really just a polite way of saying Mercenary or Hitter). Should she prove to be slower and dumber, then there were only two scenarios that started differently but but always ended the same. Gunned down then and there was scenario number one. Number two was captured to be tortured later.

Both scenarios ended with death.

Well, no, torture done right ended in death, whereas sloppy torture ended, at least for Caden, in haughty derision and escape.

But slipshod torture methods and the idiot thugs who implemented them were the only reason Caden Quinn was alive and kicking.

Erratically kicking anyway, seeing as how the side effects of electricity ripping through her body had yet to wear off.

Aside from her current circumstances, Caden Quinn loved her job.

It came with all kinds of perks. Like getting to hit assholes—which, let's be honest here, was always fun. The manhandling and stealing of incredibly old and priceless artifacts was another big perk. How many other people in the world could say they'd successfully nicked and sold the jeweled Lion of Gilgamesh?

The answer was eight. Only eight in the six hundred and seventy-sixty years after it had been cast off the mold, gifted to the visiting king, and then lost to the sands of time. And Caden was proud of the fact that she counted among that eight. Then there was that thrilling and utterly satisfying sensation that came hand in hand with outwitting a competent opponent. Above all else, Caden rather liked the nanny-nanny-boo-boo moment that sung in her mind when she flattened some meathead or slipped safely through a laser grid.

Unfortunately, there were just as many downfalls, which was perhaps why it was so very thrilling for her. Torture and death were standard in her line of work; being the one on the rack or the one to pull the trigger, it was the job. And Caden had been on both sides of the rack; she was no stranger to torture.

She'd been drowned, or close enough to it a couple dozen times. A copout method and also not as effective as one would think. And really, how many times could a thug dunk and hold a captive underwater before they realize it's not working? Fourteen times by Caden's count. Though admittedly she had blacked out for a few minutes, so give or take a couple of dunks. Some people were just thick.

Beat bloody—a waste of time for all involved, really. Seeing as how the big part of her job was being able to take a hit. That, added to the fact that she'd been taking hits since day one, made it all the more redundant. Being cut and having her bones broken fell under that same umbrella.

Foot whipping had been something new and painful as fuck. It had taken weeks to heal and even now the bottoms of her feet were nothing but white lines and slightly raised scars. She'd been burned—annoying was all that was—and starved which, in her opinion, was the worst kind of torture.

And now Caden could add electric shock to the wide variety of torture techniques she'd successfully endured and survived.

And holy-fucking-Christ-on-a-Jesus-fucking-popsicle-stick, electrocution was a whole different kind of hurt.

There were no cuts or bruises or blood. Sure, there were little red welts where the nodes had been, but that was the only external marks. Internally, it was ten shades of fucked up—fucked over—fucked sideways—there wasn't a proper metaphor to explain the horrible tremors and electric hands still ripping through her muscles. She felt like the Christmas fucking turkey and probably smelled like melting flesh.

It had been thirty minutes since they'd taken her off the rack and tossed her back in her cell (if her heartbeats were any kind of accurate measurement of time; they usually were) and her limbs were still spasming. Her muscles were weak, too weak to even push her body into a sitting position. The lava in her veins and roaring in her ears were making it hard to hear the movements of her cell buddy.

But that became a misplaced concern when she spotted his hulking figure towering over her. Bald head smudged with dirt and blood. The seventeen-day-old beard caked with the results of messy torture and living in a ten by ten cell with no plumbing or mattress. She couldn't hear the words he was saying, but if she was any judge of eyebrow positioning and ill-intentioned eyes, and Caden liked to think she was, then he was saying something threatening and probably insulting.

He'd been in residence before she'd checked in. He was American; accent and clothes were evidence of that. Big, beefy, and not exactly the sharpest cookie in the barrel. Mouth breather. Favored his right hand. Slept only when he thought she was. Smelled like shit. And that pretty much summed up all she knew about him.

As a general rule, Caden didn't make conversation or forge bonds with fellow prisoners. Leverage wasn't something she liked to hand to her enemies. That and most of her fellow prisoners were people just like her. They were people who deserved the methodical torture and less-than-stellar living conditions.

And well, he was making her point for her, seeing as how he was taking out his dick. And since Caden knew he wasn't getting it out just to get her critiques, which were numerous should he actually inquire, then she was fairly certain he was planning on raping her.

A last meal kinda thing, Caden figured.

Fucker.

Over her dead goddamn body—which probably was gonna be the case, seeing as how she had about as many fearsome ninja skills at the moment as a cadaver.

Voice: shot. Who would come running to help her anyway, Santa Claus?

Hearing: impaired. Not a real problem.

Sight: fuzzy and swimming with little dots. Laser vision would be so handy.

Muscles: still spasming and day-old-kitten weak. Fucking shit.

Weapons: nil. Her sharp wit and deadly good looks would be of no use in this situation.

Baldy was on her like a bag of bricks. Hands and tongue everywhere. Trying to pull off her clothes at the same time he was trying to grope all the good bits—counterproductive, really.

Caden fought the urge to insult him and his mother in all the languages she knew, but only because her voice box was shot from all the torture-induced screaming. So instead, the Hitter willed her arms and the trembling digits connected to them to obey and focused on first locating that loose bit of stone on her right and then gripping it.

Her shirt and bra were ripped to hell by the time she got the rock in her hand. Cold hands were bruising and rough. Controlled rage helped to still her spasming muscles. Now all she had to do was wait for an opening.

One good jab to the neck and he'd bleed out.

And there went the remainder of her shirt and bra.

Bashed in the temple would send him to hell flat out.

He was alternating between rubbing himself and pawing at her naked torso.

His own nose stabbing into his brain would be instant and not near as painful as she'd like.

He was concentrated on her jeans now, trying to find the button and zipper under all the mud and blood. Then he was wrenching them down. Smirking like a bastard, he moved to pull at her breasts again.

Brachial artery it was.

Caden steeled her muscles, shot her arm forward as his arm moved within reach, and slashed with all her strength.

For a second he faltered, blinked in surprise, and then

smirked before he went back to bruising her boobs. A thread of fear started pulsing in her mind. She'd missed it. She was going to get raped by this scum-fuck and could do nothing about it but continue to convulse. But then his eyes got wide. That fearful, oh-fuck-I'm-wounded wide and he was scrambling to stop the flow of blood. Caden let her arm fall back and chose to ignore the fact that he was bleeding out on top of her. She had won, and he was dead or getting close to it anyhow.

Losing six liters of blood a minute was not conducive to staying alive. The scumbag would be dead in a matter of seconds.

Caden watched as horror morphed his features. He knew he was dead.

Then the rage—the rage at her being the one to kill him had him lunging for her head. His fist connected with her jaw, but the blood loss coupled with weeks of torture and malnutrition softened the blow.

Panic sank in as he forgot about her and remembered that he was alive and why exactly he liked that state of being.

Four heartbeats later, he slumped.

Two more heartbeats and he was dead weight on top of her.

Dead.

Eyes glazed.

Still pumping out what little was left in his veins.

Fucker.

2

NATHAN

Nathan Savage was out of the game.

He'd been out of the game for years. *Two* years, approximately.

But obviously, the seedy underbelly of Moscow didn't check duty rosters.

Which had been his very first thought when he ventured out of Badgers Pub and waltzed right into the small but organized army. He was out of the game and it just wasn't fair. But it only took a moment to think and another to get over it and then try to dodge the fists aimed for his torso.

They'd first beat the living hell out of him and proceeded to hogtie his limbs and toss him in the backseat of a dark SUV. It had been a group effort. Nathan wasn't a small man, but they had done it with such efficiency and grace that Nathan, the six-foot-three, two-hundred-and-some-odd-pound man, felt like a kitten. A bruised, bleeding, and concussed kitten.

The second thought to flit through his mind while he was taking a fist to the face was that he was not, despite all his extensive training and ninja-like abilities, going to win.

He wasn't just gonna lose, either. He was gonna get his ass handed to him. His ass, and maybe some teeth too.

Being a citizen and all now, he no longer carried a gun. He'd figured when he had retired that he no longer needed to be armed. If by some random happenstance, he'd need a weapon, well, Nathan was more than capable of taking care of himself. Though now it seemed rather stupid of him to chuck all his weapons just so he could pretend to be a normal citizen.

The knife he kept in his boot only managed to piss off the three men he'd used it on and was promptly stomped out of his grip by a combat boot after he'd been tackled to the ground. Another couple of hits to the head, a kick here and there, and then a gun butt connected with his temple and put an end to his struggling.

Though the very fact that they took the time to capture and detain him and hadn't killed him outright was a good sign. It meant they were taking him to the boss where he'd be held, questioned, and possibly ransomed, leaving lots of time for escape. Which made for an almost comforting thought as black swallowed him whole.

When he came to, the only thing to enter his mind was how convenient it would have been if he had just got that tracking node embedded in the fat of his left ass cheek like his brother had suggested. Granted, Nathan did get into a few snags from time to time, but at the time he'd brushed it off as Maddox being his paranoid self and bad-mouthed Han Solo. Maddox couldn't help but get all up in arms and distracted if someone dared diss his role model.

Should he escape, Nathan would definitely reconsider his stance on tracking nodes.

But Nathan couldn't say that he was at all shocked by his current circumstance. It hadn't been a big shocker that some dark-side Boss Man had heard he was vacationing in Moscow, figured he was there on government business, and dispatched men to deal with him. It had been an 'Ah hell' moment when he'd rounded the corner and spotted the goons lying in wait for him, but not a shocking one.

And really, Nathan Savage was not a man easily shocked. He had a knack for adapting quickly and rolling with the proverbial punches. Having grown up with seven brothers had cured him of shock early on. The years he spent as a Navy SEAL and in Black OPs had only reinforced that bit of his personality. So being taken captive by any one of the garden variety assholes he'd pissed off while employed by the US Government did not shock him.

No, he hadn't been shocked when they'd beat him into an unconscious state. Or when he'd woken up in a moving vehicle with his feet, wrists, and thumbs bound. Or when they dragged him into a dank foreboding-looking prison in the middle of nowhere Russia. If he was even still in Russia. Or when they dumped him in a cell no bigger than a broom closet with a corpse shoved up against the far wall.

He'd taken it all in stride.

Until the corpse rolled over and moaned.

No, the corpse suddenly waking from the dead hadn't surprised him. The shock had come when he approached the figure and discerned a face.

Dried mud and blood matted her long, dark hair. Her torso was naked and covered with blood and bruises. A long crooked nose from one too many breaks sat on a slender pale face that was marred with dark bruises. Long dark eyebrows that, in Nathan's experience, were always arching in mocking amusement. High cheekbones, thick pink lips, and a stubborn chin made for a pretty face.

Caden-goddamned-Quinn.

There was no mistaking her. The long scar that cut down her jaw and trailed past her collarbone made denial impossible. Nathan had experienced more than his fair share of Caden Quinn, so he was pretty damn sure of the corpse's identity. They had butted heads more than a couple of times over the years. Well, no, 'butted heads' wasn't the word for what they did, even if her head had connected with his on more than one occasion.

She took what didn't belong to her.

The government sent him to take said items back.

She wreaked havoc.

He pursued.

She had been a constant pain in his ass and the reason for three of the many scars adorning his body. After he'd done his whole sabbatical/early retirement stint, Nathan had shaken her off like a bad dream. He figured he'd never see her again, let alone have to deal with her.

But there she was. All broken and bloodied, lying on the ground like she was one light beating away from death. Looking all kinds of vulnerable and pathetic.

There was a moment of hesitation that had Nathan feeling ten shades of shame and thinking of his mother. Sure, the bullet-shaped scar on his left shoulder was courtesy of one Caden Quinn and a sniper rifle, but that was not reason enough to let her rot.

There were a select few people, in Nathan's opinion, who deserved that kind of death.

Caden Quinn was not one of them.

Even if she had run him over with a goddamn Mini-Cooper.

It took another beat to get over the shock and another to locate something he could actually use. A bucket of water and a bowl of what looked like white snot sat next to the door. Which was a slightly comforting thought. At least they kept their prisoners fed and watered.

Lots and lots of dried blood crusted all over her. Hands, chest (that he was not looking at inappropriately), stomach, feet, and face. Christ, he was kneeling in a puddle of it. There were some cuts on her, but none were deep enough to produce that much blood. Bruises, cuts, and what looked like electrical burns sat under the layer of dried blood.

All of which were things he could do nothing about.

What he could do was clean out the cuts on her arms and stomach, hope they weren't badly infected, and wash off some of the blood.

As soon as he touched her, she jolted awake. Her left arm shot out and just about connected with his jaw before he ducked it. Her other hand reached out and clutched his left wrist. Feeling like a fool, the man tried to put his hands up in the universal sign of surrender and leaned into her line of sight. Caden Quinn was lethal with or without a weapon, tortured and weak, and even half dead. She was dangerous.

Wild, dark eyes glared up at him from under her matted hair. Nathan held very still while she assessed the threat. A blood-soaked arm moved to her side before recognition sparked in those shark eyes and confusion was scrunching her eyebrows.

"What... how in the fuck..." Her voice was hoarse, like she'd screamed for hours and her face was scrunched in confusion. Then she was scanning her surroundings, panic and frustration starting to seep into her dark eyes. She swept the place twice before the confusion disappeared and was replaced with a smirk that instantly had the man feeling defensive.

"Ah." She fractionally untensed and the wild in her eyes softened a bit. "Fancy meetin' you here."

Blood-caked hands retracted, dark eyes set on his, and still smirking like she'd won a prize, she let out a laugh. Or what he assumed was supposed to be a laugh. It kind of wavered off into a pained moan. Red fingers fluttered to her chest and then away just as quickly, like she didn't want him to be aware of her broken ribs.

"Yeah." Nathan settled for a grimace and tried not to scowl at the woman. "Fancy."

"Nathan Savage." Her busted lips curled, and she blinked up at him again. The thing about Caden was that she could turn anything into an insult; even his own name sounded like something rotten.

"Where are you hurt?" Nathan decided on ignoring her smirk and went back to searching for serious damage. She should have been dead from all that blood loss and not smirking up at him like she was privy to some secret joke.

"If you wanna keep those fingers, I'd keep 'em to yourself." Red hands swatted his and went up to cover her naked chest.

"Like you're in any state to be makin' threats." Nathan frowned at her smirking face and settled on his heels. "I'm only tryin' to help ya."

"I don't need any help and I can sure as hell still kick your ass." The smirk was now gone, and Nathan felt a tingle of satisfaction at her reaction. At least he irked her as much as she did him.

"Where are you hurt?"

"Leave me alone, Savage." Her jaw clenched and her fists balled.

"I'm not gonna leave you alone to bleed out in this goddamn cell!" Nathan prided himself on keeping a level head at all times, but he always seemed to be short on patience when Caden Quinn entered the equation. "Look at ya! You look like you're two heartbeats away from dead. It looks like you suffered some head trauma, those look like electrical burns—which means you've been tortured—so internal injuries that Caden can't do shit about, a broken rib or two, and you're covered in your own blood! You're gonna die if you don't let me help you!"

How much more did he have to spell it out? She wasn't stupid. Why was she pretending like she was?

"It's not my blood." She positioned her body against the wall like she was getting ready to strike out if he moved towards her. "I am fucking fine."

Well, that changed things. Seeing as how she wasn't the owner of all that blood, Nathan could, without a nagging conscious, retreat to what would now be his half of the tiny cell and attempt to rein in the temper that only flared up when this woman was within a ten-mile radius of him.

"Whose blood is it?" When he settled into the reality of his situation, he put his attention back on the mercenary and blushed. "Oh, sorry."

That predator gleam in her dark eyes sharpened when he shrugged out of his shirt. Surprise had her blinking at him when he tossed it to her. Nathan decided not to get offended as the surprise dissolved into suspicion and hesitance.

"Would you just put it on!" He couldn't take the suspicion anymore.

Dark eyes shot to his and Nathan was wishing he'd gotten tossed in with someone—*anyone* else. No one ever looked at him like Quinn looked at him. Like she couldn't decide what he was. A bad guy pretending to be a good one, waiting for a moment of weakness, or some kind of alien not yet accustomed to human interactions. He didn't like either thought.

And if anything, she was the alien.

What kind of life had this woman led that made her suspicious of common damn courtesy?

"Christ, it's a shirt! Not a bomb. I'll not be asking for anything in return. I'm not that kind of an asshole."

After a long minute of intense scrutiny, the merc finally came to a decision and pulled it over her head.

Nathan figured she finally decided that she could trust him or kill him outright should he prove to be that kind of asshole.

"The blood... it's my first cell buddies." Her voice was gravelly, and high sounds kept dying in her throat. "Who also couldn't keep his hands to hisself."

It wasn't a subtle threat, but Caden Quinn was about as subtle as a steeled-toed boot in the face.

"Are you all right?" The question was met with a glare and a slight shaking of her head.

Other than the coat of blood (that wasn't hers, he had to remember) and the bruises and scrapes he could see, she looked fine. She wasn't moving stiffly or favoring any limb that he could tell, so he dropped it and tried not to scowl at the woman.

Figuring he was in for a long silent night with the possibility of interrogation/torture thrown in there somewhere, Nathan settled himself as comfortably as possible against his wall and rested while he could.

3

CADEN

Nathan Savage.

Wasn't that just a kick in the head.

Caden couldn't help the upward curve of her lips at the sight of him all bare-chested and scowling. That scowl, laugh lines turned into frown lines, eyebrows bunched, and those thick lips pursed like he was eating something sour brought back old memories. Good gloating ones Caden rather cherished. The bare chest was new and not at all hard to look at.

He'd been bouncing off the front end of her car the last time she'd seen him, which, she was sure, she should feel bad about. But it wasn't like she had been aiming for him. He was the genius who'd stepped onto the road and decided to play chicken.

And screeched like a newborn when he bounced off the hood of the Mini Cooper.

Besides, it wasn't like it had hurt him all that much. Nathan Savage was a big man. He towered over her at six-foot something and then there was all that finely toned muscle packed onto his frame. Nathan was a big man, and it had been such a tiny car.

That had been two years, thirty-some-odd jobs, and five scars ago.

She heard a rumor that he was in Prague taking down a human trafficking ring a few months after the car versus man thing, but then he had dropped off the face of the earth.

Optimist to the core, Caden had figured he'd either gotten killed on the job or had been captured by one of the baddies he'd pissed off and was rotting in a dungeon somewhere.

It was nice to see that he was alive.

But maddening as all hell to be sharing a cell with him.

Sure, she liked him, well, about as much as a mercenary could like a lawman. Out of all the G Men governments had sent after her, Nathan Savage was her favorite. He was ten shades of competent, very capable in a fight, and was always either one step ahead or behind her. There was nothing to hate about him. He made her job all the more fun.

On top of that shining list of character traits, he was a good man.

A genuinely good man.

Caden Quinn knew no good men anymore. All the good men were long since dead.

Now they were all either king pins, psychopaths, sick fuckers who liked to inflict pain, selfish assholes only looking out for themselves, and general dicks. There was no other version of man. Which maybe wasn't all that surprising, considering the circles she ran in.

Nathan Savage was the exception.

And sharing a cell was maddening as hell because his presence fucked with her golden 'caught and tortured' rule.

Bunking with a bad man was all well and fine. She could bunk with a hundred bad men and not so much as blink when they went off to be executed or didn't survive the latest torture method.

Bunking with a good man, at least for Caden, was a different story.

And there he was, a good man, asking if she was okay when she'd told him she'd murdered another human being and being all scowly and good citizeny.

When all she wanted to do was die in peace. Or, well, relative peace, having to factor in the torture and all.

Well, it was not gonna be any skin off her ass.

He got himself caught, so he sure as hell was gonna deal with the consequences all by his little lonesome. She would feel no obligation to help the man. Or feel an ounce of guilt when he took a turn on the rack.

Caden would simply ignore his existence.

And she did so for about seven hours. Alternating between pretending to sleep and glaring at the wall beside his head.

But when the four heavily armed men waltzed in and whisked him off to be interrogated and probably tortured, she couldn't help the twinge of guilt and anger that pulled at her gut.

Caden attempted to squash those treacherous feelings and put all her energy towards dying.

It should've been easy, right? Hell, she'd already died once in her lifetime and it had been a cakewalk. She'd been dead for two minutes and thirty-seven seconds before the paramedics brought her back. Blood loss and blunt force trauma to the head. It's what they said after she'd been stabilized.

A miracle she was alive. A miracle she came back from

the dead. Was what they said when she came to in the hospital bed two days later.

She should be thankful that she had made it 'cause others weren't so lucky.

A fucking miracle. They said.

Point was that she'd done it before, she could do it again. It was willpower, plain and simple. And Caden Quinn had that in spades.

If she could crawl through a jungle with a gaping hole in her chest and a broken leg, she sure as hell could will herself to die.

But it wasn't working. Her brain couldn't process the request. Like she knew what death was, but her body didn't know how to quit fighting. Because fighting was all it ever did—all she ever did.

She was done fighting.

So Caden closed her eyes and tried not to think of all the pain and hurt Nathan Savage was enduring and the stomach knotting, 'what if's'. What if he didn't make it through the torture? What if they went through all the work of capturing him just to kill him?

Savage was tough. She could ignore the anxiety and guilt knifing at her gut. He was quick and intelligent, with an overabundance of bad jokes and a crooked smile. Added to the fact that the man had to be some kind of former soldier, he could hold his own.

The first time she went head to head with him had been in Istanbul. She'd been coming off an adrenaline high after a job well done with the item in her bag. Then he popped out of the woodwork, called her by name, and told her she was under arrest. Caden had been wary. Usually, they (they being governments and/or corporations) sent pencil pushers after her—not men like him. For a moment, Caden had suspected that he was another hitter trying to take what was hers, but he kept his distance and his stance just *oozed* agent.

Caden had politely scoffed at the attempted arrest and continued on her merry way. And then he engaged. Well, no, he'd tried very hard not to engage. He had pulled out his Glock, warned her against resisting arrest, and grabbed for her shoulder when she didn't heed his warning.

Shocked as shit was what she was when he blocked her blows and returned with some well-placed jabs. It would be a lie if she said she hadn't been scared and just a wee bit turned on when he proved competent in hand-to-hand combat. But he had held back: Caden figured it was because she was a girl and he was a good ol' southern gentleman and she had escaped with him lying unconscious on the sidewalk.

The clomp of heavy boots and the familiar sound of skin and fabric sliding on cement had the merc positioning her body upright and holding her breath. The clang of the lock being thrown back was a good sign it meant they had something left to bring back to the cell. It meant he was alive or close enough to it, anyway.

Two heavily armed men entered first, arms drawn and aimed at her head. She did have somewhat of a reputation amongst the seedy underbelly of Moscow, but the fact that they'd assume she'd try to escape *now*, now with four guys toting guns between her and the hallway and with no knowledge of the building's layout and no escape plan whatsoever, was insulting as hell.

She only glared while the other two dragged the shivering do-gooder into the tiny cell and dumped him in the center. They backed out, eyes and guns trained on her until the door was shut and locked again.

She was up and pulling at the heap before she fully

registered what the hell she was doing. But it was too late to feign disinterest. She was already prodding at him and smacking at his face.

"Savage." He was hot to the touch. Red welts littered his torso. "Savage!"

"Whaa-at?" He clenched his teeth and batted her hands away.

"Anything fatal?" Caden ignored the look of confusion on his face and tried to act casual.

"Nah—he just fu—freaking electrocuted me."

Ever the gentleman, he censored himself. Caden couldn't help the disbelieving smirk that curled her lips. She retreated back to her corner of the cell when she ascertained that he wasn't dying.

"Why do you care?" He stayed sprawled in the middle of the room.

The return of the heavy combat boots on the cement stayed any explanation she could concoct. Nathan let out a heavy sigh and tried to push himself up as the feet paused at their cell and the door was opened, obviously thinking they'd come back for him.

Weapons up and at the ready, three new guards stepped into the room, one trained on Savage and the other two on her.

Asshole Number One was motioning with his gun and yelling at her in Russian to get on her knees.

Her Russian was rusty, but she got the gist of it. Caden didn't have time to comply before they were pulling at her and kicking at the backs of her knees.

Caden grinned, voluntarily held her hands up, and waited as Asshole Number Two quickly bound them. Honestly, she was surprised at how easily the language came back to her.

He kept motioning with his gun and told her to stand.

She complied, ignoring the burn of her busted rib, and got to her feet.

"Quinn." It was a goodbye. He looked damn near sad for *her*.

What an idiot.

But still, on the likely chance that this was going to be it, well, she was sorry he'd gotten his ass caught. Caden grinned at the man and patiently waited for the trio to get their shit together.

"Walk," he said in Russian.

And she did. One foot in front of the other.

4

———

NATHAN

Nathan hated that smile. It wasn't even a smile. It was a baring of her teeth. All predator, no lifelike spark in those dark eyes. Like she had no soul. Like she was nothing but a sack of organs that somehow functioned. It scared the shit out of him.

When she directed that shark smile at him, Nathan couldn't help the cold shiver that crawled down his spine. He'd seen that same look on dead men, on men in firefights who had nothing at all to lose and didn't give a shit if they took a bullet to the head.

She didn't always smile like that; sometimes she smiled like she was human. He'd seen her smile in Bangkok when he'd pulled from his colorful mental archive of doozies.

And then there was that one time in Oregon. He'd tracked her from Egypt and somehow miraculously stayed on her while she took the most diluted and confusing route possible (three different modes of transportation into it, he'd figured she was shaking possible tails). She finally ended up in Portland, Oregon, and was all soft smiles talking on the phone like she wasn't a wanted fugitive.

That had changed when he had headed her off at some Ma & Pa restaurant. She'd gone directly for the bathroom; Nathan had followed, knowing he'd been sighted and expected a fight. They'd duked it out in the woman's handicapped stall. He'd promptly gotten his ass kicked and was put out of his misery, rather forcibly, by way of his head connecting with a handrail three times. Generally, they were on pretty equal footing when it came to hand-to-hand combat; Nathan was big and strong, whereas Caden was fast and ruthless.

But in Portland, she'd had rage on her side and it had been scary. Her eyes got all kinds of crazy. That shark smile appeared, and she hadn't even so much as taunted him. Usually, when they went at it, Caden Quinn was the picture of professional: calm, collected, and even jovial. Like she very much enjoyed his attempts at arresting her.

Which annoyed him.

She annoyed him.

So Nathan switched thought tracks and tried not to think of all the horrible things being done to the woman—no, genderless mercenary, not *woman*—who annoyed him.

Kyott.

The head honcho's name was Ralph Kyott.

Nathan had recognized him from his days as the government's bloodhound. Human trafficking was his main thing. If Nathan remembered correctly, the short man was originally from Boston, went down for kidnapping and murder way back when, but got back out again and disappeared. Nathan had never personally gone after him while employed by the US Government, but he had sure as hell heard of the asshole.

Caden Quinn did not fit into that picture. Her thing was high profile, high-value art, and occasionally (or well, more often than not) she'd involve herself in violent disputes. Last he knew she did not work for scumbags like Kyott.

Though that bit of knowledge was dated. But somehow he couldn't see her involved with human traffickers.

Nathan hadn't realized he'd dozed off until the sound of a door creaking open jolted him awake and got his adrenalin running. Someone aimed a light directly into his eyes and, if they were competent, a gun was on him as well. So Nathan put up his hands and didn't move until they chucked a body inside and backed out again.

"Quinn." She was slumped in a pile on the ground like she was dead. "Come on, get up."

Panic shot through his system when she didn't even so much as twitch. Usually, she was either hitting him by now or retreating from all physical contact.

Nathan bit back the rising panic, gripped her by the shoulders, and flipped her as gently as possible since he didn't know the extent of the damage, so she was on her stomach. She moaned in his arms and started cursing.

Thank Christ.

She wasn't dead.

Nathan had to take a moment to breathe that in before he went back to examining her hurts.

"What they do to ya, Quinn?" Nathan kept scowling when she didn't answer. "Come on, Quinn! Talk to me; I can hardly see anything."

The light was gone, but the moon was shining through the window bars. His hand came back wet and dark. Dammit, she was all bloody again. The back of his shirt was in pieces. Her back was all torn to hell. Like they'd whipped her until they broke the skin. Numerous times.

"Are you hurting anywhere else, Quinn?" He reached for

the bucket of water, trying to keep from jostling her too much. "Caden, answer me!"

If she could curse like she was doing, she could sure as hell answer a simple question.

"Just..." Her voice was hoarse and weak and... and something he couldn't name. "Leave me alone, Savage."

"What? No." He was growling again and ignoring her protests as he stripped her of his shirt. "Just let me help you! How are you gonna reach your back—you can't even sit up by yourself!"

"Savage!" Her gravelly all-outta-screams voice got louder, but it died in her throat and she kept on struggling to get away from him. "I don't want your fucking help! Leave me alone!"

"No, I will not. First of all, I ain't doing nothing but helping you, so stop freaking out. And second of all, my mama would kick my ass if she knew I sat back and watched you rot in here. Jesus, it's like you wanna die."

"What the fuck do you think I'm doing here, Savage?" Her voice was fading out like it was taking too much energy to form sounds. "Taking a vacation?"

It took a long moment for her words to sink in because it was so at odds with everything he knew about her. She took advantage of his shock and slipped out of his hold.

Caden Quinn was suicidal.

Well, maybe he knew that already, taking into consideration some of the insane jobs she'd pulled, but he placed her in the crazy but not *suicidal* category. It wasn't just that. He'd seen her eyes go all wild and gleam with 'what ifs' before (usually when she did something stupid and insane), he'd seen her kind of crazy before, but it wasn't just that. Now it was... it was all that fight, that innate thing that made her

Caden Quinn, that trait Nathan had figured was seared into her bones, had been drained right out of her.

It was her giving up.

The same woman who had navigated on foot through a war zone, crawled through a maze of sewers, and then took a butcher knife to the stomach, all for some golden statue of a cow.

He couldn't process it. He couldn't understand the why or how of it. So Nathan did the only thing he could do. He got mad.

"Well, that ain't gonna fuckin' happen."

She hadn't gotten far, not that there was anywhere to go. So he waited until she quit crawling and then held her down until she wore herself out cussing and kicking at him.

It took him a bit to wash off the blood and clean out the cuts. Which was surprisingly easy now that she only had energy enough to flinch under his ministrations and occasionally let out a pained moan.

"Why is your hair wet?" Nathan found his voice again as he carefully tied together the dangling bits of fabric that now made up the back of her shirt. "Do you have a head injury?"

"He..." She breathed like speaking was taking too much energy. "He wanted to see his handy work, so they sprayed me down."

"What a bastard." Nathan finally relinquished his hold on her and sat back against the wall.

"Savage, I don't need you to hold my hand. I've had much worse. So... can you just... go do your good citizenry on the other side of the room?"

"It's called being a decent human being, Quinn." How she could make even that insulting was a gift only she possessed. "And seeing as how you're now on suicide watch, you can look forward to days and days of hand holding. Or well, however long we'll be bunking together." At the sound of her disgruntled huff, he couldn't help but tack on an overly enthusiastic "Roomie" at the end.

Another groan.

"We could even make friendship bracelets."

"Yeah." She shoved his hand off hers and buried her face in her arms. "We could pluck a few tails off the rats and make real pretty ones."

"I'm sensing some sarcasm in there, Quinn." Nathan shifted so his butt wouldn't fall asleep on the hard cement. She ignored him and eventually, her breathing slowly evened out.

Nathan didn't know what the hell he was doing. He'd only once before been caught and tortured by the enemy, but it had been part of the plan. His team had infiltrated and rescued his ass before any real damage had been done. There would be nobody coming for him this time. It would be easy enough for his brothers to track his passport to Moscow, but then they'd be at a dead end. And they probably didn't even know he was missing yet. So escaping was up to him.

And he somehow had to keep Caden Quinn alive, which would be difficult if she put as much effort and will into dying as she did everything else. He couldn't write her off; he wasn't that kind of person.

Besides, he needed her. According to the very small file on Quinn, she'd escaped imprisonment a fair amount of times and Nathan believed it. She'd escaped federal custody twice from him alone. She'd escaped Marskib's dungeons. He'd seen how incredibly messed up she was when she came out the other side, and that alone was a testament to her fight. So all he had to do was figure out how to turn that frown upside down.

And then maybe they could escape.

5

CADEN

She was still fucking breathing.

A-fuckin'-live, god dammit.

The burn in her chest and back was evidence of that unfortunate state of being. Obviously, getting dead was going to be a harder endeavor than the merc anticipated. She'd been pretty goddamn sure that Kyott was gonna stop pussy footing around that last go around, but the rat bastard hadn't.

Instead, the man had questioned her. Kyott and his fuckhead goons had questioned her.

While she hung like a slab of meat from a hook and they'd lashed her back to pieces, they had fucking interrogated her.

At first, it had been about a stupid goddamn fucking statue. A statue she had long since stolen and sold to the highest bidder in Montreal. Apparently, it had gotten nicked again and Kyott, the dumb fuck that he was, thought she was responsible.

He wanted a fucking jeweled elephant. A statue she

hadn't touched in years. And when he got no other response than, 'No dumb-fuck, I don't have it', he moved on to other questions.

Like where was her stash? Everyone and their mothers knew full well she had to have a stash of art, weapons, and gold. She was Caden Quinn. Where the fuck was her stash?

Then he got down to the list of people she had worked for in the past. Harrington was of special interest to him.

Which didn't bode well for her plans.

It wasn't torture for torture's sake anymore.

Soon, though, he'd get tired of asking and remember exactly why she was on his 'To Kill' list.

Evil-little-piddly-shit sons didn't grow on trees.

The opening and closing of the cell door was what slapped her back to reality. Not Savage or his snoring. Not even the fact that he was still invading her personal space and was he—he was fucking drooling on her hand. The back of her hand was pillowing his stupid head like he could trust her not to kill him in his sleep.

Which, okay, she wouldn't kill him, but he was operating under the assumption that she was a good person and that was just wrong. The only people to trust her that much were all dead. Still, though, the fact that he trusted her enough to fall asleep around her was... refreshing.

Caden didn't know what to think about that. So she ignored his snoring, drooling, and explicit trust and took evaluation of her hurts.

The agony of her lashed-up back had all but dulled while she slept. Now it was a burning ache she could shove to the back of her mind and forget about. She could ignore the fact that every time she moved a scab broke open or the ones that were too deep to scab felt like they were ripping deeper into her muscle.

What she could not ignore, however, was the fullness of her bladder and how badly she needed to piss.

But Savage was right there and the thought of pissing into the designated bucket in the corner of the room while he was not five feet from her was an embarrassing one.

And also frustrating as all hell. She never had qualms about pissing in front of Señor Rapist. Not particularly liking that little revelation, Caden couldn't help but snarl.

"Get off me, Savage." She took her hand back as violently as possible.

Savage, the precious soul that he was, bolted upright, still drooling down his chin, and moved over her. Like he was protecting her from an attack. Unsure what to do with that, she kept snarling and wiped his slobber off her hand. Confused and pissed and… weirded out was a combination of emotions Caden didn't like feeling.

"You okay?" He was up and moving towards the food and water.

"Do you think you could maybe keep your drool to yourself? Or, I don't know, sleep on your side of the room!"

He only smiled, a smile that was not at all diminished by the swollen lip or the two black eyes, in response. The welts on his torso had pretty much faded, but the bruises were vivid against his skin. Still, though, he was not at all hard to look at. What with his back muscles all flexing and his arms stretching. Nope, no problem at all with looking at him. She was just having a problem with the looking away part. Dammit.

"What?" He caught her staring and glanced down at his chest. "Stop looking at my nipples." He placed her own bowl of white snot in front of her and moved to put an arm over his chest. "I'm cold, okay."

He took a seat by her head and swallowed his own in three gulps, shivering as it went down.

"Ugh, it's like eating Maddox's cooking. Cept less burnt." He was grinning again until she made no move to touch her own food. "Aren't ya gonna eat?"

"That'd be counterproductive."

He only scowled at that and nudged it closer, looking like he was contemplating shoving it down her throat. But he let out a sigh and slid over till he was even with her back.

Caden didn't bother fighting when he hovered over her and examined her back. She'd probably piss herself from the effort. His fingers were gentle on her back. Caden didn't like it or him, for that matter. He was annoying and god, he just had to waltz in and ruin everything.

"I have to piss."

"Okay." His hands moved to her shoulders, and Caden couldn't help but growl. "Are you—are you actually growling at me?"

"I don't need your help, Savage." Caden pushed herself to her feet and watched through narrowed eyes as the man put his hands in the air.

"You're hurt, Quinn." He was all aghast, like it was madness, allowing her to get to her two feet without aid. Like she was some delicate little flower that would collapse at the slightest breeze.

"Yeah, no shit."

Pain was the one constant in her life. It wasn't some foreign thing she'd never dealt with before. It wasn't terrible or all-consuming. It just was.

Most times, it served as a reality check; she was not a machine and she should stop pretending she was.

Other times, it was a reminder that her life was and always had been shit.

But Caden had learned a long time ago exactly how to grin and bear it. A ripped-up back was nothing comparatively. Still, though, it hurt like a bitch.

So she did what she'd always done. Pushed the pain to the back of her mind and focused on her goal. Getting to and pissing in the bucket across the room.

Easier done than said really, seeing as how it was walking and squatting.

"Anyone ever compliment you on your friendly disposition, Quinn?" He was getting snarky.

"Not anybody that likes breathin'." Which was a lie because nobody actually ever commented on any part of her shining personality.

Even before all the stealing and killing, conversation with other people mostly consisted of one-word sentences and a good arm's length of space away from her. People, Caden realized, didn't much like her.

He scoffed and, very much like the gentlemen he was, turned so he was facing away from her. Another little show of trust that Caden herself wouldn't give to another human being so freely. Which really wasn't saying much, being who she was and all.

"So... do you mind me askin' how you wound up in here?" With his back turned towards the light, Caden could make out a couple of different scars that had long since healed. He'd been shot in the back. And it looked like he'd taken a knife to the side and whirled away from it.

"My last job went south, got nabbed, and auctioned off to the highest bidder." Muscles burning, blood drizzling down her back, and feeling like a million fucking bucks, she reached the bucket.

What she didn't say was that she really hadn't tried all that hard to escape the first ass-hat. She'd gone into the first job looking to take a bullet or a knife somewhere fatal, and when that didn't happen—well, she was nothing if not persistent.

"Highest bidder? You mean Kyott paid money for you just so he could hurt you?" He was all incredulous, like he couldn't imagine such a thing. "Well damn, what'd you do to him?"

"Killed his bouncing baby boy in Ireland last year." Caden bit back the urge to explain herself to him. She did not feel guilty for taking that little pervert out and she didn't have to justify her actions to him, even if she felt like he was judging her. Dammit. "You can turn around now." What she needed was a change of clothes. She'd been in the same jeans for two fire-fights, a few tussles in the mud, and then the bleeding. Most of it was someone else's, which made it that much more gross.

He didn't respond, only watched her like a hawk while she took up a bit of concrete as far as she could get away from him. As soon as she'd settled back skyward and head in her arms, he stood and stretched.

Caden tried very hard not to gawk like a schoolgirl as the man exercised. But really there wasn't much else, besides a few rats and the gray walls, to stare at. So Caden gave up, pretending that she wasn't perving over his finely toned abs and arms and watched as he went through a few quick exercises. After a good forty-five minutes of him workin' up a sweat, he finally stretched again and took the spot by her head.

"Okay, Caden, we are gonna get the hell outta here. Together—we're both alive in that scenario, just F-Y-I. But first we gotta fix... this." He motioned towards her sprawled figure with both hands.

"Savage," How many different ways was she gonna have

to say it? "you don't seem to be comprehending this. You don't get a choice. So leave me the fuck alone." Maybe she could request a different roommate.

"Yeah, and I believe we've already been over this whole 'I'm not gonna let you kill yourself' thing." His deep voice took on a slightly elevated 'duh' tone that grated on her already fried nerves, like she was the one that was too thick to get it. "So, uh... do you wanna talk about it?"

Caden curled her lip at his stupid, sincere face and laughed outright. He only frowned and gave a disapproving look. A look that served to not only piss her off, but make her feel guilty at the same time. Maybe if she didn't engage him, he'd stop. Eventually, the man would recognize a lost cause. He wasn't stupid.

"Okay fine, I'll start." He scooted over so he wasn't crowding her and crossed his arms over his bruised chest. "I, uh... I've been retired from the agency for two years now. You may have noticed?"

He looked down all expectantly at her and Caden decided to stop looking at him as well.

"Of course, I noticed, Savage. There's been a big gaping hole in my life since you've been gone." Voice high and squeaky, like he was channeling a thirteen-year-old girl. "You were the very best and the most handsome agent on my case."

"Well, Quinn, I'd miss me too. What with my extraordinary good looks and keen sense of style, no longer a major presence in your life... I can understand you getting all emotional like that."

"Keen sense of style!?" Now he was lying through his teeth. "Savage—you are the worst dressed man I have ever —there is nothing keen about socks and sandals! Or fanny packs!"

Dammit, she'd engaged.

"That was one time!" He was scoffing and all kinds of outraged now. "My shoes were wet! And it was cold, which was why I was wearing socks! And I was playing a part with the fanny pack."

Caden couldn't help but smirk at the memory. He'd caught up to her in Liverpool and it finally came down to blows when he refused to shoot her. They'd both taken a tumble into a body of water. He'd arrested her (only because Caden panicked and froze in the water) and marched her back to his hotel. Where he'd promptly handed her off to the local official idiots to be held until the next plane to the States. She'd, of course, escaped—compared to Marskib's dungeons, damn near everything was escapable.

"Let's see... what could we talk about?" He settled against the wall, obviously readying himself for a long wait, and started in on his job. Or ex-job.

The first ninety minutes were interesting enough. He recounted every single case he'd worked on in the five years he'd been an agent. Though, much like a government man, kept names and real-time details to himself. The merc liked hearing how he went about successfully trapping and arresting other thieves.

But hour three rolled around and he was showing no sign of stopping or even slowing. Sure there'd be lulls in the one-sided conversation where he'd get up to take a lap around the small space, pause to think on the next topic, and go to the bathroom. But right when she was about to nod off, he'd start up again and slap her back into reality. As hard as she tried, his voice was too gravelly and deep to block out.

When he'd exhausted art theft, past missions, the finer points of accurate record keeping, and how he only missed being a government bloodhound occasionally, Caden was starting to get frustrated. He moved on from government work to his time as a Special Ops Soldier. And not even the good bits, it was another long list of How To's.

Proper gun care, how to correctly setup camp, evading the enemy, the importance of foot care whilst in the field, his absolute hatred for MREs and how much he missed Ellen's cooking when he was in the field. She tried to fall asleep but every time she nodded off, his voice cut through her doze and slapped her right back into awake mode.

Hour four was when her resolve to not kill the bastard started to waver. How could any human being talk for four hours straight and still have something to say? But Caden beat that urge back down, remembered that she didn't kill good men, and breathed deeply.

If she could perch on a window ledge for seven hours to wait for the leader of the Azarik to walk through her crosshairs, then she sure as fuck could listen for hours on end while he jabbered on. She would outlast him. There was no other option; she was going to beat him. He was eventually gonna run out of things to say.

She'd actually managed to doze off near hour six (six hours and her ears had grown accustomed to the tilts and twangs of his southern drawl so it became easier to block him out) and woke up to him still gabbing away. Judging by the color of daytime coming through the tiny window, she'd been out at least two hours.

He'd moved on from tedious How To's and started talking about random shit. Like how much he hated reality TV—'cause first of all, there was nothing realistic about it and secondly, it was horrible. He'd had to endure it for a whole three days when he got out of intensive care. Caden wanted to ask what the hell was he doing in the ICU in the first place but squashed the urge. Reminding herself that she didn't give a shit, and she was supposed to be focusing on dying.

"I have a problem with teal. I don't know what it is about half blue and half green, but I hate it. Even the word is ugly. Teal. Blue and green are fine by themselves, but when they are together... it's ugly."

Tater-tots were put on the earth for his sole enjoyment and don't tell anybody, especially not his brothers, but he was a huge fan of Martha Stewart. He and Ellen, well his adopted mother, watched the show together whenever he was home. A lot more recently since he'd retired and was currently mostly unemployed.

It was mostly because Jackson, one of his brothers, had roped him into this part-time Security Consultant job. But honestly, his heart wasn't really in it. Again, don't tell his brothers, because he was sure as hell gonna figure his own shit out in time. He probably just needed some time away from death.

He'd stopped briefly for the delivery of their daily snot quota. Made sure her bowl was in easy reach and started again after he'd downed his.

"I mean—come on, how many legs do ya need?! Eight, I can understand. Eight is practical when you're an insect. But eighty freaking legs! No, it's actually eighty to a thousand little legs. Nothin' needs that many legs. That's purely for scaring people. And I can admit that I do literally get struck dumb with terror. Oh man, you shoulda seen my brothers." He let out a soft chuckle, and Caden couldn't help the upward turn of her own lips at the sound.

"Every last one of 'em are these big, hardcore, highly trained soldiers. And we were all spending Thanksgiving at my parents' house. I saw a millipede in the basement—I mean, a firefight or any angry Brazilian mob I'm fine with but a zillion little crawling legs and—ugh!"

He shivered beside her, and Caden had to bite back a laugh. Nathan himself was a big, hardcore, highly trained soldier and here he was admitting to being terrified of a bug.

"Anyway, I screamed loudly and very much like a little girl. All my brothers come hurdling down the stairs. Guns drawn and ready to down the intruder. They'll never let me live that down. Ever.

"Oh, and then there was that time I peed my pants in public. Another thing they'll never stop reminding me of. I get adult diapers at least one holiday a year. Bunch of assholes." He was shaking his head ruefully and when he saw that she was looking at him, he started looking all expectantly again. Like how dare she not immediately shoot down that confession with disbelief? A man like Nathan Savage would never lose control of his own bladder.

"How did you lose control of your bladder, Nathan?" All high and squeaky again, he added a hand flourish and batted his eyelashes. Jerk.

He paused again, giving her the chance to actually ask, and Caden couldn't hold her vigil any longer.

"*You*? Pee yourself in public?" She added a gasp to drive the sarcasm home for him. "No! That couldn't possibly be true."

"Well, Caden, not that I appreciate the mockery, as I am baring my soul and all, but since you asked, I'll tell ya."

When she shifted to maneuver her body around to get some feeling back in her legs, his arms shot out to help her. Caden flashed her canines at him and moved to a sitting position out of his reach. Mostly scabs now. Her back was no longer on fire every time she moved, though she wouldn't be lying on her back anytime soon.

"This was in high school, mind you, so it was like ten times more embarrassing." He handed over her bowl, and Caden took it without thinking. "I had pneumonia in... freshman year, I think. Yeah, 'cause it was right after Ellen and Bobby adopted us. Anyway, the medication I was on was still in my system and I just... I just peed. I couldn't have stopped it. I only knew I was peeing 'cause I felt something hot on my leg and some kid started pointing and laughing at me." He shook his head again and squinched his eyes like he was in pain.

"It was, of course, in the middle of the cafeteria and one of the most embarrassing things I have ever done. Everyone, the lunch ladies, the kids in the corner, the kids in the hall —everyone saw. The girl I was dating at the time dumped me like then and there. My brothers had a laugh but beat the hell out of everyone else, that was. We all ended up in suspension. Lots of bowel-related jokes after that.

"What about you? Got any embarrassing and traumatizing high school stories?"

"Not really... I, uh... I tripped some kid in the hallway once. She wasn't hurt or anything, but she started crying and ran away." Which had been awkward and weird at the time until she found out that a rumor of her gouging out somebody's eyes had been going around. In which case, bursting into tears and running away was definitely understandable.

"*You* cried and ran away?" His head tilted like he wasn't comprehending.

"No, she did." Caden shrugged and hissed as a jolt of pain coursed through her system at the movement. "I dropped out my sophomore year so I don't really have many embarrassing moments."

Once, when she was first learning to drive, she'd accidentally driven down the wrong side of the road for like a mile, which would have been embarrassing had anyone been in the car with her, but no one had been. She'd dropped a whole box of tomatoes at one of her part-time jobs, but the embarrassment had lasted all of ten seconds before it just became more annoying than anything.

Why the hell was she sharing to begin with?

"Oh well, I've got enough for the both of us. More than I really care to admit to actually, but hey, what the hell?" He settled against the wall and started in on the list of his top fifteen most embarrassing moments.

Number seven was about the time Caden realized she was not only smiling, listening intently, but also eating the bowl of snot.

No, it wasn't his doing.

Caden just needed to switch positions every couple of hours or her limbs were gonna fall off. And fuck, it wasn't like the slop was doing anything to replenish the nutrients and shit in her body. So why not drink it? If Caden had to describe the white-lumpy-syrupy-snot as anything, it would be most like curdled milk; slightly thick and bouncy, but more liquid than anything. It actually required a combination of chewing and swallowing she was probably never gonna get used to.

It wasn't the fact that Savage was talking to her like she was a human being and not the Terminator (before his wires got all crossed).

Nor was it because another human was so openly sharing things that were obviously personal and embarrassing with her. *Her.*

It wasn't even the fact that he was once again demonstrating his weird and candid trust in her by telling her about himself.

It was not because her gut was doing weird things at the prospect of being treated like a normal, nonviolent-person-who-could-go-off-and-kill-every-living-thing-in-sight-at-any-moment-so-fucking-tread-carefully, person.

It was just that her stomach was numb and her ass was gonna take a turn on the cold cement.

6

NATHAN

It was working.

She was upright, smirking at his embarrassing stories, and eating.

If it didn't make him look so stupid, Nathan would have high-fived the shit out of himself. But she already thought that he had no fashion sense. He didn't want her to tack on 'lame' as well.

But damn, his voice was getting raw.

Water would be good, but Nathan wanted to ration it in case his captors decided against refilling the bucket. He sipped it instead and shoved it towards Quinn. She scowled a scowl that didn't really reach her eyes, but huffed in annoyance and took a sip.

High-fiving was out of the question, but Nathan was running victory laps in his mind. Seeing as how she seemed to respond to personal stories, Nathan decided that he'd share all of his colorful history if it got her engaged and not thinking about dying.

"All right, let's see." Nathan settled beside her and tried very hard not to pat himself on the back.

The man drew a much-needed breath, resettled his ass on the concrete so it didn't fall asleep, pictured the farm, and dove right in.

It wasn't hard coming up with topics and he wasn't really ever gonna run out of things to say about his family or the farm. With six brothers who were all their very own brand of crazy and a pair of loving parents, there was a lot he could talk about.

So he started with a rather, if he did so say himself, great description of the family farm. The names of all the cows, horses, and chickens. The big beautiful house he'd spent a good amount of his childhood in. How he twice jumped off the second-story roof to prove to his nay-saying brothers that he could, in fact, fly. He only needed a good amount of distance from the ground and the right kind of bed sheet tied to his wrists and ankles. The only thing he ended up proving was that he could break the same arm twice and could get maybe three seconds of hang time before plummeting to the garden below.

About how his mother sold the extra produce and such at the farmer's market and had done it since they'd moved there. How his adopted dad took them all camping at least three times a month during the summer and they'd learned to swim and fish and shoot. About playing war in the woods with his brothers. All the little nooks and crannies on the farm where he could stash firecrackers and odd-shaped rocks.

How Reid, one of his adopted brothers, had gotten himself lost in the woods lining their farm one summer. How when he'd been found, fourteen hours later, the kid had acquired a squirrel friend and didn't know what all the fuss was about because he wasn't lost. He had known exactly where he was.

How it wasn't the stupid chickens that would wake him up in the morning but one of the many strays Kade, another adopted brother, had brought home meowing straight into his eyeball until he got out of bed.

It was odd, talking about his family. Nathan never really had the chance to regale his friends with the humorous and always cringe-worthy tales of his childhood. Because he suddenly realized he had no friends. Sure, there were some high school friends and Navy buddies, but those were all people he used to know.

The Savage family as a whole, except of course for Bobby and Ellen, had never really been good at welcoming strangers with open arms or getting friendly with the locals. They preferred to keep to themselves and the village people tended to regard the Savage family with a wary kind of distrust that was, considering the boys' combined escapades, understandable.

"You were in foster care?"

He'd been talking so long and planted firmly in his own head that her voice threw him off. For a second, Nathan doubted she'd said anything at all, but she cracked an eye open and peered sideways at him.

"What?" The surprise at her engaging had pretty much pushed all other thoughts out of his head.

"You were in the system—in foster care?" She was staring imploringly at him. Damn, she was pretty. Even all beat to hell, she was pretty.

"Er... yeah." Nathan tried to focus on her question instead of her lips and forced his mind to pay attention to her words, but it was hard. Foster care. She wanted to know about his time in foster care? *That* had her asking questions and breaking her silence? "My biological parents weren't— well, my mom ODed when I was seven and my dad just used me and Holden as punching bags till the state stepped in and took us out."

Something soft and dark moved in her eyes. Maybe she had a similar experience? Which maybe meant that she was from the States. Nathan knew she had to have roots somewhere, but maybe now he could narrow the range of possibilities. That little bit of information had the man sitting up straighter and leaning in closer.

"Were they... I mean, how did they treat you? Your foster parents." Her head cocked to the side slightly and her hands were fidgeting with her shirt.

"They were nice. They actually ended up adopting me and Holden after about six months." Nathan didn't particularly like talking about his life before Ellen and Bobby, but if it got her to talking and got him even a bit of info on her, he'd write her a book. "It was terrifying at first. I mean eleven years of walking on eggshells, of being in constant fear of triggering an episode, of getting beat on... then getting put with Ellen and Bobby. It was like waking up on a different planet—like we had to relearn how to interact with other humans."

She nodded absently at him with her brow furrowed, like she wasn't comprehending what he was saying.

"Can I ask you about your family?" Maybe he was shooting himself in the foot, but he had to ask.

There was a beat of silence. Her eyebrows jerked upwards in surprise and furrowed once again in suspicion. She stared him down and Nathan tried to not make it too obvious he was still staring at her lips. He had to stop perving on a woman who was so incredibly tortured and bloody that she shouldn't have even been appealing to a fucking zombie. Maybe there was something wrong with him.

Finally, her fists unclenched and her eyebrows smoothed.

"You can, but there's not much to say." Her head settled against the wall and her eyes closed. "They're all dead."

"I'm sorry." He frowned, another two beats went by and Nathan couldn't stop himself. "Okay, so tell me about you, Caden Quinn."

Nathan scooted closer and watched as she found his face in the gloom. A sardonic little smirk pulled at her busted lips and her dark eyebrow arched at him.

"You want my back story?" There was only amusement in her tone, but her eyes shot to his and she regarded him like she was looking at an alien. Like he was some foreign thing she'd never be able to comprehend. Or maybe she was deciding on which way was best to kill him.

"Well, why not?" Nathan was nothing if not persistent. "Seeing as how you're not gonna be leaving this prison—I feel it's only fair."

"Fair." Snorting, she rolled her eyes and smirked again. "How is that *fair*?"

"What—how is it *not*?"

She did a little jerk of her head and her eyes took on that 'slightly amused but mostly just thinking that he was a special kind of stupid' look she saved special for him.

"Caden—I chased your ass for two years. Two. In those two years, I've arrested you twice. Both times ending in your escape and my being forced onto a 'vacation'—which thanks for, by the way. Oh and also you've shot me *twice*, whereas I've only fired warning shots at your ass."

Ass, good word choice, really. She had, in fact, shot him in the ass. Nathan hadn't been able to properly sit for weeks after. His brothers, aside from Reid, had themselves a grand ol' time coming up with butt jokes and making fun of him.

"Oh, and I guess taserin' doesn't count?" Dark eyes narrowed, and she shoved a finger in his direction. "Don't go pretending like you're the victim here—you've tased me like seventy times."

"Okay, exaggeration." Nathan was starting to feel like a girl in his tone and head motions. "I've tased you three times —*three*. Once in Cairo. That one time in that Burger King in Korea, and then in Manhattan. That's *three*."

"Yeah, well, I only *grazed* you." The smirk pulling at her lips curled wider. "Warning shots, you could say."

Grazed? Grazed. She had freakin' sniped him. Sure, it hadn't hit bone or anything fatal, but the scar on his left shoulder was proof enough that she hadn't just grazed him. Her eyes flicked to his shoulder for half a beat and Nathan was pretty damn sure he saw something like guilt flit through her eyes before it was quickly pushed out and replaced with an 'I'm not impressed' look she'd obviously spent lots of time perfecting.

"Point is that I know nothing about you—aside from the very basics. Do you wanna know what was in your file when I first started trackin' you? A sketch of your face, a list of sightings, jobs that you may or may not have done, and a list of possible contacts."

"Sounds... like a file?" Caden quirked an eyebrow at him again.

"Yeah, a very nice file. Except it's not like you fell outta the sky. No matter where I dig or who I question, there is nothing on you." It had been frustrating as hell.

Thieves, good thieves, were not at all like their Hollywood and cartoon depictions. They were highly intelligent and highly organized beings. But that did not exempt them from having social security numbers and families. There was never, in all the cases he'd worked, zero on the criminal.

Except, of course, for Caden Quinn.

"Really?" Surprise colored her tone almost bordering on shock, which had Nathan all ears.

"You sound surprised?"

Had there been some secret file with her name on it that he hadn't found? Was his government secretly keeping tabs on her? If that were the case, why would they send him in practically blind? Maybe it was a departmental thing no one, even though they all swore under the same flag, purposefully tipped their hand.

"Well yeah," shrugging, she settled against the wall again with only a little wincing, "but I guess I really shouldn't be."

"I can't tell if that's a jab at the government or you're genuinely surprised that they didn't have more on you."

Her face closed off and Nathan's spidey senses were screaming. There was something. Something she thought the government had on her.

"You can't?" Eyes blank and head tilted like she didn't purposefully just evade his question.

Frustration. The woman was frustration itself. But Nathan was retired now, so secret files or no, he wasn't ever going to see them. So instead, he carefully filed away that little tidbit and went back to his original intent.

"So how bout it?" Eye contact made and breath held, Nathan waited as patiently as he could.

She regarded him for a moment, bit her bottom lip, and narrowed her eyes at him.

The thing about Caden was not that she was the only criminal who had gotten away, but she was the only one who consistently had him tied in knots. Mostly because he had and could get nothing on her. But she was also one contradiction after another.

Other thieves he could understand because they made sense. Their pieces fit together. Even if he didn't have the whole story, he could still make sense of them. But with Quinn, it was frustratingly different. Every time he interacted with her, she gave him a whole new jigsaw puzzle piece that didn't fit with any of the ones he already had.

Where other thieves were tightlipped and angry when Nathan popped up, she was all eager smirks and very verbal. The fight in her, the thing that kept her crawling through ditches, razor wire, and bullets with what was left of a dead man handcuffed to her and shrapnel logded in her hip, was like nothing he'd seen. But there she was, half dead already and not giving a piss about it.

"And what exactly do you want to know?" Shoulders relaxed slightly, fingers uncurled, palms turned up.

"How 'bout your real name?" It was one of those top-of-the-list questions.

Lips pursed and those dark eyes were on him again. Her arms folded across her chest and Nathan, once again, held his breath. Finally, she let out a long sigh, and her arms unfolded.

"Ava." It was soft and heavy with all manner of unsaid things behind that one word. "My name is Ava."

"Ava. That's pretty. Where'd you get Caden from?"

"It's my middle name." Her shoulders relaxed, and she kept her eyes on him.

"So if by some miracle we—" her eyes narrowed on his and Nathan rolled his eyes, "—*I* got outta here and looked up Ava Caden Quinn I'd find you?"

"Nope. Quinn's not my surname. It's Collins."

Nathan did not like the fact that she'd told him so casually. A first name wasn't bad—there were probably a million Ava's in the States alone, but a surname added to it made it that much easier to find her. And she'd given it to him without even so much as twitching.

The mercenary was obviously set on dying.

"Ava Caden Collins, huh?" Nathan kinda liked the sound of it. "Well, where'd you get Quinn from?"

The smirk fell from her lips and Nathan watched as fists formed.

"Somebody dead." Her face closed off and her eyes got cold. Those thick lips pursed and her eyes strayed to the ceiling.

"Oh." He decided to change the subject. "How 'bout that scar on your chest? How did you get that?"

"You'll have to be more specific." A small smile pulled at her lips and her hand fluttered abstractedly towards her chest.

"The long one between your..." Nathan was no blushing virgin, but Caden tended to bring a color to his cheeks. "Your breasts."

"Broadsword." Her left hand touched her chest, and that smirk returned.

"Are you serious? A broadsword? I mean how?"

"I was commissioned to retrieve a..." She slanted her eyes at him and her lip curled. "Certain object. The dude in possession of said object had himself a broadsword and some skills. Ended up shooting that fuck-head in the leg and the arm and the other leg—he wouldn't stay down." She shook her head. "Got it, got out again, went home to sew myself up, and learn some fencing."

"Wow." He sat back and watched the smirk go soft a tiny bit.

A smile small pulled at the corner of her mouth and Nathan suddenly got the impression that those stories, the ones of how she narrowly escaped death, how she ingeniously stole a priceless artifact, how she walked away the victor in a death match, was her 'I jumped off the roof of my house cause I was a silly kid' stories.

"I know, it was crazy. I mean, I'm good with knives and daggers—they're small and practical. A broadsword is not. Why would that be his weapon of choice? What was he thinking?" She shook her head ruefully and smirked wider. "What about you? Any weird scars?"

"Uh," he jerked his attention away from her lips and focused on answering the question "not really. Mostly just combat scars. Actually, I was once attacked by an angry flock of chickens. I've got like little dots all over my legs from their beaks."

"Damn." She smiled at him and Nathan could only stare blankly at her. "What'd you do to the chickens?"

"I was using them as target practice." Nathan felt a niggling of guilt at the confession and the sudden urge to explain himself.

"So you deserved it." She smirked again and folded her arms across her chest.

"Yeah, I did." He couldn't have her thinking that he was some heartless chicken killer. "I was like twelve and stupid. I don't shoot at chickens anymore."

There were a few questions the ex-agent in him was burning to ask. Like how old she was. Where she grew up. Why the hell wasn't she in the system? And could he maybe have some of her DNA? Where had she received her training? How exactly had she robbed a thousand-pound statue of a naked guy in the middle of the damn day in Cairo?

But Nathan didn't want to burn any bridges by spooking her, so he decided to keep them subtle and as non-threatening as possible. Although, she had thrown out her last name all willy-nilly, so maybe, she'd happily give up more information.

"How'd you get into... I mean... why are you a mercenary?" Nathan watched a rat squeeze under the door and briefly tried to imagine the rat tail friendships bracelets.

Gross was the only thing that came to mind.

"What else should I be, Savage?" Her voice turned tired and her palms turned up. Like there had never been any other option, and it was impossible to fathom being anything else.

"I don't know... a businesswoman... an astronaut—just why a merc? I mean, there ain't many women in that line of work. It's dangerous and violent and I don't see the allure—especially for a civilian."

Honestly, he couldn't see her as anything else, but he needed to know how she'd gotten there. How she decided to skip everything else and go straight for the thieving and killing.

"I had bills to pay." Knuckles turned white and that hard something was back in her eyes.

"And you don't anymore?"

The sound of combat boots stomping down the hallway had her straightening and almost frantically shoving at his arm.

"What?"

"That ain't dinner—they don't come for another three hours." She was hissing and spitting and still shoving at him. "Get on the other side!"

"Why?" Though he was already up doing as he was told.

"Shh!" She was scowling hard and looking pissed off. "Don't talk to me."

The boots stopped at the door. He watched as the merc stiffened and carefully kept her eyes off him. A clang of the metal lock being thrown back and the door opened. Two men rushed into the room and forced him up against the far wall with just enough room around his neck to draw shallow breaths.

A third man, Kyott, waltzed with an amused and slightly surprised look on his face.

"Well, I'll be damned." He stooped to grip a handful of Caden's hair and drag her to her feet. "You're still alive."

"Walkin' and talkin'." Her voice was carefully pain free and mocking, like she was unimpressed with his torturing abilities.

"Well, let's see if we can't change that."

7

———————

CADEN

aden had been through this same ol' song and dance many times before. Not just as the torturee but also the one doing the torturing, so it went rather like a checklist in her head.

Display an arsenal of clever little torture devices.

Rid victim, aka the asshole stupid enough to get caught in the first place, of torture-hindering apparel.

Bind said asshole.

Attempt to reason.

Torture.

They'd done spectacularly so far.

She'd gotten a good view of the torture devices (a strategically placed set of knives and, hell, she wasn't gonna bitch at their lack of creativity) when she'd been pushed into the room.

Number one, check.

She'd been stripped of her jeans and tied to a chair that was bolted to the floor.

Check and check.

He'd asked her politely and in the best way he knew

how to be reasonable. All he wanted was a location. That was it. There was no need for this mess. If she only told him, then he'd let her go back to her cell. Didn't that sound easy?

Check.

And when that hadn't worked, he'd started cutting into the soft flesh on her inner thighs, always asking the same question.

"Where's the boy?"

She was grunting and growling and focusing on breathing. On inhaling the cold dank air and letting the exhale be her release. Really, physical pain wasn't all that torturous. Sure as fuck hurt, but it was just that, hurt. It really only served to fuel the rage in her belly and put names on death lists. As heart-stoppingly painful as torture was, she could handle it.

And really, it served as a frustratingly demoralizing reminder that she had yet to achieve any kind of progress on the whole 'getting dead' front.

She was bored. Pissed and hurting, but bored all the same. Or maybe *bored* wasn't the correct descriptor. Maybe it was defeated or enraged or couldn't-be-bothered-to-give-a-flying-fuck. One of those or all of those, it didn't matter.

That wasn't to say that getting a knife to the soft flesh of her inner thighs over and over didn't hurt like fuck, but it was now just... just a stall. And she was so fucking sick of the stall.

Here, Caden was in the hands of the man who'd recently suffered the loss of his firstborn. The killer of that little shit-fuck-weasel was sitting right in front of him. He had a knife. He had a gun and he still wasn't killing her.

No, instead he found a reason as to why she, the murderer of his son, should still be breathing.

"Just tell me where the safe house is, Quinn, and it'll stop."

Fucking—fuck!

Caden was trying her damndest to get dead. How fucking hard was that supposed to actually be? How many times had she dodged a well-aimed bullet or deflected a killing blow? How many times had she been on a gurney flat-lining? How many people had she killed, there and breathing one moment and gone the next? It was simple, right? But somehow, a woman that had killed more times than she wanted to count and had practiced dying (the whole dead for two minutes and some odd seconds thing when she was young), couldn't even get this fuck-wad to off her.

It seemed as hard as she tried to get dead the Universe or Aliens or Gods (whoever the fuck was pulling the strings) were trying just as hard to keep her breathing.

It was just... she was done.

First with Nathan, the only good man she knew, getting tossed into her cell. And now with this problem Kyott pulled out of his ass. A problem she, and only she, had the answer to. It was frustrating and disheartening.

Which to any other person on the surface of the planet may have been a flashing neon sign reading, 'Quit your goddamn bitchin' and pointless efforts and get on with your pathetic fucking life!' from said Puppet Master, but to Caden, it was another challenge. Another fight she had to win.

But maybe that wasn't true anymore. Caden was always fighting for something. But now... what the fuck was she fighting for now?

She had nothing left.

"Quinn, pay attention." Kyott brought her back to the

conversation with a deep cut to her underarm. "All you gotta do is tell me where he is and I'll let ya go back to your cell. Hell, maybe I'll even think about hiring ya on."

It took a long moment to find her voice and beat back the waves of white-hot pain smothering her nerve endings.

"You do have a position to fill now, don't ya? Seeing as how Liam's... well, he's not gonna be jumping outta his grave any time soon, is he?"

Her intention was to remind the fuck-wad why she was in the chair and then maybe he'd finally get the job done. But it did not have the effect she was intending. The man only smirked and let out a short incredulous huff like he found her amusing. Apparently not a whole lot of love in the Kyott family.

"Ya got some balls on ya, you know that?" The flat side of the bloody blade hit her cheek a few times. "For a woman who's said to have survived well—fucking *everything*—you don't seem too keen on staying alive."

Well, mother fucking hallelujah, give the man a prize.

"Is that—" He jerked back like he'd been stuck and the knife went with him. "Is that what this is for you, Quinn? You wanna die? That's it, huh?" He gave a sadistic little chuckle and patted her cheek with the knife again. "Well, how 'bout this? You tell me right now where he is and I'll kill ya. As messily or quickly as ya'd like—I'll kill ya."

The 'he' in that sentence was the son of a rather dangerous man she'd worked for six months back. She'd acted as the kid's bodyguard while they moved base camp and again when Harrington decided his son needed a more secure and secret location. The 'he' was eight, named Trevor, and liked Oreos on his pancakes.

"How 'bout it?"

Caden was many things, a killer chief among them.

What she was not, in any way, was a snitch. Especially where a kid was concerned. She did not kill innocents. Sure, there was the random beat down should said innocent come between her and her job but never kill. Despite his parentage, Trevor was an innocent.

It wasn't a big mystery why Kyott was suddenly so interested in Harrington. They were always comparing dick sizes and trying to out evil the other. The fact that Kyott was now going after Trevor either meant Harrington had done something similar or he was making a play for the scum-bag crown.

"What do you think?" She couldn't catch a break.

After a moment of what looked like contemplative concentration, a smirk curled his lip and he moved within head-butt range.

"Wrong answer." With that, he stabbed down, impaling her forearm and then the wooden arm of the chair before leaving it there and turning back towards the table. White hot searing pain jolted up her arm and smothered everything else.

It was moments like those that Caden dearly wished she'd been tossed into a vat of toxic waste at birth; telekinesis would be mighty handy. Unfortunately, Caden was not a mutant, and the knife was not gonna magically unsheathe itself from her arm and plunge into Kyott seven or eight times. So Caden focused on breathing. On drawing breath and letting her exhale be her release.

Inhale.

Exhale.

He turned back around, syringe in his hand, and flicked it a few times, looking rather smug. Caden guessed that it was either some kind of poison or sodium pentathol. Her money was on sodium pentathol though, seeing as how he was interrogating her. Poison wasn't a thing a man like Kyott would spend any kind of time on if there was a gun readily available.

Inhale.

Exhale.

There was a pinch on her neck followed by a cold burn under her skin and the merc bit back a growl; she hated being drugged and the loss of control that came with it. She'd been drugged before, of course, a few times, but only ever twice before with sodium pentothal—the Truth Drug. In Caden's seasoned opinion, it wasn't so much the Truth Drug as the *Talk* Drug. All she had to do was talk and keep talking. It wouldn't take long to infiltrate, considering her body mass and the lack of sustenance in her belly.

Kyott, looking ten shades of pleased with himself, moved back to the table and positioned himself against it so he could watch as the drugs kicked in.

"Oh, here, I'll take that back." He grinned sheepishly and leaned over to pluck the knife out of her forearm.

Inhale.

Exhale.

It took a good five minutes to set in properly, which, by Caden's count, was a whole minute and forty seconds longer than it took the last time some ass-hat had injected her with it. Hell, maybe she was building up a resistance.

Slowly Caden could feel her muscles loosen. The burning pain from all the cuts and slices subside and a sense of ease settled in her head. Like she wasn't being tortured and maybe Kyott wasn't so bad. He was trying to make a living like everyone else.

"How are you feeling, Quinn?"

The all-around pain dimmed to a dull roar in the back of

her mind and allowed Caden to focus on the man in front of her. Yellow flicked in the corner of her eye.

"Oh, you know peachy." Weirder than peachy, though. More like her lips had been rusted shut for a while and Kyott had oiled them to working condition again. Like the Tin Man in that creepy ass movie with the flying monkeys and the floating heads. "Fuck, if those flying monkeys show up, ya'll are on your own. That's like giving wolves wings —'cept wolves don't throw their shit. Oh god, could you imagine? Shit raining from the sky while you're getting dived bombed by ill-intentioned monkeys wearing creepy fucking uniforms? Who thought of that? That's like some twisted Beetle Juice shit right there."

Yellow flickered again and Caden tried to decide what exactly she'd said aloud and what she hadn't. And what the hell was that yellow thing?

"Quinn." Hot hands gripped her face and suddenly she was seeing pores and nose hairs she didn't want to see. "Focus, Caden, I need you to tell me where Trevor Harrington is."

"Focused. I am so focused. Well, maybe not as much as you want me to be, but definitely more focused than that time in Belgrade. No monkeys there, no. They had this guy —who only had one arm—on a unicycle juggling flaming knives. Now *that* is some serious skills. I would *not* want to meet him in a unicycle fight. Shit would get intense real quick and he'd probably skewer me with a flaming machete. But wouldn't that be a way to go? I mean how many death certificates read, 'death by flaming machete lodged in gut whilst fighting a one-armed man on a unicycle'. Not many is my guess."

This was nice. She'd never gotten to tell anyone about the one-armed, unicycling man before.

"Quinn."

"As soon as he was off the stage, though, I was focused. Like laser-focused. Well, okay no. First, I tracked the one-armed guy back to his apartment so I could find him later and have him show me how to unicycle. But after that, I focused." Caden Quinn did have a work ethic after all. Stealing and maiming first and *then* the extracurricular activities. "Completely forgot about that till now. I never actually gotta go back there, either. G-men started popping outta the ground once someone recognized me."

"Where is Trevor Harrington?"

"I don't know. Emotionally, he seemed pretty scared when I left. Though he was doing that brave kid thing, too. Putting on a smile and trying to pretend like his palms weren't sweating. I mean, he didn't have his dad with him and his mom *just* died from a car bomb. That was all nice and protective of Harrington to move his kid, but he was leaving him alone so he wouldn't have to deal with the kid's grief. That's not good parenting."

"No—physically, where is he physically?"

"Umm, I'd say... like a hundred-thirty, hundred fifty—kid's got some girth on him. Comfort eating, and no outside time, plus his genes ain't the best. I mean, you've seen Harrington. You know what I mean." The yellow turned into a head of hair. A yellow set of locks, she somehow knew. "Though he was much less fat when he was younger—more muscle-y. Once he made Bossman, he let himself go. Not a good choice considering his career, though."

"Trevor Harrington, Quinn. Where the fuck is Trevor Harrington!?"

"Ezzy?" The word was like a punch to the jaw. It sent her reeling and grappling for something to hold on to. "Ezzy."

The owner of those yellow locks. It couldn't be her, though. "Ezzy!"

But there she was. Standing in the corner. Her head jerked up at the sound of her name and her blond locks fell over her shoulders. Her cheeks were pink and healthy. Like she wasn't dead and buried. She waved jazz fingers and smiled that smile she used when she was trying to be patient.

"No! Trevor Harrington!" Kyott, not particularly blessed with an overabundance to begin with, lost his patience and slapped her across the face.

Panic set in when she couldn't see Ezzy for the long moment it took her drugged brain to catch up with her eyes. But she blinked away the haze and turned to watch her baby sister stand in the corner, fingers impatiently plucking at her backpack straps, biting at her bottom lip, and making a concentrated effort not to glance down at her watch every few minutes.

Just like she'd done when they were kids.

Caden would be coming off a shift and Ezzy would be waiting in a corner booth, pretending to read or focus on her homework, but was really counting down the minutes. Caden couldn't help but smile at the memory of her impatient sister. Ezzy smiled back. Looking all kinds of alive and ready to get going.

"Quinn, where is the safe house?" He moved back into headbutt range, blocking her view of Ezra. Rage lit in her veins and pushed a half-strangled screech from her throat. The merc took a moment to calmly draw a steadying breath, snap her head forward, and break the bastard's fat nose. He screeched and stumbled back, bringing Ezzy back into focus.

"Fucking," pissed, Kyott returned with a bone-cracking

right hook to her nose, "bitch!" and when that didn't fully satisfy, he brought the knife back into play.

A muffled sort of burning cut into her side this time. It moved to her thighs and then the soft under part of her arms. She had the presence of mind enough to know that the drugs were softening the pain and that they'd hurt like hell if she woke up again, but it didn't matter because there was Ezzy, alive.

Like she wasn't actually six months dead and buried.

She was alive and waiting on Caden's ass to hurry the hell up.

How did she get out of her grave? Caden had watched the coffin lower into the ground. How was she alive? Why was she even fucking questioning it? Ezzy was alive! There had been some horrible mistake—Ezzy wasn't actually dead. She smiled again, and Caden felt her heart sink.

Kyott would see her. He would see her and do terrible, horrible things to her. No, she couldn't let that happen. Caden had never let anything from her dirty world touch her baby sister and she sure as fuck wasn't gonna start now. She had to focus on keeping his attention.

She had to.

Ezzy was right there, all bright-eyed and innocent, sticking out like a sore thumb. But he was turning to trade knives and panic was closing her throat up.

He didn't see her.

She was standing right there, but he didn't see her. Ezzy grinned again. All kinds of triumphant and proud. The same smile she'd broken into when she had successfully lied to a cop or a landlord when they were kids. The same smile she'd worn when she'd gotten her PHD.

"You cunt!" Another slash of white-hot pain, hit to the gut, and he was done. Kyott stormed his way to the door, passing within a foot of her baby sister without seeing her, and screamed at the meatheads standing guard.

"Get her outta here!" Big hands were on her, pulling at her—rough, too rough. It hurt. But her stare stayed on Ezzy. Ezzy the innocent. Ezzy the dead sister. Not the only sister she failed, not the only person to be dead because of her. Caden tried to walk but she was so... tired and couldn't get the message to her feet quick enough to keep up with them.

Pain.

Something hurt. *She* was hurt, right?

Ezzy. Ezzy was hurt or no, not hurt. But she was going to be if Caden didn't get out of her drugged stupor.

She was cold, but her skin was warm. Something was burning her cold skin. Her blood—it was her blood that was burning. She had to snap the fuck out of it.

Ezzy was still there, trailing along behind them, looking like a bright little flower in the middle purgatory. She needed Caden sober.

Caden pushed away the heavy fog, kept her eyes wide, and forced her feet to catch the floor. By the time she found her feet, the big hands were shoving and pushing again. Her face found the cement before she could right herself, but that didn't matter; wasn't like her face could get uglier.

"Ezzy!" She flopped over and almost started balling in relief at the sight of her baby sister standing by the door swinging her arms, a sign that she was getting more impatient by the second.

The burning wasn't so bad anymore. She was cold all over now but maybe that was worse. Her mind was screaming some kind of warning at her, but it didn't matter —nothing fucking mattered. Ezzy was alive.

It was okay. It was gonna be okay. Ezra was alive, and Caden was there to protect her. She'd be okay.

Everything was all right now.

So cold. Cold, but not dead. Not green and pale cold—not dead cold. Not yet. Had Ezra been cold when she died? Had she felt pain? Did the constant mix of drugs dull her death?

No. No.

Ezzy was dead, right?

Caden had held her hand and watched the life leave her big brown eyes. She'd seen her pretty little sister white and green with death. She'd raged at the doctors and screamed and threatened and cried—too young—not fair—she hadn't even lived—she couldn't fail Ezzy too.

No.

Ezzy was dead.

8

NATHAN

Nathan Savage could do many things. Hunting, sewing, dressing combat wounds, he could do the damn mamba, cook a mean bowl of spaghetti, and was more than proficient in a wide array of combat styles.

What he could not do was escape by himself. Not from lack of know-how, but from an inability to leave Caden Quinn behind.

It was sun up now. The sun had been in the sky for a good hour and she still wasn't back.

No—nope. He wasn't gonna think about the merc and all the horrible things they could be doing to her.

He was gonna think about his escape.

And not about the little bits of fabric littering Quinn's half of the cell. A dark blue fabric that, Nathan figured, used to make up her shirt. He would not think about the scum-sucking bastard who'd assaulted her. Quinn had protected herself and killed him. Which was maybe why he liked Caden so much. She was no damsel. Still, though, the thought of some ass-hat knocking her around made him feel all pissed and protective and weird. He didn't like it.

So, instead of dwelling on the weirdness, the ex-special ops soldier focused on the task at hand: finding and utilizing a lock picker. There was not much of anything in the room. Hunks of rock that had been knocked loose from the walls, a rat carcass in the corner with what looked like rat-sized bites out of its middle, the pee bucket, and a puddle of blood that had yet to soak into the stone.

Which meant there was absolutely nothing he could add to his Escape Plan inventory.

An Escape Plan that had yet to actually take a plan-like shape in his head. There was really nothing to it beyond, 'Open Door'. The next step would be figuring out how to actually pick the lock. He could pilot a helicopter and disable all manner of explosive devices, but apparently, breaking out of a tiny room was beyond his capabilities.

Useless, he was fucking useless!

And frustrated.

And anxious.

Scared—scared shitless that she wasn't coming back.

That thought set the man to pacing the ten-by-ten-foot cell again and gnawing on his bottom lip.

They'd taken her hours ago.

Escaping. That's what he needed to concentrate on. He somehow had to get Caden on board with the whole living and escaping thing. She was getting out of this god-forsaken dungeon.

Period.

Nathan would drag her by the ankles, kicking and screaming if he had to.

Maybe he could knock her out and toss her over his shoulder... while he single-handedly took on the guards and all the security measures while simultaneously trying to find an out.

Yeah, *that* was a solid plan.

No, he needed her awake and functioning if they were ever going to make it out alive. She was the brains, or would be the brains of the escape. Not to mention half the brawn. But that would depend on how she fared this new round of torture. Another thought that gnawed at him. The longer they were imprisoned, the harder it was going to be to escape.

But she would survive. Caden Quinn always survived.

Ava Caden Collins, actually. It made him almost giddy to know it. To have all of her names. It was like Christmas.

And well, that was a nice bit of silver lining to all this torture and kidnapping.

The ex-detective in him had already plugged some pieces into the puzzle that was Caden Quinn, but he hadn't really gone over what he'd learned yet. So the man went about organizing it over and over in order to ignore the fact that Caden was not yet back and the sun was climbing higher.

Name: Ava Caden Collins. Another excited chill ran down his spine at the fact that he finally had her real name.

Age: late twenties, early thirties, maybe?

Family: all deceased.

He was almost ninety percent sure she was from the States. Possibly spent some time in foster care. High school dropout. Was fluent in at least three languages that he knew of, plus he was pretty sure she was speaking Russian a day ago. So that made four. Notorious and skilled thief. Hyper-intelligent. It wasn't dumb luck that enabled her to penetrate highly secure facilities and pilfer whatever she wanted.

Now that he had her actual name, he could probably find whatever she thought the government had on her.

At last, heavy footsteps sounded in the stillness. Nathan about jumped out of his skin. It took him two seconds to cross the room, sit against the wall with all his limbs in full display, and splayed his fingers in the air before him. He was the picture of compliance.

Nathan didn't speak Russian, but it wasn't hard to decipher, "stay still or die," what with the guns trained on his head and all. He kept his hands up and tried not to visibly grimace when Quinn's face caught her fall. The gun-toting duo exited as quickly as they entered.

"Anything fatal, Quinn?" She was on her hands and knees, long dark hair dragging on the concrete as she crawled to the far wall.

She didn't have pants on, which was odd 'cause she'd left with a blood-stained pair on her legs. Nathan wouldn't let that implication take hold until he ascertained her state of health. Then he could go batshit crazy.

She reached the wall and flopped against it like she didn't have a bone in her body. She wasn't looking at him. She was mumbling, whispering words he couldn't piece together to form anything intelligible. He couldn't understand her. The sound of broken half-whispered sentences crawled into his ears and under his skin. It prickled all the little hairs on his arms and made his vision blurry.

"Quinn, talk to me!" It came out screechy and panicked, like he regressed a couple of decades and was his awkward pubescent teenage self again.

Her head jerked up at the sound of his voice, like she was just realizing he was in the room. Broken nose; blood tracked down her lips and dripped off her chin.

"Caden... you all right?"

The merc didn't acknowledge that he'd spoken. She kept staring at the wall behind him, dark eyes glazed and unfocused. Fear crept up his spine at the sight of her sprawled, limbs splayed like she wasn't in control of them, and her whole body shivering.

Kyott had done something horrible to her. He'd never seen her so... so affected by the torture before.

The bright morning sun shining through the tiny window did a pretty good job of highlighting every bruise, wound, and cut on her. And there were many, too many. She was red, drenched in red, her own blood. It took a beat for him to process what he was seeing. Dozens of long red lines cut into her skin, all seeping red. Inner thighs, the backs of her calves, and all up and down her arms.

"Holy Christ." Maybe it wasn't as bad as it looked. Maybe they were all surface wounds that would heal easily. "Quinn, are you..."

She was either drugged or so far gone that she was completely out of it. Her eyes were dull and glassy; her breathing was concerningly slow and deep for just getting off the rack. Could be too much blood loss or the effects of some kind of sedative in her system. Nathan was hoping for the latter.

"Ezzy." Focused past his shoulder and smiling that soft smile he'd only seen on her once. "You shouldn't be here."

A slight slur in her words like she was too tired to bother with forming her vowels correctly. Drugged was so much better than bleeding out, not by much, but still it was something to be thankful for. It was a short-lived relief, however.

Drugs plus mercenary add in the torture and a dash of strange surroundings and he had himself a very out-of-it lethal killing machine who wouldn't think twice about dropping him if he made a wrong move.

"Caden, it's me... Nathan Savage." Not even a batted eyelash in his direction. She kept smiling that soft smile at the wall over his shoulder. "I'm gonna try my best to wash out your cuts, all right? We don't want them to get—"

"I'm so tired, Ezzy." She wasn't whispering anymore. Her usually guarded eyes turned desperate and terribly helpless. "I don't... I don't want to... hurt anymore. I can't."

He was witnessing an utterly personal and vulnerable moment. She couldn't defend against him, not with the drugs in control. She couldn't turn away and pretend, like a normal person, that she had something in her eye. Stripped bare of all her emotional and mental defenses, there she was, Caden Quinn.

The broken and defeated version of her anyhow, pleading for someone, someone important to her, to understand why she had given up. Why she was allowing herself to die?

Nathan didn't know what to do. Under any other circumstances, he would have quietly left the room and let her deal with her own shit without the feeling of someone watching over her shoulder. He wanted to retreat to the other side of the room and cover his eyes to grant her some kind of privacy, but he couldn't.

Despite the urge to cover his ears and wait it out, a bigger part of him was furiously engraving all that she was saying into his brain to go over later, burning it into his memory so as not to forget a single syllable. It was a compulsion for him where Caden Quinn was concerned. Any and all information he could get, he would. He was already going to hell, anyway.

Although retreating to his side of the cell and pretending that he wasn't mentally scribing every second of her unguarded confessions was probably the smartest thing to do, at least until the drugs wore off, it was not an option. He wasn't putting such an effort into keeping her alive just so she could die of an infection.

"Caden, I'm gonna have to touch you to clean out your cuts." Oh god, he was going to lose a vital part of his anatomy, he just knew it. "I'm cleaning out your cuts, okay? It's gonna sting, so please try not to take off my head—or anything else, okay?"

"I... buried you..." Her head lolled to the side, and her sliced arms wrapped around her middle. "... all I got are headstones now..."

He didn't know where to start. There were so many cuts on the drugged woman—no, mercenary. It was a very important distinction. A drugged and injured civilian woman was about as lethal as a wet cat. A drugged and injured mercenary was a whole other can of worms; ninja worms trained to kill and would do so at the slightest provocation.

She didn't acknowledge he'd spoken. She was muttering again and staring at the wall like there was someone there. He touched her hand, ready to deflect the inevitable blows, but she didn't even so much as twitch at the contact.

Not good. Caden Quinn avoided physical contact, save for fighting, at all costs. She either hit or retreated.

Even when the cold water touched her skin, she didn't react. Only kept muttering to that spot on the wall. The cuts were deep but clean. She needed stitches for a few, but nothing fatal. It was only when he pushed her shoulder to get a better view of her back did she react.

As soon as his hand hit her ribs, she bolted up, shark eyes slammed into place and the edge of her hand connected with his throat. Gasping and sputtering, Nathan reeled back to avoid more hits. She slid out of his hold.

Knees bent, soulless eyes now focused on him, the threat in her drugged state, she circled him.

"Caden, it's me. It's Nathan." He stood and watched in resignation as she circled him in the tiny room. "Nathan Savage... I'm not gonna hurt you... Caden."

She swooped in and landed a quick jab on his stomach and then just as quickly slipped out of range.

The only thing getting through the haze was the pain and that he was the one delivering it. So Caden, being first and foremost a fighter, would annihilate the threat so she could safely get back to convincing the wall to let her die. Nathan wasn't too keen on getting his ass beat, but he didn't want to fight her and add to her injuries, either.

"Ava, hold on! It's me!" Maybe her real name might get through. "Ava!"

It did.

She stilled for a long moment. Nathan watched as she caved in on herself. Shoulders slumped, head bowed, knees stiff.

"Ava." He'd never seen her look so... so what?

So pathetic and beaten down.

But that only lasted another second before she was snarling, actually snarling, and gnashing her canines like some kind of rabid animal, and charged at him.

"Caden! I'm not gonna hurt you! Stop!" He dodged a cat paw to the chest and a well-aimed kick to his crotch. He forced her back and tried to swerve away from the hand aiming for his throat.

She slid in and jabbed at him again, but Nathan (being less tortured, starved, and not drugged) was, for once, faster. While she was going for his solar plexus, Nathan side-stepped, gripped her wrist, and pulled her flush against his chest.

"No! No! No, no, no, no... no..." The hoarse screams slowly dissolved into whispers.

He tried to be mindful of her back and newly acquired hurts, but it was hard with her working against him.

"Shh, it's gonna be alright Caden... It's gonna be all right." He held tighter as she tried to claw off his back when her elbows and knees proved ineffective against him. "It's gonna be all right." He wasn't lying, just being optimistic. She wasn't the only one that needed to hear it.

"Don't! Don't touch me! No!" She struggled and bit and fought and screamed a silent scream that chilled him to the bone. He continued to talk in a calm, soothing voice and kept his hold firm as she thrashed and bucked to get him off. Eventually, she exhausted all her energy and slumped against him.

Nathan decided against letting her go and instead carefully lowered them both to the hard cement without relinquishing his hold.

A sad thought occurred to him when her bloodshot eyes blinked up at him in confusion—like she hadn't just tried to kill him. He wondered if anybody had ever tried to hold her before, protect her from the world, or tell her that everything was going to be okay. But he remembered the scars, battle scars that were vivid on her skin, and the slightly faded ones far too old and similar to his own to be anything but childhood nightmares. He knew, with a horrible twisting feeling in his gut, that no one ever had.

"Quinny! Go, baby! Run!" A strangled scream that froze the man's blood had him adjusting his hold against her renewed fight. "No! No! You run!" It was a terrified command filled with so much anguish Nathan couldn't begin to imagine what she was seeing in her drugged state.

"No! No!" She started thrashing again and Nathan about

lost her, but he kept her between his arms and watched in horror as tears started streaming down the Hitter's face. "No. No... no no no no... she's just a baby—please no... no..."

Something inside of him broke at the sound of her terror and desperation.

"No no no no..." She was begging. Caden Quinn was begging. "No, no... I'm sorry..." Tears rained down her cheeks and her body jerked in silent sobs.

He only pulled her closer and tried to find comfort in the feel of her heart thumping against his chest. She was alive, at least. Nathan didn't know what kind of hell she was living in her head or even the hell she'd already been through. What he did know was that Caden Quinn always survived. She would survive this as well.

Hell, knowing some of the places she'd been and the things she'd done in her life, Nathan couldn't help but admire the hell out of her. Maybe there was some pity there as well. Pity that he had what she didn't a family and something to live for, but mostly he marveled at the things he did know about her. They all pretty much added up to form one descriptor.

Badass.

She was a badass.

There was really no other explanation for the sobbing woman in his arms.

9

CADEN

Surprisingly enough, it was actually uncommon that Caden found herself jarred awake, adrenaline already pumping, instincts set to kill, and blindly groping her weapon. It was uncommon (though not rare) because Caden was awesome at her job. Which went hand in hand with covering her ass well enough to feel secure in the fact that no one would actually be able to find her in order to kill her in her sleep.

It wasn't rare because Caden didn't live a nine-to-five-pick-up-the-kids-from-the-Y-and-more-toilet-paper-while-you're-in-town type life. What with the professional violence and the frequent grand larceny and all.

What had her going for her opponent's exposed neck and coming to with what felt like a shot of adrenaline to the heart was the feeling of someone big and muscle-bound attacking her. Not just attacking her, but on-fucking-top of her. And shit, she'd already fought off one scum-bag this week. Wasn't there some kind of quota?

Muscles: tense and weak—like she'd lost too much blood. Arms and legs pinned. Fuck.

Weapons: not a damn thing. Double fuck.

But her senses came back to her in full force and she remembered exactly where she was, which wasn't an altogether happy thought, and then recalled who was attacking her.

Or not *attacking* her.

Hugging—it was hugging.

And it was weird.

Nathan Savage had himself wrapped around her body as if he moonlighted as some kind of human blanket. Both of his muscle-y arms were wrapped around her middle and she was smashed face first into a whole lot of torso. Keeping her mouth firmly closed against doing anything... untoward (like maybe licking him), she settled on getting an eye full of his chest hairs and an up close and personal view of a white and fading scar. One of his legs, which now seemed like it was about as big as her whole body, was thrown over hers while the other was wedged under her knees.

The sensation of being held and not pinned was foreign. Disconcerting in all honesty. She wasn't a cuddler by nature and not too big on the whole touchy-feely thing in general. The last person she'd held without the intention of injuring or killing was Ezzy.

Caden kind of liked it.

He was warm and softer than the cement. It felt... nice.

The Hitter hadn't realized how absolutely bone-cold she'd been before Savage had tried to absorb her into him like some kind of freaky alien. Now she was warm and dreading the moment when she'd have to move away from him in pretend disgust. Maybe even get a solid hit in, just to reiterate.

Though why he was holding her in the first place or why she had no recollection of the previous night was cause for some alarm. Judging by the state of her pounding head and the dry scratchiness of her throat and eyes, Caden would have to say it was drugs and more torture. Which was most likely why she couldn't remember shit and probably why Nathan was wrapped around her.

Dread knotted her stomach at the thought of what might have happened in that state. Caden and drugs never mixed well. She could barely consume alcohol without becoming a raving lunatic set on destroying anything and everything in her sights. She had to have attacked him.

Oh god, had she killed him?

The rhythmic thud of his heart and the warm flush of his skin against hers squashed that panic attack before it could sink its teeth into her gut. From what she could see (given that she had very little wiggle room) he looked well enough. A few new dark bruises marred his torso and were those scratches on his side? Christ, she hadn't actually scratched anyone in years and years. Stabbed, kicked, punched, jabbed, and shot—yes, but *not* scratched. What the hell kind of night had it been?

Why her pants were gone was another panic-inducing alarm bell sounding in her mind.

Though she knew without a doubt that he hadn't fucked her while she was out.

She trusted him.

The realization of that fact sent a shock wave through her system. Nathan Savage was a man she trusted. A man she liked. A good man who didn't deserve to be tortured to death with her as a cellmate.

It was at that moment Caden decided she would get the man, who was drooling in her hair and wrapped around her as if she wasn't the villain in their story, out. He was a good man and deserved a good life. She'd get over herself, make a plan, escape these godforsaken dungeons, and get him home to that family he talked so softly about.

She tried to shift out of his hold, but he was heavy. Two hundred and some odd pounds of sleeping muscle was not like juggling kittens. Not that she'd ever juggled kittens, but it sounded easy enough. They weighed like what, an ounce, maybe? Two ounces if it was dead weight. Stood to reason that juggling them would be easy. It wasn't a perfect metaphor but shit, she couldn't think straight with Savage all mashed up against her.

Then the rest of her aching body (not just the bits mashed up against Savage) made themselves known. The migraine exploding out the back of her skull reminded her exactly why she hated being drugged.

Instead of focusing on the drooling ex-agent, she mentally catalogued her hurts and the events leading up to her current state of being.

The last thing she remembered was—what did she remember? She'd told Savage her real name. Which now didn't seem like the best move. He'd wanted to know why she wasn't some accountant's housewife with the picket fence and two-point-five children and... nothing.

She'd been drugged; though she didn't know what exactly they'd pumped into her, she did have a few educated guesses. Given the freshly tortured state of her body, she assumed (and this was being ridiculously laughingly optimistic) that she hadn't given up anything. Physical pain usually didn't break her, but with drugs in the mix, she could never be sure what she'd do.

Her head hurt. It pounded and slammed against her skull like it was trying to get out. Blood was pulsing in her ears, adding to the ache in her head. Her throat was raw and burning, like she'd spent hours screaming.

Had she head-butted granite? Her head was not a third fist, and she had to stop treating it as such—she was gonna go brain dead. The rest of her, brain aside, was in working order. Though every inch of her was throbbing and stinging all at once. She felt crusty and itchy and warm. And dammit, her nose was broken again.

But she was warm, and that kinda made it less horrible. Which was a cringe-worthy thing to admit, but the merc only started making a show of pushing him off when he started to rouse.

"Caden?" He blinked down at her and Caden had to physically restrain herself from the sudden inexplicable urge to reach up, tug his head down, and kiss those pretty, sleep-swollen lips. "Are you... lucid?"

"Yeah." She tried to shove away from his torso, but he didn't let go. "Would you get off me!"

"Here." He was up and setting her up straight before Caden could right herself. "How are you feeling?" His hand was on her forehead before she could get a word out. "You thirsty?"

She didn't actually nod or make any indication whatsoever that she did in fact want the water, but regardless of her silence, the bucket was in her face. She reached for it but stopped when she caught sight of the state of her arms and legs. Underarms, inner thighs, and even her hips were all slashed up.

"I tried to clean 'em up. They aren't fatal—I mean, there's some that need to be stitched, but we have to keep them clean to keep from getting infected." He smiled, but it looked more like a grimace. "Speaking of which, I should look at your back."

"Okay."

He opened his mouth, but then blinked in surprise and shut it again. "You should probably eat first, though."

Caden tried not to feel awkward with his fingers on her back. So she focused her energies on wording the 'Okay, let's ditch this popsicle stand' sentence, so it sounded less like she'd lost something and more like it was a decision she was happy about. But he was done with her back and had moved to the front half of her and it became increasingly difficult to worry over sentence structures when his fingers were on her thighs.

"All right." Screw it, she'd just go for it. "Let's get out of this shit hole."

A startled crooked smile spread on his lips but then just as quickly disappeared when his brows furrowed and his blue eyes turned wary, like he was afraid to hope. Instead of answering, he only bit at his lip and kept on dabbing at the oozing cuts on her flesh. It wouldn't take long—he could only hold out for so long. It had to be burning him up.

Caden schooled her expression, trying very hard not to smirk evilly at the sight of his jaw flexing every few seconds. Like he had to actually bite his tongue to stop his questions from pouring out. Finally, he tossed the rag and settled on the cement in front of her. As soon as he opened his mouth to start the inevitable interrogation, she spoke.

"Can you set my nose?" It was very hard to keep the smirk off her face at the sight of his clenched jaw and the questions burning in his eyes. It was killing him.

"Uh." Big calloused hands hovered over her face for a good sixty seconds. They almost made contact twice before they dropped again to his sides. "I can't."

"Why the hell not?"

"I don't want to hurt you." Like he hadn't tasered her into oblivion countless times before.

"Savage." Was he serious? "How many times have we fought? How many times have you gut-socked me?"

"Yeah, but this is different. Now... you're all broke. I don't want to break you more."

"Are you serious?"

"Caden, look at ya." He gestured at her, making sure to keep from touching her. "A gust of wind could take you out."

Well, now he was exaggerating.

"Ugh." Caden steeled her nerves, raised her hands, and took three quick breaths, and when that didn't spur her into action, she blew out three more. "Shit. Please, Savage, I promise I won't die."

His lips formed a thin grim line, but she could tell he'd relented by the sagging of his shoulders.

"Fine." Warm fingers settled on her cheeks. "On three, okay?"

"Okay." Caden huffed again and pressed her head firmly against the cold wall so she wouldn't puss out and jerk away from him.

"One." Fingers lined up on both sides of her nose.

"Two." Fuck. It would hurt like all hell.

"Ya know what—you can't even tell that it's broken." Fingers still hot on her skin, he grinned down at her. "I mean, you're still hot. Let's not do this."

"Savage." Caden couldn't help the growl in her voice. She couldn't do it herself.

"Fine." Another grimace and then resolve. "Three."

Pressure. A wet-sounding snap. White hot mother-fucking pain engulfing her face.

"Ahhhahahaa!" She tried to grip her face, but his hands were still there. "Son of a mother... fucking-cunt-sucking-donkey-fucking-shit-bag!"

His hands left but came back three seconds later with a

cold wet fabric that was nothing short of holy salvation on her face.

"Thanks." Caden plucked the fabric off her face when the pain subsided and examined it. It was a larger piece of her shirt that had been ripped to shreds.

"Sure." He moved out of her personal bubble and settled on the concrete in front of her once again.

"So you think I'm hot, huh?" She could feel fresh blood trailing over the crusted blood under her nose. Her eye sockets had to be pure black and blue at this point and not an inch on her wasn't bruised or sliced up. Hot didn't quite cover it.

A slow smile pulled at his lips, and he dissolved into laughter when she waggled her eyebrows at him.

"Well, right now you look like a zombie straight out of a bar fight. But somehow you still manage to be attractive."

Well.

Fuck.

What did she say to that?

"Why the sudden change of heart?" The attempt at casual interest was not at all working for him, but it saved Caden from trying to form a reply.

"I don't see Kyott killing me any time soon—turned into a torture fest interrogation of sorts the last couple of go's." She shrugged and tried to push the flare of pain to the back of her mind. "And I can't very well leave a person like you to fend for yourself."

"A person like me?" His lips pursed and his hackles raised. Caden tried to suppress the smirk, pulling at her lips at the sight of him all defensive and riled. "You mean the well-dressed former Special Ops soldier?"

"That's the kind." She couldn't help but smile back at his stupid, contagious grin. "It was Special Ops, huh? SEAL?"

That's what was so familiar about his fighting style. But that bit of information did nothing to help her understand how he went from soldier to desk jockey in a completely separate part of the government.

"Hooyah." He chucked his arm in the air and smirked at her.

"I don't understand that transition... did you get injured?" She watched his expression morph into one of exhausted guilt. He opened his mouth, closed it, and then opened it again.

"No, nothing like that... I couldn't... do it anymore. The things that we were doing—the things that I did—it was too gray area." He sighed and rubbed at his face.

That was something Caden could understand. Or, then again, maybe she couldn't. Despite the big ol' gray areas that all but blotted out the map of her life, Caden didn't suffer the same moral compunctions as the ex-soldier.

Sure, she felt guilt; it knifed at her gut whenever she found herself in some dark, lonely corner of the world. And then there were the nightmares of all the things she'd done that ate away at her soul. But that wasn't the same thing as removing herself from the situation entirely like he'd done. She'd actually done the opposite.

There was nothing Caden had long since proved she wouldn't do for family.

"Bringing thieves like yourself," he paused for dramatic effect or to smile at her again, she wasn't sure which. "to justice... well, there was really no gray area."

But he'd quit that too. Caden forced herself to shut up and stay on target. Swapping backstories and braiding each other's hair wasn't gonna get them anywhere. She needed to focus on coming up with some kind of escape plan that had him at least walking out alive and not on the Lifetime movie special that was Savage.

"What were you doing in—"

"Nope—no more little heart to hearts," Caden cut him off and ignored her hypocrisy.

"So you get to ask all the questions?"

A hypocrite was, by leaps and bounds, not the worst thing she'd been accused of being. She could deal.

"Yup—if and when I get your ass out of here, we will go our separate ways. You don't know me and I don't know you. Comprenday?"

His lips formed a thin mutinous line, but Caden glared with all her glaring might, which was a considerable amount taking into account people's reactions upon getting up close and personal with it. He eventually sighed and folded his hands in his lap.

"All right, so what's the secret? How did you escape Marskib?"

The merc blanked her expression out of reflex, barely suppressed a shudder, and then promptly locked down that madhouse before it really got away from her and released all her pent-up crazy.

Usually, just the man's name didn't conjure up long-buried memories of all the things that had been done in those dungeons, but she figured the torture was wearing on her.

"That was a trial an' error run. With a whole lotta error." Nonchalance was key in hiding weak spots and, happily, it was something she'd perfected over the years. "But I eventually escaped."

There were a lot of things Caden was scared of: getting a limb chopped off, airplanes, small talk, old people, contracting some rare disease, and normal people—maybe *people* in general.

What terrified the living hell out of her like nothing else did or could was Marskib. Definitely something to be dealt with later (preferably in the dark, under covers, and gripping her favorite knife) and not in front of Nathan holds-a-drugged-and-lethal-mercenary-like-she's-an-actual-person-and-not-a-killing-machine-oh-and-look-at-my-perfect-ass Savage.

"All right so, the two golden rules of escaping are: accurate mental lists of everything—times, protocols, guards names anything you can get. Second: know the terrain, building layout, and all the little toys they've got to keep us in here." She watched Nathan take it in like he was engraving it on his skull. "They've got the home team advantage. You see any CCTV on your way in and out?"

"No." He shook his head.

"Me either. No video surveillance means more manpower as well as more guns. This isn't an actual prison —more like a half-assed upgraded hospital. Kyott's too small a fish to be getting all land grabby yet. So he's renting our room, which is both good and bad 'cause the flunkies running this chop shop aren't gonna be focused on us. Plus, we've got their patterns, times, and routines down. Which makes Kyott the wild card. We don't want him waltzin' into an empty cell and having them gun us down before we get any kind of mileage."

"So, fast and stealthy, then?" He quirked an eyebrow and nudged the water bucket at her again.

"That's what I'm thinking. Usually want to avoid direct confrontation but... well, it's either die by torture and thereby infection or die fighting. And you seem like the die-fighting type." She'd thought that'd sound a lot less corny out loud.

"A trait we share." He smiled that crooked smile at her, and Caden couldn't help roll her eyes and violently obliterate the butterflies in her stomach.

Fucking *butterflies*!

Like she was some kind of teenager with all that hormone imbalance and pent-up sexual frustration.

It didn't take all that long to plan. Their options were few and far between. It took maybe ten minutes in all to plan, two minutes to cringe over, and maybe sixty seconds to get over and focus on the point zero one percent chance of success. At least it was something. Which, unfortunately, left a whole lot of time for Nathan to do his talking thing.

"So, can I ask you a question?"

"Savage—no more little heart-to-hearts—I believe I already covered that bit. Me and you, we are not friends. So the conversation topics are restricted to: weather, rats, and escaping."

"Ahh!" He actually flinched back and looked hurt. "We —me and you," he mimicked her hand movement and raised his voice a few octaves, "we are friends."

"How do you figure?" What exactly went on in that weird brain of his? Was everything cupcakes and rainbows?

They were not friends. They were cellmates, plain and simple. Any affection he was feeling towards her was because they'd been forced to... coincide over the same emotion-heavy adrenaline-filled experience. And vice versa. Right?

"Caden, you told me your real name." Like that was some kind of stepping stone. "And you have mine. I like you. You like my abs."

"They are your best feature." Caden refused to blush at having been caught staring again. Damn it.

"Next to my intelligence and sparkling personality, you mean?" Curling his arm and flexing his stomach, he quirked an eyebrow. "Right?" Oy.

"Yeah, definitely what I meant." She couldn't help but smile when he chuckled.

"You know about my six brothers. I know the story behind one of your scars. *We* are friends."

"Whatever." Because she could think of nothing to say in rebuff, Caden scowled at the giant and frantically tried to rack her brain for the reasons that they were not friends. There were reasons. Good, legitimate, logical reasons. What the hell were they? "Shut up."

It was then that the former soldier smiled like he'd won the lottery, which did funny, fluttery things to the Mercenary's stomach. So Caden decided the best possible defense was to ignore him and pretend to sleep.

Fucking butterflies!

10

NATHAN

"Can I ask you a question?" Considering how perilously close Nathan was to squealing and clapping his hands together like an excitable preteen, the squeak in his voice was forgivable. He was trying very hard to keep it casual, so maybe she could overlook the personal nature of most of his questions and answer.

"Shut up, Savage." She huffed and finally decided to stop pretending to sleep.

Sure, the actual plan of escape wasn't all that... reasonable in the whole 'staying alive' scheme of things, but at least it was something. What actually had him repressing his squeals of glee and going for the more manly and acceptable nod of approval was the fact that Caden Quinn now had two feet firmly on the right side of the veil.

It was like... hell, he didn't have a proper comparison for the swirling sense of relief and victory in his chest. She'd quit her kamikaze nose dive and was set on escaping.

"Come on—it ain't gonna be that personal." Try as he might (okay, so he didn't at all) to swallow all the questions burning his tongue, he just couldn't keep quiet. If there was even the slightest chance that he'd get any kind of info on her, he would. She flopped an arm over her eyes and then hissed as her cuts pulled, but otherwise ignored him.

"Okay, how about a trade?" Nathan watched her lips purse and couldn't help but wet his own.

"What is it you think that I want from you?" She lifted her arm and narrowed her eyes at him.

"I'm sure there is something you want to know about me, or my job, or how I keep this body so delectable." He tried for a sinuous hand glide down his front but hit his bruised side and tried not to visibly wince. She only rolled her eyes at him. There was something. She was biting at her lip and looking even more apprehensive of him—like she was trying to figure out why the hell he cared so much. "So how 'bout it? An answer for an answer."

She mulled it over, chapped bottom lip under her teeth.

Damn it, he was fixating. She was gonna notice and then get all uncomfortable and defensive around him. The man focused on her hands instead. Dry, bruised, and scraped knuckles. Raw wrists. Busted fingernails. Red crusted in the tiny crevices in her hands. They moved out of his line of sight and pushed her upright.

"Okay." She sat forward. "What's she like?"

"Who?"

"Your mother." Her eyebrows arched up, and she eyed him as if he was slow. Like, who else in the world could she possibly be talking about? "Your adopted mom."

"My mama?" Nathan blinked and paused to glance down at her face, half in surprise and half in suspicion that he was being mocked.

"Ya know, your southern drawl gets really pronounced

when you're surprised." Another half-smile that didn't reach her eyes pulled at the corner of her mouth.

"I don't know..." Nathan shrugged and tried to figure out where the hell that came from. "She's a mom, ya know?"

He'd expected a question about busts or other thieves—hell, even something more about his Special Ops days. Not questions about his mother.

"No."

Surprise kept him quiet for a long moment.

"You don't have a mom?"

"I..." Her voice was hesitant and after a moment, she let out a resigned grunt and continued. "I think she either split or died before I was old enough to remember her. My dad never said anything about her—other than that she was a whore, of course."

"Oh." Nathan absorbed that and tried to fit it in with the short and vague history of this woman. "You didn't ask about her?"

"You didn't purposefully draw attention to yourself in my family." Her voice turned grim. "So no."

"Why not?" The old scars, the ones under all the others, on her back and neck and arms popped into his head and suddenly he understood why she wanted to know.

"Are these your questions, Savage?" She let out a pointed huff and wrapped her arms around herself.

"Oh, no. Sorry—I—my mom. She's—" How did he explain his mother? "She is the mother of seven boys—no girls, all boys. Adopted us all, her and my dad couldn't have kids, so they did foster care and adopted. And we were hellions." God, they were the worst kids. "She is always doing something—yelling mostly, cooking—though we'd beg her not to. But even her cooking is better than three weeks in the middle of nowhere on nothin' but water and MREs."

It was really ridiculous how horrible his mother was in the kitchen. It was like she didn't have taste buds and lost her concept of time when she put something in the oven. They'd actually developed a system that involved plastic bags tucked into jeans and frequent visits to the bathroom and then raiding the kitchen for snacks when they were supposed to have been sleeping.

"Our complaining got so bad when we were little that Bobby, my adopted dad, took a bunch of cooking classes—he still does, actually. They were supposed to take them together, but Ellen refused to take 'em." That dark thing that was so hard and impenetrable in her eyes melted and she seemed almost warm. "She said that Bobby had been living with her cooking for years and he was still alive, so it couldn't be as bad as we were making out. But Bobby's the designated cook now and everyone's much happier."

Hell, he'd talk about his mama all day if she was going to be all human about it and not the hollowed-eyed robot that was her default response.

"It was always a controlled chaos at home when we were kids—still is, really. She is always in motion... she's tough, bossy, loud, and stubborn. And god help ya if you forget your manners."

"She's sounds... nice." A small smile pulled at the corner of her lips.

"I don't know if *nice* is the proper adjective for her, but she's something." He grinned at her and she smiled back, looking... wistful. It kind of killed him.

"How many questions do I get?" What he wouldn't give for mind powers. How many times had he pressed into the back of his closet or hid under his bed and fervently believed that he'd had the ability to turn invisible when he was a kid? Now he'd give his right arm to read the Hitter's mind.

"Is that one of your questions?" Her eyes narrowed and instantly cooled again.

"I just needa gauge what I should ask."

"Damn, Savage—there ain't that much to know about me! There's gotta be something wrong with you—no one in the world asks as many questions as you! Is it some kind of compulsion you've got no control over?"

"Is that one of your questions?" So it wasn't exactly mature to mimic her, but he was starting to feel a bit defensive.

"No."

"How many?"

"A few." She huffed at him, looking almost as annoyed as he was.

"As in two, three, four...?" It was like pulling teeth trying to get anything out of her.

"A few,"she growled and shoved to her feet.

"What are you—do you need help?"

"I swear to god Savage, I'm gonna bust your kneecaps if you keep doing that." Scowling, she gingerly tested each limb.

"Doing what?"

"That—that—that good ol' boy scout let's help this woman across the street and rescue fucking puppies *thing* that you do!"

"You mean trying to help you to your feet?" Was she insane?

"Yes, I am not a quadriplegic—I can get to my own goddamn feet without your help." Slowly, as if testing her limits, she moved one arm at a time until they were both over her head. It was at that point the ex-special ops soldier's brain turned to liquid and poured out his ears.

She stretched for a full minute and Nathan had a hard time remembering just where the hell he was and why it was so imperative for them to leave. So it was doubly easy for him to forget about how incredibly annoying and frustrating the woman was.

And holy Christ, why was it now that he was zeroing in on the fact that she was indeed a woman?

Usually, her ten-foot-tall-grenade-munchin'-assassin swagger and the body armor she wore pulling jobs and going into combat hid it. But clad in only his tattered t-shirt and purple panties, he could see every feminine curve.

There had to be something wrong with him. She was all kinds of tortured and beaten and there he was, getting hard just watching her stretch.

So Nathan did the only thing he could do in defense: flopped onto his back, stared at the ceiling, and thought of how unsettling and creepy small children were. And how unpleasant electrocution felt. And that one time his dad had worn a speedo to the beach. And when that wasn't working, he dug deeper and thought of combat, firefights, good men dying, and the smell of burning flesh. Absolutely anything other than how Caden Quinn's long legs would feel wrapped around him—or straddling him.

Holy hell. He had to pull it together.

Questions—he was supposed to be asking a question. It was a onetime offer that he wasn't gonna waste. Somehow, understanding how she stole a statue was no longer at the top of his list. There were so many he was burning to ask.

Like, where did she come from? Asking about her childhood would most likely incite some kind of violence. What had she been doing in Oregon? He'd had his suspicions, but he needed them confirmed. Who the hell had failed to slit her throat—was it even a combat wound—how had she survived that? Who was Ezzy? What was that horrible nightmare that made her, the inhumanly stoic mercenary, cry and beg?

All of which were personal questions, and she'd either respond by sucker-punching him or ignoring him altogether. Although she'd asked about his mother so maybe he could assume that she'd be up for answering family-related ones as well.

Under control now, Nathan turned to watch as the woman moved to the far side of the cell, by the half-eaten rat, and breathed deeply for a bit. Without opening her eyes, she moved slowly and deliberately: block, duck, hit, dodge, hit. Katas, she was going through routine martial arts moves. She repeated it twice, faster each time, before it finally struck home for him.

She wasn't the innocent little civilian woman turned mercenary that he'd assumed for years now. Holy hell, because she was a woman, he hadn't even thought to entertain the notion. How many times had he simply brushed aside or ignored the obvious? Mentally, the man connected the dots and then resisted the urge to kick his own ass.

First: because, well, it was physically impossible and being all drama queen about it wasn't going to change anything.

Second: there was that time in Greece and then Syria and hell, even that time on the borders of Canada. But Christ, why the hell hadn't he even caught on in Syria?

He'd caught up to her in Syria, was waiting on the other side of the window for her when she emerged, winnings in hand, and arrested her for the third time. He hadn't had time to report in before a car bomb (unhappy civilians protesting their government's rule via homemade bombs and Molotov cocktails) went off. She'd been barking out orders left and right and making barricades while he'd laid there with half the car door sticking out of his leg. They'd made it out okay, but the newbie agent she'd been hand-cuffed to did not. By the time the full-out civilians versus soldiers mayhem moved streets, she'd escaped.

"Where did you receive your training?" Attempting to swallow that pill, the one where he'd blatantly ignored the obvious for—hell, how many years? He wanted to know under which flag she'd served. Maybe Israel?

"The United States Military." Her lips pulled into a grim line and she moved faster in her routine.

"What?" And Savage was once again shocked by the mercenary. "How do we have nothing on you, then? I don't..."

"I spent a couple of years in the army before I got snatched up by CIA Black OPS. Spent five years as a govern-ment-sanctioned attack dog. Five years doing all kinds of... wet work for god and country. One of our missions went to hell; we were set up from the start. Didn't have a fucking chance in hell. And then you know how it goes. Big Brother denies any involvement and either scrubs you from the database or names you a rogue agent." She'd stopped moving and just stared at the wall beside his head, eyes glazed, reliving the horror.

"Someone in management sold us out. We... my team—everyone was slaughtered. They blew us up first; I took five pieces of shrapnel to the heart and back, and then they moved in to deliver headshots to anyone still breathin'. Garth, he'd had his leg blown off—blood was spurting everywhere, and little bits of his leg were dangling. He couldn't fucking walk, let alone crawl. But he somehow got to me and shoved me over the bridge. He was always doin' shit like that... always putting everybody's life before his own. He was my team leader... he was a good man. They all were."

Once again, Nathan was awe-struck by the amount of sheer *fight* she had. No matter what she faced or how dead she was supposed to be, the woman always came out on top. Nathan felt a swell of pride at that thought and then promptly shook himself.

Admiration, yes, he could understand. All you had to do was meet the woman to feel awe. But pride was something he shouldn't be feeling when it came to Quinn. She wasn't his family or a colleague. The man should not be feeling pride at the thought of the things his woman had done and survived doing. Because she wasn't his woman. She'd probably beat the living hell out of him if he ever let that thought slip.

But Nathan did not lie to himself; it was an integral part of what made him so adaptable. So he laid it out quite clearly in his mind. Sure, he was attracted physically to the woman—who the hell wouldn't be? But he liked, he realized with a degree of surprise that was almost unsettling, her as a human being. Always had. Damn, it was impossible not to like her.

She was tough with all kinds of sharp angles and could probably kill him with a flick of her pinkie finger. Which maybe would have put off another man, but it seemed to have the reverse effect on him. She was funny, even if she didn't realize it, and quick-witted. The level of intelligence she possessed was equal parts intimidating and thrilling. Her fight, though, the thing that made her Caden Quinn through and through, was probably what clinched it for him.

"Woke up on the shore later being operated on by this in-fucking-sane—fuck, I don't even know what he is. He claims he's got a PHD and was a surgeon, but he also has an invisible friend named Marty and lives in a cave to keep the aliens from finding him... so who knows? I eventually got out of that mother fucking jungle."

He didn't just *like* her. Hell, he was half in love with her. He'd always been half in love with her. Maybe it was when she'd hit him with the car, or the first time she grinned at him with that 'come and get it' look. Maybe there was no *half* about it.

"I'm sorry about your team." Nathan knew firsthand all about betrayal and death.

"Me too." Her face twisted into cynical angry lines; her lips curled and her chin jutted out like she was resisting the urge to speak. "You know what the real kicker was, though? After he slaughtered my team... he informed the families— my sister that we'd fallen in combat. Not MIA or even rogue, just dead." Rage crawled into her voice. "Do you know what dead does to people? I was too late—she'd already—fucking dead—like I'd failed—like I didn't keep my promise."

"What did she do?" He was pretty sure they were talking about Ezra or Quinny. From what he'd gathered, both were dead and he could probably guess what her sister had done after being told of Caden's death.

"Tried to kill herself."

Tried. As in, she tried but didn't succeed. And hell, it seemed suicide was a Collins family motto. Did none of them have anything to live for outside of each other?

"So, does that mean—is she still alive?" Maybe he'd misinterpreted. Maybe there was actually something in her life that wasn't tragic and horrible.

"No."An empty laugh that had his skin crawling burst

from her lips. "Think I'd be here if she was still... She found out she had cancer during the same visit. Breast cancer. I came home and there she was, wrists all bandaged and cuffed to the bed like some kinda... Breast cancer. I mean, after everything thing she's been through, after everything she's survived—how is it fair that she gets—" Rage melted away and she was back to being nothing more than a sack of organs that somehow still functioned. "She fought it for a while, a few years. She'd be in the clear for a few months, but it always came back. She... I buried her six months ago."

"I'm sorry." Nathan could say nothing to make it better, so he didn't try. He couldn't fathom losing one of his brothers. He understood the dangers of each of their jobs and knew there was a possibility that any one of them might not make it home, but still, it was a foreign concept that he did not want to even consider.

But to have to watch as one of them withered with cancer. To watch for years as they fought and fought, only to lose and die before their time. Before they could make fun of each other for going gray and getting wrinkles and pot bellies.

"She's dead." Something in her voice jerked his attention back to her. She all but fell to the ground. "She died. I haven't told anyone—there was no one to tell. I was holding her hand. Promising her that she wasn't gonna die—that I would make the doctors fix her. She's dead."

Like she hadn't accepted it before. Like she hadn't let the truth of it touch her. Like she'd been on autopilot for six months and her mind was just catching up with the rest of her.

She sat still for a long while and just stared at the cement below her. Nathan wanted to hug her or maybe just hold her hand, but he knew she'd attack him if he tried to touch her. So he did the only thing he could. Nathan scooted on his ass until he was right beside the mercenary, shoulders almost touching, and waited. She tensed beside him, but when he made no move to touch her, she relaxed.

"She was four when her mama tossed her at our doorstep." After a long minute, she curled her fists and lifted her head. "She was always so smart. I mean, Quinny was the brave one and Ezzy was the genius. She could read and count money by the time she was four—I shit you not. If I was too beat to move, she'd swoop in, at age four, make dinner, put Quinny to bed—pay the damn bills even. Honor Roll every year, all top marks and honor classes. She graduated at fourteen and got scholarships. She had just broken up with her boyfriend when..."

"She sounds nice." What could he say to a heartbroken sister that could make it hurt less? Nothing. "I'm sorry for your loss."

"She was nice," Caden acknowledged and shot him a grin and then slid back the barest inch as if just realizing he was all but on her. She shifted awkwardly and cleared her throat. "It's about time for 'em to come."

Nodding, the man gave her space and moved to the other side of the tiny room. Mentally stowing all the sudden realizations and the Quinn backstory for later, Nathan stretched his limbs for a bit. He had to focus. They were going to get out and then he'd be able to put his full attention on wooing. Or maybe he should just drag her to his home and let his mother at her.

"See, this is the part I don't understand." Nathan felt the need to express some kind of distaste as he positioned himself on the concrete.

"What don't you understand? Lie there and convulse.

Try to work up a froth." She frowned at him and stood straight.

"What are you gonna say? I mean, I understand that you're a woman and therefore seem like the lesser threat, but how the hell are you gonna get them to come in? As appealing as your feminine wiles are—don't you think they would come in earlier if they were going to come in at all?"

If it went the way she'd predicted, Caden, being the more injured and handicapped of the two, would be the one taking all the risk. Which made absolutely *perfect* sense to Nathan.

"It doesn't matter what I say—all that matters is how I say it and what language I say it in." Caden turned to grin at him from her position at the door. "And hope to hell they aren't Irish."

"You speak Gaelic?" Was there anything she couldn't do?

"Eh," she shrugged and then grimaced at the movement. "Enough to get by. I can ask where the bathrooms and sand-wiches are."

"Ya know, Quinn, you're kinda amazing."

She cocked her head, smiled, and shrugged her shoulders like she was conceding the point. Two sets of boots sounded in the hallway, right on time. Nathan watched as she pivoted, stuck her face in the square cut into the solid metal door, and promptly turned into a quivering mess of snot, tears, and sniffling.

It was a soft and scared voice he'd never expect to come out of her mouth. She sounded delicate and fragile and very much like a damsel in distress

Nathan did his part by working up a good froth and letting it drool down his chin while he jerked and shook and won a fucking Oscar in seizing. He'd wanted to play the part as already dead, but Caden had insisted saying there was a difference between already dead and getting there.

Nathan kept on seizing as they yelled at the helpless woman.

He couldn't see her as it was but she was still doing a very convincing freaked out woman.

"Do you speak English?" A heavy Russian accent sounded over her fake sobs.

Caden didn't answer in any language he could understand. She just kept repeating the same phrase over and over.

"Back away." Metal creaked on metal and adrenaline spiked in his system. She'd done it. Nathan would have smiled if he wasn't foaming at the mouth and trying to convince the slop dealer and his guard that he was dying.

Cold metal nudged his side. He kept on convulsing. A steel-toed boot kicked him. Nathan could see the man's face when he leaned over to peer at him. "Can you speak?"

Nathan shot up, shoved the barrel of the AK-47 aside (so as to avoid getting gut shot), and jerked it out of the man's hold. The guard reeled back, tried to regain his balance, and threw a clumsy fist at Nathan's neck. Nathan blocked the blow with his forearm and sent a right hook to connect with the man's jaw. It was a solid hit, but he must have had a reinforced jaw because the man didn't go down; he just kinda stumbled around for a bit. So Nathan helped him to the ground by aiming a kick at his kneecap. It crunched under his bare heel and the man let out a pained screech before he collapsed.

"Wait!" Caden was at his side, gripping his arm. "He called it in." She bent to retrieve the AK-47 and pointed it at the moaning man's head. She said something threatening in Russian.

Nathan wasn't sure what that meant, but he could connect the dots. Something about calling it in and a time frame to do it in.

"Odin." One.

The guard did some especially pathetic groaning and bleeding, but otherwise remained still.

"Dva." Two.

Shaking his head, he started sputtering and looking terrified.

"Tri." Three.

"Okay—friend—okay?" He held up his hands and nodded his head like it could save his life. "Friend. Please, do not kill me. Okay? Friend. Okay?"

He kept on nodding, took a deep breath, and called it in. As soon as he was done, his hands went back up and Caden bashed him in the temple with the butt of his own gun.

Both were big men. One man, however, had some girth on him so Nathan got to stripping him of his dirty jeans, weird sweater vest thing, and his shoes. Christ, it would feel so nice to wear things like socks and shoes again.

"You think these will fit you?" She tugged off the unconscious man's boot and chucked it in his direction. "They sure as hell ain't gonna fit me."

Step one: get clothes and weapons. Check.

Step two: stealth it out and hope no one is the wiser.

Not a real rock-solid plan, but it was the only one they had. Suited up and armed, they started for the door.

"Wait," Caden halted abruptly, and Nathan had to move left to avoid plowing her over.

"What?" He breathed, trying to listen for the approaching threat, but all he could hear was the steady beat of his heart in his ears.

The Hitter whirled around, got on her toes, gripped a

handful of his hair, and dragged his head down to kiss him full on the mouth. Nathan froze in shock, but that quickly dissolved when her teeth nipped at his lip and she fisted his hair.

The torture, escaping, men with guns, rats—it all melted away and a fire lit in his gut. It was hot and hard. There was no gentle and sweet with Caden. Dazedly, Nathan wondered where the gun that had been in his hand went but that didn't matter because her tongue was in his mouth lighting a fire that went straight to his dick.

She pulled away first, panting and grinning up at him like she was privy to some secret.

"You can put me down now."

Nathan was surprised to realize that he had her shoved up against the wall with his knee between her thighs. Apparently, he had no control or presence of mind when it came to Caden.

Guilt ate at him; here he was, losing control and shoving her around like she hadn't been beaten and cut and whipped within an inch of death. Taking deep breaths to calm himself, the former soldier removed his hands from her body and reluctantly set her back on her feet.

Caden Quinn had just initiated physical contact. Initiated *intimate* physical contact. With *him*.

There was a god.

Unwilling to be the one to break contact first, Nathan stayed where he was (which was all up close and in her personal bubble) and cocked an eyebrow at her.

She only shrugged, "Just in case," and pushed past him.

That brought reality right back, like a punch in the face.

11

CADEN

"Would you stop fucking grinning!" Every time she glanced sideways at him, he was smiling that crooked 'pleased-with-himself-I'm-so-hot-and-look-at-these-great-abs' smile. It took a concentrated effort on her part to keep her own lips in a firm line.

They were strolling down the halls of the hospital-turned-makeshift prison, waltzing into an almost certain doom, and there he was, grinning like they were skipping down the rainbow bridge headed for Middle Earth.

Or no, she was getting her Hobbits and Norse gods mixed up, but it was understandable seeing as how high school had been a long time ago, and even then she barely even attended before she'd dropped out. The point was, he had to stop grinning like an idiot. It was doing weird things to her stomach, weird fluttery things she refused to acknowledge as butterflies—because they weren't fucking butterflies.

"What?" He only smiled wider as his eyes strayed down to her lips.

"You know *what*. Stop!" She mentally shook herself,

about-faced, and strode further down the hall before she gave into the insane urge to kiss him again.

The first part of the plan had gone off without a hitch. Now they only had to make it outside, commandeer a vehicle, and drive off into the sunset. All the while remaining undetected and hoping like hell a firefight didn't break out because they were woefully outnumbered and laughably outgunned.

"Do you like Mexican food?" He caught up in two strides and was once again at her elbow, still grinning. Caden decided her best defense was to not look at him and concentrate on the escape at hand.

Savage had the AK-47 slung over his shoulder. An automatic that was unreliable, at best, taking into consideration the frequent jamming of the model. The smaller handgun she'd pilfered off the guard only had one extra clip, good for close range, and that was about it. She kept that tucked into her baggy jeans. The pen knife she found on the bigger man's body was in her left hand and making her all kinds of wistful for her own weapons.

"I can't even look at a burrito without getting queasy—not since that mishap in Mexico." Maybe 'mishap' wasn't the right word for the six months she'd spent in the sweltering heat that was the Yuma, and the scant seven minutes it took for it all to go to hell.

"How 'bout Italian?"

Briefly, she entertained the possibility of her captors having her gear. And shit, if she was going to go down that road, maybe they'd even catch themselves a leprechaun. It was using its magical rainbow abilities to clean the assortment of knives and guns she kept on her person when she wasn't imprisoned. Wasn't that a nice thought? Maybe she'd get a unicorn with built-in GPS, too.

Drugs left over from the last torture session had to be the reason she was feeling all light-headed and weirdly giddy. Or maybe Savage just brought out her whimsical rainbows and fucking daisies side.

In any case, it was not her current captors who had her weapons. It was the shit-buckets who'd sold her in the first place. They would have already either pawned them off or pocketed them. Not an altogether pleasant thought. In fact, it was kind of sickening. Her Karambit was most likely being used as a nail file in the sweaty fist of some idiot who didn't know his ass from his hat.

"Eh?" Discomfited at the proximity of the man and the way his heat was soaking into her skin, she shuffled to the left and tried not to scowl. "Sure."

A door opened up at the end of the hall. A short, uniformed man stepped out. They'd passed a few already, but the others had been too occupied in conversation or on their phones to notice. This guy was a loner and already glancing down the hallway at them.

"Do you like dancing?" Nathan leaned over and got all up in her personal bubble again with his body heat and his intense stare.

It was unnerving and frustrating.

The man at the end of the hall zipped up his fly and started towards them.

They were in a situation and he was busy picking out curtains and naming their nonexistent children.

"Savage." Caden made sure to keep her face pleasant and her tone light—the man was three feet from them now and squinting as if he was trying to place their faces. Fuck. "Focus."

"I'm multitasking." Lopsided grin on megawatt, he lunged, with more grace than a man of his size should have, clipped the side of the guard's head, and the man was down for the count.

Boxing one-o-one: hit them hard on a pressure point, the blood flow to the brain is momentarily cut off, and the body responds by shutting down.

"What are you doing!?" Caden resisted the urge to swat the annoying ex-agent upside the head. "Now we have to hide another fucking body!"

For a second, the mercenary was struck by her own words and just how incredibly... standard they were. How much different would her life be if she never had to say those words? It was a normal occurrence for her to be standing over a body looking for a nook or cranny to stuff it into, but did other people—normal people—have to hide bodies or ever voice that sentence? Probably not.

"I'm getting you shoes." He shoved the body over and started tugging off his laced-up combat boots. "He's small, like you, so I figured..."

"I'm not small," was all Caden could work up in response, seeing as how all her mental efforts were focused on battling the sheen of tears that'd sprung up in her eyes.

What the actual fuck?

The fact that he took out some random asshole to get her shoes should not be making her all emotional and crazy. What the hell was wrong with her?

Lack of sleep and malnutrition.

That's what it was.

"You are small. Small and lethal—and sexy as hell." He was grinning again and holding out the combat boots.

"Would you stop—you're just embarrassing yourself." Caden tried hard not to smile at the giant, but it was difficult when he was smirking at her and trying to be all charming.

"Ya know." The boots were a wee bit too big for her, but

they'd work. "I'm starting to think I was wrong about this being a prison." It almost felt weird to wear shoes again.

"I'm starting to think so, too." Nathan was frowning and staring down at the body, now bound, gagged, and stuffed in the bathroom he'd come out of.

Everything she'd predicted so far was off. They'd been on two floors now and there was the random guard or two. They'd found no holding cells or even rooms that remotely resembled the one they'd been in. Then there was the lack of torture sounds coming from other jailees. Which only led to the assumption that there were no other prisoners.

She had been right about the CCTV, though. The concerning thing about that was there were no patrols to make up for it. Sure, they'd passed the odd guard or two, but they hadn't looked like they'd been actually guarding.

"All right, fuck, let's go." There was no turning back now, and she was sure as hell getting Savage out.

Another flight of stairs and two corridors later, they finally found an out. Double doors with big square windows cut into them that shone in the sunlight like the holy fucking grail. Between them and the doors were guards. There were three of them, standing around a computer laughing at something on the screen. They were all wearing the same thing, all armed, and all looked capable.

"Okay." Caden stepped back into the stairwell. "I say we try walking right past 'em. Hell, they probably won't even look up."

"I think." His face was torn between concentrating on the making of a plan and his mounting concern for her well-being. Caden could see the internal war he was waging with himself whenever she breathed too shallowly or leaned too far over for his liking. She tried to suck it up and blank her expression so the man wouldn't throw her over his shoulder and try to escape all by himself. "Okay, how 'bout you stay here and I'll take care of it?"

"Pfft." Was he joking? "And how exactly are you gonna take care of it? You don't speak the language and you have no money to do any kind of bribing. I mean sexual favors, maybe, but I can hardly see you getting on your knees."

"Well, that all depends on who I'm kneeling for." He paused to arch a suggestive eyebrow at her and Caden willed her face not to flush. "Don't worry, I've got it."

"What are you gonna do? Question 'em to death?"

"Caden, I feel like—and this is just a vibe that I'm getting —that you underestimate me."

"If you shoot at them or start a shoot-out, you'll bring the whole damn house down on us." What was he not understanding? Was it a man thing where he had to prove his macho-ness?

"I understand and I won't. Don't worry."

"Nathan!" Caden was snarling and pissed. "There are three of them, *three*. You, mister macho man, are gonna need this woman's help. Now shut up and—"

"Ya know, I've noticed that you only call me Nathan when you're concerned for me."

"Shut up." God, she could punch him.

"Look, you stay right here and be impressed." He grinned and stepped out into the lobby.

"If you get yourself killed, I'm not even gonna bury your ass. I'm gonna fucking write, 'TOLD YOU SO' on your dead damn forehead and everyone's gonna laugh at your ass."

"I can live with that."

"You wouldn't be living in that scenario, dumbass! You'd be fucking dead."

"Kiss for luck?"

Caden only glared when he bent down and offered his

lips. After she made no move to kiss him, he only grinned, took her hand, and pressed his lips to it.

The thief leaned the AK-47 against the wall for support and lined up the head of the meanest-looking asshat. Stupid Savage. He was thinking she was some dainty female who needed protecting. Fuck that.

They didn't notice him, which was hard to believe because the man was huge, until he was right on them. They looked up in unison, amused grins dissolving, replaced with confusion, and they almost had time to be suspicious, but then Savage was taking them apart.

Guard one went down first with a hit to the balls and then a quick and efficient snapping of his neck. Guard two went for his gun about the same time Nathan's hand slammed into his throat. He sputtered and gasped and reached for his neck like he was trying to hold it together. Guard three had his gun out of its holster by the time Nathan rounded on him. Savage stepped in close, grabbed the gun hand, disarmed him by yanking the Glock out of his hold, and proceeded to bash the same gun against his temple. Number three went down without a sound.

"Show off." Caden could do nothing but smirk at the man who'd just downed three guards, unarmed and tortured. It wouldn't be entirely truthful if she said she wasn't turned on by his obvious skill.

Okay, a lot turned on.

Hell, if he'd done it shirtless, she'd have probably thrown him down and had her way with him on the spot.

Nathan grinned and righted, looking all too pleased with himself.

"So..." He grabbed the biggest guy's feet and pulled the dead weight behind the desk. "Now, do you wanna have my babies?"

"Oh my god—shut up." Well, at least he hadn't done it because he was some kind of sexist asshole. He'd wanted to impress her. Which, maybe, would have been kind of sweet if they weren't in such a horrible-high-stakes-one-mistake-and-die kind of situation.

She left the hiding of the bodies to him and moved towards the far side of the room. The mercenary peered out the slit in the concrete that passed for a window and memorized the layout of the ridiculously expansive courtyard. A football field-sized courtyard that had absolutely nothing for cover. No big rocks or trees or dilapidated vehicles or even a goddamn outhouse.

They were fucked.

What the fuck was Kyott into nowadays? This was not his usual MO.

They had to get by a small army undetected and that was all before the gate entrance, where three armed guards stood at their posts checking the IDs of the passengers coming in and out of the compound.

Completely fucking fucked there as well.

"Okay..." Nathan joined her and looked rather discouraged after a quick scan of the courtyard. "Well..."

"We're fucked," Caden supplied helpfully.

He turned his attention back to her and smiled that crooked, playful smile of his.

"Look at that, we're already finishing each others sentences."

"Savage." She should never have kissed his dumbass.

"Hey, you opened this can of worms and it just so happens to be a can of worms I like."

"Ew."

"But maybe pretend I didn't equate our would-be love to worms."

Caden couldn't help but laugh at the sight of his cringing face.

"Okay, Casanova." Caden turned back towards the window. "Here's what I'm thinking. You see those SUVs over there?"

Three black SUVs were parked on the left side of the building.

"Yeah?"

"Well, let's get to one without getting caught and hijack it."

"Okay, but what about the three armed guards on patrol at the gate, and then there's a shit load of men that will rain fire on our asses when we get stopped and spotted at the gate."

"I don't know. I'm fucking making this up as I go along. I'll happily take any suggestions." He shook his head and motioned for her to continue. "We can make a new door in the walls. Hopefully, it's not reinforced steel. Or run them over and hope those SUVs are bulletproof."

"Suddenly," he went back to the three downed bodies and went through pockets and wallets, "I'm not feeling so confident."

A slightly muffled voice came out of a radio on one of the bodies.

Caden's blood started to race. They were so fucking dead. She reached over, ripped a radio from the pile of bodies and dragged Savage, as much as she could drag the two-hundred-some odd pounds of man flesh, towards the door.

"Yeah, join the fucking club." She checked her handgun and made sure the AK-47 was loaded and strapped to her back. "They just found us out. We've gotta do this now."

The radio blared again.

"Okay, this might be your last chance to get another smooch." His eyes were concentrated on their surroundings and he was checking his weapons at the same time. "Thought I should make ya aware of that."

"How 'bout we make it past that gate—not sporting body bags or toe tags and I'll kiss ya 'til you're blue in the face." She would do a whole helluva lot more than just kiss him if they survived, but he didn't need to know that.

"Promise?" He checked his clip, glanced up, and touched her shoulder. Like he was trying to convey something. Like he was saying goodbye. Like he was saying good luck. Like he was trying to put a lifetime's worth of words into one touch.

Which was so much more intimate than a kiss. And had the effect of pissing her off, scaring the shit out of her, and confusing her all at once. So she did the only thing she could do in defense: turned away and pushed through the double doors.

The sunlight was almost overwhelming. Grass was crunching under her stolen boots. The fresh air was in her lungs. For a moment, she felt... alive. She felt a surge of sun-fueled adrenaline and had to repress the sudden urge to giggle and go off skipping through the green green grass.

But then all hell broke loose and the giddy feeling building in her gut was effectively snuffed.

As soon as they'd pushed open the double doors and stepped into the sunlit courtyard, gunfire had rained down.

Reflexes, as tortured and malnourished as they and his whole body were, forced him to react almost instantaneously to the gunfire by diving for cover. And shit, there was no cover. The wooden bench that was so weatherbeaten it shouldn't still be standing would have to work.

They'd opened fire.

Someone had found them out. Nathan had trouble wrapping his head around it. It had been radioed in not even sixty whole seconds ago.

Sixty seconds, *if* that, was all it took for the entire compound to get the message, pinpoint their location, organize a plan of attack, and then execute said plan?

Guns were discharging left and right.

Nathan glanced to his left to check that Caden wasn't shot full of holes. She wasn't right beside him. She was glowering at him, no doubt cursing him in all the languages she knew, four yards away. Apparently, they had dived for cover in different directions.

While Nathan had gone for the first barrier he'd seen, she'd used those thinking skills Nathan had yet to fully develop and dived in the direction of the SUVs. She was using one of those outside cement ashtrays that doubled as a trash can for cover. It was too skinny for any kind of proper cover, but she was angling all the important bits of her anatomy out of range as much as she could.

All Nathan could think for a terrifying moment was that Caden was gonna get dead, and he was going to get goddamn shot again.

Something was weird, though. It took the trained SEAL a whole thirteen seconds to realize what was happening. Or what was *not* happening.

It took him another seven moments for that tidbit to sink in. They'd opened fire but were not, in fact, aiming their weapons at the escaped prisoners. They were aiming for the helicopter hovering overhead and the giant holes in the gate encircling the perimeter that was now smoking and aflame. They'd inadvertently timed their escape perfectly with invaders. Maybe it was a rival gang or the authorities. Who the hell cared?

All Nathan could do was grin. Either he was the luckiest bastard in the world or... or nothing he *was* the luckiest man in the world.

Caden was moving, obviously already having caught on. She was fast and single-mindedly focused on the SUVs. Nathan moved to follow, keeping his automatic up and ready. He didn't want to get shot by either party. The invaders would mistake him for his captors because he was dressed like them, and the ass-clowns guarding the compound would shoot him if he took off the clothes. Neither option was preferable.

A word of what the guard was saying caught Nathan's attention. He searched out the shouter in the chaos and was surprised to find the guy was looking straight at him. Something about the way the man was yelling and pointing and looking directly at him was ringing alarm bells with Nathan.

He could only barely speak the language, and even that was to ask where the bathrooms were. Other uniformed guards were diverting their attention from the firefight to him. It didn't take a native speaker to understand that they'd spotted him.

It took him only a moment to weigh his options and another to utilize the AK-47 and spray a few bullets their way. Mostly just to let them know that he was armed, and that he wasn't their biggest concern at the moment. They mostly hit the ground or scattered, but the message was sent.

He moved forward but stopped short when cold metal, which could only be the barrel of a handgun, pressed against his neck. Nathan froze and watched as another guard, this one sported a pair of big ears and a hooked nose, stepped into his line of sight and directed his weapon at Nathan. He said something in Russian and then shouted it again after Nathan didn't respond.

Finally, Dumbo motioned for Nathan to drop his guns.

He complied. He moved slowly, dropping the AK-47 and putting his hands up, so as not to scare them into killing him prematurely. He wasn't going to do their work for them and rid himself of all the weapons he'd collected. Maybe he'd get lucky and they'd miss a few.

The gun barrel resting on his neck moved and a single hand was patting him down, removing and tossing his pilfered weapons to the side. Dumbo was speaking more Russian, but Nathan didn't bother to pay attention. He was focusing on the guard behind him and waiting for his moment.

It would have been convenient if Caden swooped in, armor shining, white steed whinnying, and save his ass, but she was most likely dealing with her own assholes.

The gun was on his left shoulder now and the single hand was on his left thigh. Nathan took his chance (figuring he could survive a shoulder wound much better than he could survive a bullet through the neck) tucked his shoulders down and catapulted his body forward.

Using his head as a battering ram, Nathan slammed into the guy's gut. Dumbo bounced off of him and hit the grass, gasping and wheezing.

Pivoting and reaching for the knife he'd stowed in his boot, Nathan straightened.

Lined up his shot.

Tried to remember how exactly he was supposed to compensate for the uneven weight of the weapon.

Cocked his arm.

And was hit square in the chest with a sledgehammer.

Nathan was familiar with that particular full-body jerking. It was very much like being hit with a sledgehammer wielded by some beefed-out giant. The second guard had his gun leveled on him and—had that gunshot come from his gun or someone else's? It had been a while since he'd been graced with the oh-so-pleasant sensation of being shot but he remembered the feeling all too vividly.

Another too-close-to-be-any-other-gun-but-the-one-aimed-at-his-torso shot sounded and another sledge-hammer hit him right in the ribs.

Damn it all to hell, he'd been shot. *Twice.*

13

CADEN

aden had never walked the straight and narrow. From early on, she'd been a thief and a liar. Out of necessity, more than a lack of moral fiber. Her father had been a drunken, violent bastard with random fits of sobriety, which meant his three daughters went hungry and cold more often than not.

Caden had been four years old before her sisters came into the picture when she first began stealing. Food from grocery stores and when she couldn't make it to town, she'd break into her neighbor's homes and raid their pantries.

She'd begun stealing in earnest when Ezra's mother chucked her on their doorstep. When her sisters came under her care, things changed. Things she had never spared two thoughts to before, like rent, bills, and consistent meals, became all too important. Caden had acquired many alternative skills at a young age—chief among them was stealing cars.

At first, it had just been her dad's pickup truck to get into town; occasionally she'd hijack a neighbor's when the need was urgent. A skill that had morphed into a more profitable form of grand larceny when they'd escaped foster care and Ezzy had gotten into college. One of many skills from her misspent youth that had a lifetime guarantee. Which was why Caden hadn't hesitated when she'd seen the SUV.

The fact that they were not being shot at or had even been detected was a shock. She had to have a moment to get over it. Hell, it was like reality had flipped and her usually low reserves of luck were now disproportionately high. Like the Luck Gods suddenly decided to stop being stingy dicks and instead decided to liberally bequeath luck unto their subjects. Savage was most likely in good with them—him being likable and charming and all.

Wow, she had to shake the whimsical shit and maybe not play kissy face with Savage before doing important stuff. It was fucking with her head.

She'd gotten to the SUVs without so much as a sideways look. Much to her annoyance, Savage had dived the opposite way when they'd stepped out. He'd corrected his course, but he was still a good yard or two behind.

The roar of the battle going on around her was a sound she'd grown accustomed to through the years. The pop of bullets discharging and the sharp smell of cordite brought back memories.

Memories that froze her in place.

Memories that crushed her from the inside out until she was gasping for breath. Screams, familiar screams of men she lost long ago, had her white-knuckled and shaking. Big ol' beads of sweat plastered her forehead and dripped into her eyes.

Normally, she could hold her shit together in a firefight. Flashbacks didn't hack away at her defenses. She probably had some mild form of PTSD acquired from way back when, but she'd always been able to work around it or push through it.

Then again, she wasn't exactly at a hundred percent. Fuck, the blood loss coupled with malnutrition was most likely the cause of her sudden display of weakness.

She had a fucking mission.

Nathan Savage.

Nathan Savage and getting his ass out safely was her sole purpose. He was her mission and she sure as fuck was going to see that through. Thoughts of him and his big, dumb grin galvanized her into action. She forced herself to take a deep, calming breath and keep moving. To ignore the long-dead screams. To shove back the portraits of blood and gore and loss her brain was trying to paint all around her. Caden stomped the familiar screams and the horrible gut-wrenching death back into their dark corners and shoved the memories to the back of her mind.

Savage.

She had to get him out.

The SUV was locked. Caden knew how to jimmy a lock and she was capable of being all kinds of subtle when breaking into a vehicle. She figured that there was a time and place for subtlety. But now, in the midst of a firefight with a chopper hovering overhead and explosions rocking the ground, was not the time. Which was why she located a big hunk of rock and then proceeded to smash in the driver's side window with about as much subtly as Savage's choice of socks and ties.

It was at that point Caden turned to see just where in the hell he was. Her blood congealed when she located his muscle-bound frame in the fray. For a long terrifying moment, all she could do was stare in shocked horror. A gun was pointed at his chest.

The first bullet hit him, and his whole body jerked at the impact. Rage colored her vision and took control. Cold and methodical was how Caden fought. It was how she kept alive. It got the job done. But a red haze had settled over her vision and raw rage had the reins now.

She closed the distance in seconds flat, but not before the fucker got another shot off. Caden reached him just as Savage disarmed him.

Disarmed or not, the fucker was dead.

She used an already downed body as a step up and got a grip on the man's shoulders. With quick, ruthless grace, she made footholds in the fuckwad's back by kicking and digging into his flesh. She gripped his chin, jerked his head up and to the left, and pulled with all her might. He crumpled and tumbled to the ground, with Caden straddling his back.

"See," Nathan stumbled around, trying to stay upright, "you love me." He was holding his arm; red was seeping through his fingers. He hit the ground on his knees, still grinning.

Caden was in no mood to debate with him. She launched her body at the stupid man; knocked his legs out from under him with her weight and fell with him as his back met the ground with an "Ooph!"

"God damn, Caden," he wheezed and sputtered. "Can't wait to get in my pants, huh?"

"You stay here. Play dead. I'll be right fucking back." After a moment of hesitation, the mercenary glanced back down at him and leaned over to get right in his face. "Don't die, Nathan." She took a breath and tried not to sound too pathetic. "...please."

He was bleeding. Caden couldn't make herself look at his bullet holes. Not yet. Not when they weren't even out of the goddamn compound. What if they were fatal? What if he died? What if she never woke up in his human blanket again? What if he stopped grinning that silly grin? What if he became another headstone she had to visit?

"I won't." He flashed his pearly whites and Caden about let loose with the waterworks. "We've still got some smooching to do."

She could do nothing for a whole thirty seconds but smile down at the ridiculous man. She had to blink to clear the blur of tears in her eyes and forced herself to concentrate on the small signs of life. The way his chest heaved up and down, the pulse that beat on his neck, all the tiny lines creased in pain around his mouth and eyes.

It took her too long to refocus. What the fuck was she supposed to be doing?

Out.

They were getting out.

With all the single-minded intensity of a shark on the hunt, she charged through the firefight, intent on only getting to the SUV and getting back to Nathan.

It took too long. Every step forward felt as if she was taking two backwards. When she'd finally reached the SUV, she had to refocus on popping off the cover on the steering wheel column and then focus on not locking up the starter. On finding the right wires, on stripping the plastic coverings, and breaking the steering lock. In all, it had only taken three minutes, but to Caden, it felt like an hour.

"Nathan." She stepped out of the driver's side and peered down at the man. "You're alive." It wasn't a question, it was a command.

He was white and still holding his arm. A puddle of red had gathered under him and he was blinking drunkenly up at her. When he caught sight of her, his pain-stricken face cracked into an all-out smile, like she was the only thing he'd wanted to see.

"I'm alive." He was slightly slur-y. "I told ya—I ain't dying 'til later. Much later."

She had to stop the blood flow. He was losing too much. His shoulder was spurting blood. His leg had a bullet hole too, but it wasn't spitting out blood like the other one. The bullet must have hit an artery.

"Fuck." She stripped the downed men strewn around them of their belts and shirts. "Are you hit anywhere else, Nathan?" She hadn't seen any other holes in him, but that didn't mean shit. "Here—keep pressure on that."

"Not 'til I've had ya for a good long while, at least." He was grinning still. "You'll love livin' in Texas. Maybe we should get a dog."

Ignoring his gabbing, the mercenary made her tourniquets with the belts and shirts she took off the bodies. She'd done it enough before to do it quickly and well. She cut his sleeve off at the neck and made sure that the bullet had gone straight through before she put the first tourniquet a good three inches above the seeping bullet hole and wrapped it around until she had just enough to knot. He moaned in pain but kept on jabbering when she moved to do the same to his leg.

"You'll love my mama too. Bobby'll take to ya."

"Okay." Her hands were shaking now and her eyes would roll in her head if she turned her head too quickly. She was low on energy. "Let's get you in the car."

"I may faint on ya, Caden." His eyes were closed, and he looked even paler and green now. He was sweating and swallowing like he was going to puke.

"I got ya." Caden stood and put their weapons on the floor of the car. "Just maybe try not to puke all over me."

There were still people dying around them, but the cover of the SUV provided a barrier between the two. It was almost like they were in their own little bloody, horrible world. Caden took a moment to catch her breath and attempt to still her shaking limbs before she reached down and helped drag Nathan to a sitting position.

"No promises—will you still love me if I yak on your new shoes?" He got to his feet and swayed. Caden caught him and wedged her shoulder under his. They took the two steps to the SUV together. He swayed again, and then suddenly he was dead weight.

"Holy fucking Christ." Grunting and shoving and pulling and cursing, Caden finally got his heavy ass into the back seat. "What are you like, seven hundred pounds?"

The world spun when she righted herself, but Caden swallowed the urge to vomit and closed her eyes. Ignoring the white-hot pain coming in waves from just about every-where on her, she felt for his pulse.

It was quick but steady. He'd only passed out.

She got to work digging through the dead men's pockets for cash and credit cards. She got lucky and found a bag of Skittles in one pocket and a granola bar in another. Finally, she plucked a couple of guns and knives off the corpses and returned to Nathan.

"We're leaving Nathan—we're gonna get you back to your family and those brothers. You're gonna be just fine." Talking helped to fight off the nausea and the dizziness. "You're gonna be alright."

She popped a handful of Skittles into her mouth and all but drowned in the saliva that magically appeared under her tongue. The hair on the back of her neck prickled, and the thief experienced an 'ah fuck' moment while she was trying to chew the mouthful of candy. She twisted to get the enemy in her sights, but it was too late.

The man was a good three feet away, pointing a Beretta at her chest and shaking his head at her movements.

"Toss it." His voice was low and gruff, but she heard him in through the din of gunfire.

Caden complied with a growl.

"Move away." It took a moment for her to understand that he meant to move away from Nathan. "Now." Again, she had no choice but to comply. If only he'd step closer, she could make a grab for his gun. Caden made an effort to look soft and female and anything but a threat. "Further."

He spoke English, though they were in Moscow, with a drawl so she could safely assume that he was an American. He was tall and lean. Narrowed blue eyes above high, prominent cheekbones made for an attractive face. Dressed in all black, a belt laden with all manner of weapons, a bulletproof vest protecting his chest, and cargo pants completed the gun-for-hire look. What the fuck were American soldiers doing invading Kyott's compound?

When she was a good three feet from the SUV, he moved closer, not towards her, but towards the SUV. The man, clearly thinking she wasn't too much of a threat, took his eyes off her and looked towards Nathan. A frown pulled at his face and he moved in for a closer look, gun still pointed at her chest.

Mine.

The thought resonated in her bones, sent a lightning bolt down her spine and rage ignited in her gut.

Taking advantage of his diverted attention, Caden took the three long steps into his personal bubble, aimed for kidneys, and hit Kevlar—*fuck.*

Shit, she knew better than that. Of course, he'd be

sporting armor. She had to focus. Had to get her attention on taking the fucker down and not on Savage and the two bullets he'd taken.

A closed fist rammed into her already busted ribs, sending a shockwave of pain through her and making fuzzy dots pop up in her vision. Before she could recover, an arm snaked around her neck and secured her in a chokehold. Caden turned to shove her elbow into his stomach, but he caught it and twisted it up behind her, effectively taking one appendage out of the fray.

Fuck that. She could function with one arm—she'd done it before. But fuck, it was going to hurt. She braced for pain, gripped the fingers of the arm that was locking her in a chokehold, and felt him tense behind her.

"Don't—"

Too late. The mercenary pushed away and turned at the same time, a twist of white-hot pain and the snap of her own bone cracking under the pressure put her left arm out of commission, effectively popping her arm out of its socket and possibly even breaking it. She'd broken at least two of his fingers and darted out of his now slackened hold. She spun round to face him and shoved the heel of her palm into his nose.

He turned his head just enough to keep from getting brained by his own nose. It snapped under her hand with a spurt of red. He stumbled back in an attempt to get out of her reach, but Caden kept on him. She tore the gun out of his hand and then lost her grip on the goddamn thing. It went skittering to the left, but she remained focused on taking out the threat instead of following the weapon.

Using her good arm to keep him off balance and in a haze of pain with a barrage of pressure point hits, she backed him up until he'd tripped over a fallen body and hit the ground. She broke in her new shoes by breaking a couple of his ribs with a few swift kicks (just to make sure he stayed down) and then hopped over his fetal-positioned body to get back to Nathan.

Caden all but flew into the driver's seat, put the thing in gear, and only allowed herself to scream out the pent-up hurt when the compound and all the gunfire was in her rearview mirror.

They'd made it past the gate.

Now all they had to do was make it out of Russia, get some kind of medical help that didn't include any kind of police reports, and not die while they were at it.

14

NATHAN

Nathan was unceremoniously slapped awake.

"Caden." It was a whoosh of breath that left his gut when he shot upward and slammed head-first into something horribly hard. "Fuuu-dge."

He groaned and slowly lowered his aching body and head back down, not bothering to open his eyes, until the dizziness settled and the nausea didn't overwhelm him.

"You okay, Princess?" He could hear the smile in her voice.

Relief sagged his shoulders at the sound of her low, husky voice. She was alive. They were alive. Captured again or not, she was alive. He cracked an eye open and located Caden in the cramped space. She was hunched by his shoulders, sitting on the floor of the car she'd stolen. A bone-melting kind of ease had him breathing deeply and smiling. She'd gotten them out.

"You'd think you'd treat a princess a wee bit better. Maybe, ya know, and this is just a thought, you could have kissed me awake—like any proper knight in shining armor knows to do."

Nathan felt more than saw the utter stillness that settled over her after he spoke. No tiny movements, no fabric moving against skin, not even the sound of her breathing. He swiveled his pounding head in her direction and listened intently for any sign of a hidden enemy.

Her dark eyes were locked on his. That frozen darkness in her eyes shifted and softened just a tiny bit. She looked... vulnerable and innocent. Nathan was careful not to show any kind of shock on his face, not wanting to startle her out of this new mood.

The stillness in her melted and she leaned forward until the space between their lips could no longer be counted in centimeters. Nathan drew a shaky breath, watching as her dark eyes focused on his lips. Blood, sweat, and cordite hung in the air. He was in pain, or he should have been feeling his newly acquired bullet holes, but with Caden's lips so close to his, all he could feel was anticipation and a sense of awe.

For a breathless moment, she pressed her busted lips to his. It was soft and sweet and short, but Nathan felt the touch in his bones. It left him breathless and excited and triumphant and possessive and all kinds of things that made his head swim.

She moved away the barest inch, wavered like she wanted to kiss him again, but then sat back on her haunches. That hard thing in her eyes was firmly back in place.

"You've been out for half an hour—maybe." All business again, she opened the door and managed to get out only using one arm. "We're in a barn. I doubt anyone's followed us. You're looking kinda shock-y. Here." She put an open bag of Skittles in his hand and turned her attention to the pile of weapons on the floorboard of the SUV.

"What happened to your arm?" Nathan sat up, slower

this time, so he didn't bash his head against the SUV's frame again. "What'd I miss?"

"You didn't miss much. You fainted. I loaded your heavy ass into the vehicle, I got into it with this asshat, and I dislocated my arm. I thought about knocking over a mini-mart, but decided that we'd squat for now." She selected a Colt, a hand cannon with stopping power, from the pile of guns she'd collected while he was out. "I'll be right back."

"Wait—where the hell are you going?" Nathan tried to stand, but he was too slow. She was already at the door. "Caden!"

"Stop yellin'! I'm going to make sure the house is empty." She offered a smile, not the shark smile he was used to, but an honest to god reassuring smile that had him stumbling to regain his balance.

He was feeling pain now. It was like he'd survived getting run over by an eighteen-wheeler. Sharp pain was radiating from both his shoulder and his leg. When he put weight on his shot leg, lightning bolts of white-hot pain would shoot up his leg and set his nerves on fire. Sweaty and clammy and shaking like a leaf. God, he needed to nap. And shower. Especially if he was going to do any seducing. He couldn't do any wooing smelling like blood and guns and dirt, at least not if he was planning on succeeding.

Nathan went still, pushing the searing pain to the back of his mind, and mentally took inventory of all his hurts. His limbs were shaking, not just trembling, but actually shaking. He was cold and getting colder. Nathan recognized the signs of shock and promptly swallowed a handful of Skittles. The sugar would combat the adrenaline crash.

The man absorbed his surroundings, looking for a makeshift crutch. The only light in the place was the sunlight shining through the walls. It was a standard barn with stalls and hay bales. A loft on his right with a ladder leading up to it, wood slats under his boots, and high ceilings. It looked as if it hadn't been used in years.

Caden had obviously driven through the double doors on the far end of the building, effectively hiding the vehicle. The SUV had no bullet holes, not in the doors or the tail, which maybe meant they hadn't even been pursued out of the compound.

He spotted a broom in the corner and limped his way to it. He could flip it over and prop the blunt end under his arm and hope that it would hold up under his weight.

"Nathan!" Her voice was sharp and almost panicked. "Oh." She located him in the gloom and visibly untensed. "Don't—don't" Nathan watched her stutter and then scowl accusingly at him like he was somehow the cause of her speech problems. "Don't wander off. Don't go where I can't see you."

"Quinn, I'm a middle-aged grown-ass man." Was she serious? How did he even respond to something so ludicrous? "I'm not gonna get lost. Well, I might, but I'll be able to handle it."

"Yeah, well, the last time you wandered off on your own, you got shot. *Twice.* That's two, count 'em, *two* near-death experiences, and all because you didn't stay with me. And we're still not outta the woods with your bullet wounds either, so you may still die. So, you're staying in my line of sight or I'm gonna knock ya out and drag your ass around."

Nathan didn't possess the energy to fight with her, besides the fact that the whole situation had been one big near-death experience on top of a big ol' pile of near-death experiences shared by both parties. *She'd* been the one to be in a near-constant state of peril. Not him. But it was nice that she cared enough to start making demands of him.

"Is the house empty?" He limped slowly back to where she was stuffing her pockets with their weapons, the makeshift crutch holding up under his weight. She spared him a cursory glance, still looking reproachful.

"Yep, looks like it's been vacant for a while. You think you can make it—it's a ways to the house."

"Yeah." He wasn't feeling up to even walking, but there was a bed at the place she wanted him to go. A bed and a shower and possibly even food. "Let's do it."

It was almost pitiful the way they jointly hobbled together out the door. If he'd had the energy, he'd have laughed outright. He was limping along, trying to manage the broom under his good arm and trying not to jostle his other arm. Caden, bleeding and bruised, was laden down with weapons. She was favoring her right side, limping, and one arm hung limp and useless whilst she kept her handgun up and at the ready.

There was nothing but wide open spaces all around him. The grass was green but sparse. There were more dirt patches than anything. An old dilapidated tractor sat on the far end of the field. A few old rusted-out vehicles were scattered across the lawn. The house itself was tiny. The brown paint was peeling, but it looked as if it had been kept up. By the time they reached the front door, they were both out of breath and sweating.

"The bed's all the way down the hall, first door on the right." She grunted when they'd struggled through the door and into the living room. There was a layer of dust and a level of coldness that told him the owners hadn't been home in a while. Nathan could only manage to grunt in response and move to do as she instructed, automatically absorbing his surroundings.

The room was small and packed with all manner of

random things. Knick-knacks mostly, books, and clothes. It was organized and tidy, but still compact. The bed was big enough for the both of them.

Caden grunted something, placed most of her weapons on the bedside table, and then turned on her heel and went back out the door.

Nathan took that moment to carefully chuck his shot and battered body on the bed. It was soft and there were blankets. And goddamn pillows. How long had it actually been since he'd slept on a bed? How long had they been imprisoned? It felt like ages. Nathan shifted into the bed, trying to melt into the mattress, and all but moaned at the sheer pleasure of having something with a bit of bounce and cushion under his ass.

"Here." She was back with two cups anchored to her body with her right arm, the left one still hung loosely at her side. Nathan took the cups and watched as she sunk onto the bed beside him.

"There any more Skittles?" She glanced over at him after a few minutes of joint heavy breathing. Her voice was low and slow, like it was taking too much energy to form words.

"Yeah, here." He shook out the rest in her trembling palm. Her knuckles were busted and blood was crusted into all the little lines of her palm. "We should see about those cuts."

"Sleep first." Grunting and struggling, she pushed her body up so her back was resting against the headboard.

They were both experiencing an adrenaline crash. Nathan could see the exhaustion in the lines of her face; her skin was gray and pinched in pain. His face most likely mirrored hers, but there was a warm kind of giddi-ness that was taking hold of his gut and breathing life back into his limbs. They were free. They were alive. They were mostly in one piece. And hell, she'd kissed him again.

But what they needed most was a nap. Some actual food would be nice, but he doubted he would be able to keep anything with actual substance down. And a bath, preferably together. Though Nathan doubted he could do anything more than just flail around. It was a nice thought.

She shifted uncomfortably and then, wonders of all wonders, a soft, he'd even go so far as to say *affectionate*, smirk pulled at her lips when her eyes locked on something at the end of the bed. Nathan followed her line of sight, trying to identify the thing that put that softness on her face.

"What are you smirking at?" The TV on the dresser? The stack of books propped beside it?

"I was... do you remember that one time in California? LA, I think it was." There was more energy in her voice now. The sugar was kicking in.

"LA? I never chased you there." Had he? Nathan racked his brain trying to pinpoint just what the hell she was talking about. He'd been to Los Angeles a total of three times and none of those times had he been chasing Quinn.

"No." She grinned down at him. "I saw you in Chicago and thought you were tailing me, so I double-backed and followed you."

"And then followed me all the way to LA?" Damn, how had he not seen her? Had he actually been horrible at his job? "I knew you had a thing for me."

"I didn't have a job lined up." She shrugged all nonchalantly like tailing the guy who'd arrested her twice and would have done so again without hesitation was normal. "And even if I did have a teeny tiny little smidgen of a thing for you—it died a painful death when I saw you dance."

"Dance?" He racked his brain for a party he'd attended in LA. None came to mind.

"I mean, I couldn't hear the lyrics, but I could just tell what song it was by the dance you were doing." Her voice was all kinds of amused like she was trying really hard not to laugh in his face.

And suddenly he knew exactly what she was talking about. "Oh my god." Nathan could feel heat rise to his face. His ears burned with the sudden rush of blood. "Oh god."

"All the single ladies, all the single ladies," she sang, and Nathan blushed harder. "Are you always that into the music or was that—"

"Okay, first of all, stalking me is unfair. And secondly, it was on the TV. And, you know what, women aren't the only ones who can shake their asses. I rocked that song."

He had seen it on TV. The beat was catchy as hell and it had looked like fun. He had been bored and waiting for the gala to open.

"Yeah, you did." She laughed out loud, holding her ribs with her good arm. The husky, slightly pained sound shocked him out of his embarrassment. Hell, if she was going to laugh like she had a soul, he'd make a fool out of himself all the time. "The hip popping alone. God, I laughed for days every time that song came on the radio."

After her laughter died down, Nathan felt his embarrassment return. How many other dances had she seen him do without his knowledge?

"Shut up, ya big stalker. At least I don't stalk people."

"Ah!" she snorted in disbelief and turned her indignant, dark eyes on him. "Yes, you do. You stalked me all the time."

"That was my job! Occupational hazard. 'Sides, the most embarrassing thing you've done while I watched was... hell, I don't know—pick a wedgie."

She laughed again, this time more wheezy and pained than before.

"I'll have you know I am a *lady*. Ladies don't pick wedgies. Stop making me laugh. I might pass out."

Then she smiled. A real, soft-eyed smile that had Nathan swaying where he sat. Maybe it was the blood loss. But hell, she smiled, and he about fainted.

"Want me to pop your arm back in?" It took him longer than it should have to find his voice again and change the subject, but he finally got himself under control.

"You up to it?" She motioned to his shot-up shoulder and sat up when he nodded.

Nathan had dislocated his shoulder before. He knew how incredibly painful it was to do and how much more painful it was to push back in. On top of the fact that she may have broken it as well just made it that much worse.

She clenched her jaw when he picked up her hand and pulled it up until it was straight out. All the good humor in her face was gone now. She braced herself, teeth clenched, lips pursed.

"You ready?" He rested her arm on his chest and stretched his good arm until it was even with her shoulder.

"Just do it." It was a snarl.

Making sure her arm was perfectly straight, he drew his hand back, watched as she squished her eyes closed, and slapped her shoulder. He could hear the crack of the bone snapping back into the socket and feel it under his palm. The merc went completely white, eyes wide open now. They rolled in her head and she slumped where she sat.

"Caden." Nathan knew she had passed out, but that didn't stop a cold finger of panic from crawling up his spine.

He found a pulse and made himself calm the fuck down because her pulse was there and it was steady, if a bit fast.

Taking a deep, calming breath, he resettled her on her back, figuring her ribs were causing more pain than the lashes on her.

He needed to get his shit together. He needed to make phone calls and get them the hell out of dodge. They couldn't survive another capture. Well, Caden most likely could because she could survive anything, but he wouldn't last. Not with two bullet holes and no medical attention.

All the things he should have been doing were second to the thoughts of Caden Quinn and just exactly how he was going to pursue a relationship with the notorious thief. Nathan wasn't a 'wham-bam thank ya ma'am' kinda guy. Fucking went hand in hand with relationship-ing.

If she didn't want him. Well, that would suck something fierce. She'd kissed him but, Nathan figured, it was mostly because she was about to dive headfirst into mortal combat and why the hell not just kiss him? He'd cross that bridge when he came to it, though, no use borrowing trouble. Either way, he'd still have to bring her home to his parents. Ellen and Bobby Savage had a way about them that could heal all wounds.

He just didn't know how it was going to work. It helped that there wasn't a whole hell of a lot known about the woman, but still. He was an ex-soldier, ex-government man, just exactly everything that did not mix well with a thief. His family was all pretty much the same, law-abiding citizens and all that. Actually, it was worse because the family business was specifically targeted at the lawbreakers.

The hair on his nape stood.

Fuck.

There was no telling noise that made his senses go on alert.

Shit.

The house was quiet. No betraying creek or cloth on cloth shifting.

Damn it.

There was someone in the house. He could feel it.

Silently, the ex-soldier threw a blanket over the unconscious mercenary, stuffed the Beretta in his pants, and palmed the Colt. He hadn't had time to pick escape routes, and it wasn't like he could throw Caden over his shoulder and run away. Ignoring the searing pain ripping his muscles apart, he positioned himself at the foot of the bed and waited for the invisible enemy to show themselves.

One second, the doorway was empty and then it wasn't. His finger tightened on the trigger before recognition sparked. Nathan chucked down his gun and sagged in relief.

"Jackson." Nathan should have been surprised to see his brother sweeping the room with his barrel, but he really couldn't muster up the energy to do so.

It was Jackson. The goddamn, surly, marvelous son of a bitch. Which meant a Savage Security team was in company as well. Hell, maybe all four teams.

"Clear," Jackson barked into his headset and turned his attention back to Nathan.

Reid and Holden were tailing him. Which meant Dax, Maddox, and Kade were coming in from the rear.

"You asshole," was all Nathan could muster at that particular moment. Relief and elation were smothering every other emotion.

His brother cast a disapproving look before he motioned for Reid to see to him and Holden back out to notify the rest. Holden sent him a searching look and scowled at him before quickly doing as he was ordered.

"You did it anyway, didn't you?" He tried to sound

offended and pissed, but it came out all relieved and grateful. Not at all what he was trying for.

"What—the tracking node? Of course, I did." Like embedding a tracking node in the flesh of a family member was the most natural thing in the world and he was daft for even commenting.

Nathan had fought that fight before and it never came to anything other than the knowledge that his brother was obsessively paranoid and protective. So he decided to bring the topic back up when Caden wasn't dying and he had some food in his belly.

"Well, then what the fuck took you so long?"

"You said you weren't gonna do this again." Reid, the family medic, was shrugging out of his backpack and looking all accusatory and disappointed. Like Nathan had purposefully sought out trouble and got himself captured. "Just like you said, you were gonna stop drinking soda."

"Not me." Nathan dodged his brother's hands and motioned towards the lump on the bed. "Caden, she's hurt. She passed out. Some of her ribs are broken. Her arm might be too."

"Trucks ready. Area is clear." Holden glided back into the room and nodded towards Jackson before turning to once again scowl down at Nathan. "Some vacation. What the fuck happened this time?"

Jackson stepped aside to talk into his radio and then his cell phone. Holden slapped his uninjured shoulder and more bodies filed into the tiny room.

"Reid, if she's awake, don't touch her without letting her see you first. Tell her who you are."

Nathan couldn't turn his head without suffering a shock of pain, so he couldn't see if Caden was awake or not. He didn't want Reid to lose a hand or get dead.

"Nathan! God dammit!" Suddenly Nathan was engulfed in a bear hug and being painfully squeezed. "I thought you were dead this time for sure."

"Ease off, Maddox—shit. I'm injured." Nathan pushed the man away and couldn't help but smile when Maddox threw his head back and laughed. It was more relieved than amused Nathan could understand. Maddox stepped back and bumped into Dax and Kade, who'd slipped in the door behind him. Apparently, they all had to see for themselves that he was alive.

"What the hell happened to you?" Nathan tried not to visibly cringe as he took in Kade's two black eyes, puffy broken nose, and the slight hunch on his left side.

"Your girlfriend is what happened to me." Kade, the six-foot-something, highly trained, ex-comando, was snarling and glaring.

"Caden?" When had they even crossed paths? "Why the hell didn't you tell her that you're my brother?"

"Oh gee, I don't know Nathan—it didn't come up in conversation. Oh wait, maybe that was because there was a firefight going on and I didn't know who was the enemy and who wasn't." The man's teeth were flashing with every other word. "And fuck, I thought the family resemblance would speak for itself."

The sheer amount of indignant sarcasm was, in Nathan's opinion, uncalled for. Aside from the fact that they were both tall and beefy and carried the surname, there were a few distinct differences. The one Kade was referring to was the fact that he was black, while Nathan was almost painfully white in comparison.

"She beat his ass, too." Dax was grinning from ear to ear. Gleeful that Kade had finally been so thoroughly beat. "I saw the whole thing—I was surprised he didn't assume the fetal position and cry. I woulda."

"I wasn't expecting her to break her own damn arm." He glanced surreptitiously out the window. "Now, can we get the fuck outta this goddamn country? Shit always goes south in Moscow."

Reid giggled from his position near Caden and Nathan arched an eyebrow in question as did the Savages around him.

"Coriolis effect." Reid craned his head to the side and just waited. Like why the hell didn't they know what he meant and why the hell weren't they laughing at an obviously funny joke? After a moment when no one so much as cracked a grin, the man shook his head, muttered something under his breath about stupid Neanderthals not getting a simple joke, and returned his attention to Caden.

"It's okay, Reid, maybe someday you'll be a real boy—"

"Oh kiss my ass, Maddox." Reid scowled. "It ain't my fault you're too thick to get a joke."

"A joke has a punchline, not some random ass reference to inertial force." Maddox was rolling his eyes.

"Oh, so you understood the reference, but just decided to hop on the bandwagon and pretend like you didn't get the joke." Reid was angrily stuffing his supplies back into his pack.

Nathan breathed in the sounds of his family and allowed his muscles to relax. His brothers were there. He didn't need to know anything else for the time being. Caden was going to be okay. He was going to be okay. They'd escaped.

"What joke?" This time, Kade chimed in.

"Can she be moved, Reid?" Jackson cut in, voice growly

and raspy, shutting down the argument and glaring at them all collectively.

"Yeah, it looks like it. You wanna carry her, Dax?"

"Sure. Wanna put her out first? I don't want her coming to and freaking the fuck out on me." Dax shouldered his automatic and started forward. Nathan snapped to attention again.

"Be careful. She's hurt badly. Her back, thighs, and arms are all cut up and her ribs are broken. Just be careful."

"Yeah, Nate, I'll be careful." Dax patted his shoulder and Jackson stepped into his line of sight.

"Can you walk outta here, or do I need to get a stretcher in here?" Eyes stern and scowling as per usual, Jackson scanned him, frown deepening.

Nathan maneuvered to watch as Dax toted Caden's limp body out the door. Panic slithered up his spine again. Shouldn't she have woken up already? Was it bad that she was still out of it? Was she going to wake up?

"Yeah." Nathan took a deep, calming breath and stood to follow Caden out the door. "I can walk."

15

JACKSON

Jackson Savage was pissed off. He wanted to throttle his fool brother. He wanted to kick Nathan's ass up and down Russia until he figured out he couldn't just up and leave and take a fucking vacation.

Okay—well, said like that, it sounded unreasonable, but, fuck, Jack had told him not to go unarmed. But had he listened? No. No, he hadn't and now here they were in bum-fuck middle of nowhere Russia retrieving his ass. Jackson was well aware that his stupid brother was going through some shit, but getting himself caught and tortured was not the way to go about solving those problems.

Not that Nathan had done it on purpose. Or shit-sticks. Maybe he had.

Well, fuck, that thought was an unsettling one.

Jackson could do nothing but internally growl as that idea settled its claws into his brain and froze his blood.

If Nathan had gone to Russia with the sole purpose of getting himself... punished, was the only word his brain was supplying, then they were in more trouble than he'd thought. Jackson had thought his brother's mental health was... well, fuck, he'd thought Nathan was just fuckin' fine. Definitely not to the point of seeking out punishment like some damn monk.

But then again, maybe he was just thinking too much about it. Surely, he or one of the fifty thousand people in the Savage clan would have noticed the signs of depression or PTSD. Fuck, they all suffered some form of that shit and no one was exactly shy about what they needed or what they thought someone else needed in their family. In fact, everyone had an opinion about every-fucking-thing under the sun and they would gladly shove their opinions down the throats of anyone within earshot. Nate's possible depression would not have escaped the notice of his parents, his six brothers, and that of the fifteen other people employed by SI. There was just no fucking way Nathan was that far gone.

Or maybe he was just really good at hiding it.

Jackson remembered the scrawny, angry kid that Nathan had once been. Back before Ellen and Bobby had gotten a hold of him. He'd been all elbows and knees and rage. Kid Nathan had not been good at hiding his emotions or controlling them. Adult Nathan was much better at the emotional shit but just as crap at hiding what he was feeling. Jackson racked his brain for any instance where that didn't hold true.

Nathan was by far one of the most emotionally stable Savages. The man laughed easily, channeled his rage into healthy outlets, and voluntarily talked about the shit that bothered him. And then turned around and forced his brothers to do the same. Nathan cried every single time he watched *Steel Magnolias*, and didn't try to pretend like there was something in his eye when Holden made fun of him.

Which had to count for something when considering

mental stability, right? So, his adopted brother was mentally sound.

Right?

Fuck, he didn't know. He was so swamped with work from all fronts. It was a fucking miracle if he could discern his ass from his hat at any given point. Maybe everyone else was just as self-involved and just didn't realize Nate was slipping.

"You okay there, Jackie-pooh?" Maddox's question shook him out of his reverie and back to the present.

"What?" Jackson hadn't meant to sound that snappy and pissed.

Or maybe Nathan just did what Nathan did best and found trouble. It was a well-known fact that Nathan was one big walking disaster attractor. If a stray bullet went off in a hundred-mile radius of the man, it would invariably defy all laws of gravity, reverse its trajectory, and hit him. If there was a dog within that same radius, it would go rabid, find him, and bite him.

Goddamned Nate and his goddamned inability to stay out of trouble.

"You're all but foaming at the mouth." Maddox kept his face forward and focused on the sky. "You've been growlin' like a damn dog for last the thirty minutes."

"I have not—it's been five minutes tops. Where is he?" Every word he spoke came out as a growl, but that was normal now. He barely even flinched at the sound of it anymore.

"It's not that big of a plane, Jackie-pooh." Maddox didn't bother to glance over at him, just kept piloting the plane like it was his job or something. "Just follow the sounds of Holden ripping him a new one for daring to take a vacation."

The accompanying eye roll had Jackson feeling all kinds of indignant and defensive. Maddox well knew how much he, Jackson, had not wanted Nathan to leave the safety of the compound. And he also knew just how much Jackson had been against Nathan's little jaunt to Russia in the first place.

And he'd been right, dammit!

He'd been so incredibly right about everything that they'd had to infiltrate Russia, without attracting the notice of the Russian government or with the blessing of the United States government, and invade a whole goddamn compound. All because he'd been so right and Nathan had refused to listen to him.

Maddox said something in Cajun and Jackson couldn't help but roll his eyes. How hard could he smack the pilot without endangering everyone on the plane? Daisy was a better pilot anyway. They could survive with just one.

"Don't be getting all spitty and angry and whipping out the Cajun like I don't know that you're threatening me. I can get pissy in my native tongue too—" He jerked his head around and narrowed his eyes before pitching his voice low and all intimidating-like. "¿Querrías bailar conmigo?"

"Pfft." It was only then that Daisy, Maddox's co-pilot, decided to speak up. "You can try."

"What?" Maddox glanced sideways at her, grinning like an idiot. "You got something to contribute, D? Did I not threaten him correctly?"

"You asked him to dance—that's a weak ass threat if I ever heard one." The petite woman giggled and Jackson suffered a small sense of disorientation at the sound. "Unless it wasn't a threat? Maybe I should leave you two alone and see what I can do for three minutes while you...

dance." Maddox threw his head back and laughed outright. Jackson only growled some more.

Daisy looked like sunshine and flowers and everything that was nice in the world. It was such a contradiction to her skill level and the sheer lethality of the woman that Jackson always had to remind himself that she was a warrior. Her guileless smiles and sunny demeanor did not equal soft innocence and complacency.

"Three minutes? Oh, you wound me, woman! Four minutes at least. You know how long it takes me just to unlace my boots?"

"Two minutes." She nodded solemnly, and Maddox laughed out loud again.

"Okay, well, you can play out whatever twisted fantasies you harbor for me—I know there's a lot, but I said it all menacing-like. I went old west on his ass."

It was at that point Jackson decided to take his leave. They were doing the witty, sexual innuendo, bantering thing again. Which were three things Jackson didn't do. Well, maybe *couldn't* was the better word.

"Jackson." Maddox finally turned around to face him. "Wait."

"What?"

"Just admit that the only reason you're on the warpath is because you're emotionally damaged and don't know how to tell him you love him and that you're happy he's safe." He said it like it was the truest thing in the world and it would be madness if anyone disagreed with him. Dick.

Unfortunately, all Jackson could think to do in rebuff was to mimic the asshole in the highest falsetto his damaged vocal cords could manage.

"Nice comeback, Jack." Maddox's deep, stupid laugh followed him out of the cockpit and into the lounge area.

"Shut up."

Jackson didn't think he was being unreasonable.

Nathan attracted trouble. Was it too much to expect that knowing it, Nathan would live accordingly? Like maybe, and this was just a thought, he wouldn't vacation alone and unarmed to a country where he was well known as an American G-man?

Granted, there weren't a lot of places left available to him to visit, but fuck, what was wrong with staying home? Or at least staying within the continental borders? No brutal torture there and it was a hell of a lot less likely that he was going to get shot in good ol' Redhawk Ridge, Texas. Standard shit, right?

Kade was sprawled in the cushioned seat with his head thrown over the headrest, an ice pack plopped on his face. He was favoring his right side, and to all accounts, he looked asleep. Kade was charged with watching the woman, and Kade was a man that took every one of his duties seriously. So Jackson knew the man wasn't asleep. Kade, no matter how tired or beat, would never fall asleep on the job.

"You gonna live?" Jackson examined his brother with a critical eye. Kade looked bruised and battered, but alive.

"No," was the grunted reply.

"Reid give you something for the pain?" At the sound of his brother's disgruntled voice, Jackson couldn't help but grin. It was almost funny. Kade hadn't gotten his ass so thoroughly handed to him in a long time.

"Nah, he's seeing about Nate." His normally deep voice was now all nasally and hilarious.

"Where are they?"

"In the back. If you listen real hard, you can hear the dulcet tones of Holden yelling at him. Although Nate's so high right now, he's probably seein' pink elephants. Why, you want your turn at him?"

Sure enough, Jackson could detect the sounds of deep growls and consonants in the air. He couldn't decipher any actual words. Knowing Holden, there was lots of cussing, colorful phrasing, and ranting going on.

"I'm not being unreasonable." So what if his voice was all defensive and squeaky? He was *not* being unreasonable. Kade only let out a tired sigh, but otherwise remained silent. "What? You think it's ridiculous to expect Nathan to go to a foreign and hostile country armed?"

"No, I think it's unreasonable that ya'll need to jump up his ass for doing normal Nate things. The mission was a success. No one's dead or wounded—well, not fatally. And Nate's alive."

"I'm not jumpin' up his ass. Nate knows that he is a trouble magnet—it's not unreasonable to assume that the idiot would live his life accordingly." What was unreasonable was how many times he'd said the word unreasonable in the past three hours.

"Pfft." Kade snorted and then moaned in pain, obviously forgetting about his broken face and how vibrations in his nose could hurt like a bitch. "Every fucking one of us is a disaster magnet—it comes with the last name. It's only more obvious with Nate because he can't help but get shot every six months. Now stop acting like he's some newbie and start treatin' him like an adult who's capable of making decisions and accepting the consequences of those decisions."

"I treat him like an adult." Okay, so maybe that was only half true. When Nate was shot full of holes and looking like he was gonna keel over any second, it was easy to forget that he was thirty-something and capable of being an adult. "And shut up—since when do you spout pearls of wisdom?"

"Only when asses and heads are indistinguishable, grasshopper. You really oughta jot those pearls down." He grinned and rearranged the ice pack on his face.

"You oughta jot your ass down." Jackson knew, and was reminded frequently, that he was shit at comebacks. It was something he'd embraced long ago.

"God, Jack." His tone was pitying and ashamed all at once. "It's embarrassing that people know we're related."

"*You're* embarrassing." In his experience, 'witty' was just another word for being a dick. He could be a dick without all the frilly words just fine.

"Stop. Just stop." Kade was groaning again.

"She woke up yet?"

The woman in question was on the couch, curled into a tight ball, protecting herself even in sleep. She was a big ol' ball of blood and bruises. Baggy clothes hung off a too-thin frame. Long, dark locks were matted with blood and mud. Her face was all but indistinguishable with its multitude of colors, puffiness, and open wounds. Her nose was broken. Her left arm was positioned at such an awkward angle that made Jackson think it was broken as well. Long stripes of red colored the back of her gray-green shirt and it didn't take Jackson much effort to discern what that might be.

"Nope."

"Ya know," Google and his brothers could collectively kiss his ass, Jackson could manage being a dick all by himself, "she doesn't look like much." Which was an outright lie. Sure, she looked broken and bloodied, but that just added to the whole assassin vibe. Unlike Daisy, this woman looked capable of extreme violence.

The slight, happily, didn't go unnoticed. Kade's head jerked up, the ice pack slid off his face and into his lap.

"You sure this is the same woman?" Jackson watched in

satisfaction as Kade's lip curled and his eyes narrowed into slits.

"Yes, I am fucking sure, asshole." He all but seethed each word.

"All I'm sayin' is," Jackson very deliberately scanned the woman and then arched an eyebrow in Kade's direction, "that she don't look like much."

It had the desired effect. Ten shades of offended and defensive, the man came out of his seat and jabbed a finger at him.

"Really? Do you think I did all this," he gestured to all of himself, "to myself? You think I fell down some stairs?"

"Well... I mean, is she even tall enough to land a punch? And how much damage could it really do?" For the life of him, Jackson couldn't keep the smirk off his face. Kade, of course, noticed and realized he was being played.

"You're such a jackass," Kade grunted and returned to his seat.

"Has she woken up yet?" Reid, lugging his pack and looking mildly annoyed, stepped into the cabin and made a beeline for the woman. Holden was on his heels and scowling.

"Where's Nate?"

"Reid knocked him out with lots of drugs," Holden grunted and flopped into the chair beside Kade.

Jackson didn't want to sit and wait for Nathan to regain consciousness. He wanted to get to the ass-chewing pronto. But from the sounds of it, Holden had already done such a good job. Jackson decided he'd bide his time and strike when conditions were optimal. Maybe he could get his hands on a megaphone.

"What is her name?" Reid didn't glance up from his

examination of the woman, but then Reid rarely made eye contact.

"Caden, I think," Kade volunteered, gently placing the ice pack over his face again. "That's what Nate called her."

"Caden?" Reid's tone was clear and firm. A tone he saved only for the battlefield and patients. "You're safe here. Can you hear me, Caden? You're on a jet headed for the States. You're safe here, Caden. Can you hear me?"

Everyone went silent when Reid paused to let her answer. She remained curled in a ball on the couch, breathing shallowly but evenly. Her eyes still flickered under her lids and her face was tense but relaxed in the way only sleep could do.

"My name is Reid Savage. We're not in Russia anymore. You are safe. I'm going to help you out the best I can and to do that, I'm going to have to touch you, okay? Nathan told me about most of your injuries; unfortunately, I can't do much about any of them until we get home and back on solid ground."

"Reid, she's out, she can't hear you." Holden sat forward and watched as Reid settled on the floor in front of her and started pulling things from his pack.

"What I can do is clean up your back and all the cuts on your arms and legs. Alright, Caden?" Reid ignored him and kept on talking to the comatose woman. "I'm just going to be looking for infections and doing what I can for the smaller cuts. I'm going to have to remove the back of your shirt. Holden, he's Nathan's brother too, he's going help me out, okay, Caden?"

"I love how comfortable you are volunteering me for things, Reid," Holden grunted and stood, stretching, and waited for direction.

"Heat me up some water. We have to get this shirt off

her. It looks like the wounds reopened and then dried to the shirt. We're going to have to soak the shirt to get it off her without ripping chunks of her skin off." He blinked and glanced back at the woman, as if just realizing she was within earshot. "It only sounds scary but we can do it without hurting you, okay, Caden?"

Holden was already heading towards the bathroom. Kade removed the pack from his face and went to help Reid remove the pieces of clothing that weren't stuck to her skin. Reid just kept narrating, like the woman could hear him.

The SAT phone had rung every hour on the hour since they'd landed in Moscow. It was all Jackson could do not to chuck the damn thing on the ground and stomp the shit out of it.

"Fuckin' fuck." Jackson loathed cell phones and the convenient way they made him available at any time and anywhere. What sadistic asshole invented with phones?

SAT phones in particular pissed him off. They just ensured his availability no matter what hellhole he was camped in or far away from people he was.

People.

Fucking people.

The very word made him shudder in terror. Okay, that was a wee bit exaggerative, even for him, but close enough.

If only he had someone to field the calls, or fuck, take all the calls and do all the stupid paperwork and deal with all the people. Now that was an idea Jackson could get on board with. Dax would agree; he was worse at the people thing than Jackson was.

The phone rang again, eliciting another colorful metaphor.

Maybe he could put an ad out in the paper when he got back to town. Were there people who liked that kind of shit?

Answering phones, talking to people, and doing paperwork? His common sense told him no, but people were weird, so who knew?

Jackson decided as the phone rang in his hand that he would find that weird-ass individual and pay them anything they asked.

This call, however, was a call he could not avoid. He'd seriously pissed off certain high-ranking officials with this mission.

Though Savage Security didn't contract out exclusively to anyone, there were some problems that might come back to bite him in the face if he didn't handle this correctly. He had a few connections in the government, connections he wanted to keep. There would be no financial difficulties if some contracts were terminated and certain contacts lost, but Jackson liked to keep the contacts and contracts Savage Security did have.

So regardless of his hatred for cell phones and talking to people in general, he could not let the phone ring. Ignoring it would not make his problems disappear. He was gonna have to man up and press the stupid green button.

With one last growled curse, Jackson quit his mental bitching and answered the goddamned phone.

16

CADEN

Caden came to with a jolt of adrenaline spiking in her blood. A jolt she barely kept under control. Alarm was marching up and down her spine and making her feel all kinds of cautious. Like maybe she shouldn't open her eyes and alert anyone to her newfound consciousness.

The only thing that came to mind in the first few seconds of awareness was Nathan Savage and the fact that he was no longer beside her. She didn't have to open her eyes to know he was gone. The last few seconds of memory on him was almost comforting. Shot in the leg and shoulder: not fatal. But that had been before she'd passed out.

Now, she didn't know what the fuck was going on or where the fuck he was. Those breathing sounds filtering in through the roar in her ears were not Nathan's. Judging from the sounds and smells of the place around her, they were not in that same tiny house she'd passed out in.

Captured a-fucking-gain.

Didn't Kyott have anything better to do? What was the payoff for him? Aside from her getting dead. But didn't he already pretty much say he didn't give a shit that his son was dead? He'd offered her a job, for fuck's sake.

Or maybe she was in a hospital, judging by the almost sterile aroma and the annoyingly consistent beeping.

The second thought to rip through her mind was that she was still alive. She was still alive, and that was... okay.

Good even.

Maybe improperly trained henchmen and their combined inability to kill her wasn't the nightmare it had been before. Maybe the feeling in her gut wasn't entirely displeased with still being able to draw breath.

She'd deal with that bag of cats later. Caden focused her mind and tried not to feel the sharp, burning pains coming in waves from just about everywhere on her body. The blood roaring in her ears quieted, and the merc made a concentrated effort on pushing the pain to the back of her mind. She could complain about it later. She had to focus.

Eyes shut but not squinched, her movements still but not stiff, and breathing deep and even, Caden blindly took in her surroundings.

Freshly cut grass. Surprisingly pleasant. Weird.

Baking bread. New form of torture? Working.

Sweat and old blood. Hers? Most likely.

Cloth on cloth shifting. Other inmates? Guards?

Metal plinking. Cuffs? Didn't sound like the right kind of metal though.

A dog barking. Attack dog. Not fun.

Soft humming. Not in her vicinity and therefore not a worry at that particular moment.

Pages turning every couple of minutes. Bored henchman reading? Huh.

Bodies shifting. Two? Three?

No Nathan.

There were no Nathan sounds or smells. His deep, even breaths were gonna be forever burned in her memory. The smell of him, although not entirely pleasant, being mostly sweat and blood, she'd grown accustomed to—even felt comforted by. He was not drooling on her, or squashed all up against her like some kind of human blanket. He wasn't there.

No Nathan.

Caden only just kept her lips from twitching down at the thought. A swell of something angry and dark was gathering in her gut.

Optimistically, he'd gotten away.

Realistically, they hunted his ass down and shot him where he stood.

Or maybe... maybe they'd hunted him down and just imprisoned him again, which meant he could be rescued.

Unlikely. But a girl could dream.

Guilt and grief swamped her.

No. She didn't know anything for sure. Assuming making asses of all parties and all that, wasn't that an ancient proverb or some shit? Caden shut it all down. She put thoughts of the most likely dead Nathan in the deepest corner of her mind; yet another thing to push aside until a later date, until she could safely sob all over the place without any witnesses.

Finding out if Nathan Savage was alive and kicking was the plan here. Escaping and somehow getting the upper hand was vital to that plan.

She had to focus.

Soft and firm mattress under her back. How thoughtful.

Bare feet. Cold toes. Her new boots were gone.

No belt.

Loose sweatpants and an equally baggy shirt. Someone

had changed her clothes, which was equal parts alarming and annoying.

There were, however, no cuffs on her wrists or rope or zip ties. It was almost disconcerting. Idiots.

IV in her right arm.

Well, all right then, she could work with that. Caden felt a small surge of cruel satisfaction at the feel of it. They'd given her a weapon.

Ailments: A few broken ribs. Possibly a few fractured. Painful, but nothing she couldn't fight through.

Lashed up back. Annoying was all that was.

Left arm was broken and useless. Dammit.

Three fingers on her right hand were out of commission. Gripping would be painful.

Bruising, *lots* of bruising.

Neck felt okay.

Head trauma? None. How nice of them.

Broken toe, maybe two. She'd kicked that asshole too hard with improperly fitted boots.

Overall maneuverability: thirty to forty percent. Agility was equally as shitty but still not undoable.

Blocking was gonna be a bitch. Making any kind of physical contact was gonna be painful as fuck. On top of the fact that she'd be doing it all one-handed. What fun.

Caden took a moment to find her resolve and fan the inferno in her gut. Nathan—that was her objective. Find Nathan and/or extract information on his whereabouts. Kill the bastards who gunned him down. Find the shit-fuck who ordered it and murder.

And the escaping too. Escaping was essential to the last part of the plan.

The woman made sure to keep her fluttering eyelids

slow and drugged-like when she blinked open her eyes for the first time.

Bright. Too fucking bright.

Two figures. One seated, three feet from the bed. One standing, no, *hovering* over her.

Another blink revealed an open window, maybe seven feet from the bed, and alerted the hovering figure of her wakefulness. He made a surprised sound in his throat, leaned over to look into her face, and Caden took her opportunity.

Steeling herself against the inevitable onslaught of pain from her injuries, she gripped the tube pushing saline into her veins, ripped it out of her wrist, and palmed the needle. One breath later, she vaulted off the mattress, shoved the side of her hand into the hovering figures throat, slung her working arm around his shoulders, kicked out his knee to throw off his balance, and jabbed the needle into his neck. Or close enough that he'd be all soft and willing to please.

Dizzy.

Adrenaline was beating out exhaustion, but only just.

Pain. Lots of fucking pain.

Three, maybe five minutes until she'd collapse.

"Shhh," Caden didn't recognize her own voice. It was all gravelly and groggy. "Be calm," she warned in Russian. She put pressure on the needle to get him to stop hacking and sputtering like he was drowning.

The one in the chair had startled into a standing position. He was big and beefy. The left side of his face and neck was all scarred like he'd gone a couple of rounds with a blender on puree. Jeans, shirt, weapons. One gun that she could see and maybe a couple of knives somewhere on him. His hands were up in more of a placating gesture than in a show of surrender.

"Don't come near!" Caden had threatened the same thing a couple of times in a few different languages before, so she didn't have to think hard to find the right words. "Move away or I'll hurt him!"

Another figure was perched on a chair on the other side of the room. He was quiet and watching her with guarded, calculating eyes.

Fuck.

She'd heard three bodies. Why hadn't she thought to look? The mercenary adjusted her hostage, so he was between her and the seated one and her back was at the wall.

"There ain't no need for that, ma'am." English. Southern. His accent was thick and his eyes showed surprise but not panic. "We aren't—"

"Stay back! Keep your ass where it is and I won't kill him." English, being her native tongue, was much easier to threaten with. "Toss your weapons. Both of you."

"Look, ma'am—"

"Listen, Harvey Dent, shut the fuck up and put down your weapons or I'll make a new breathing hole in your friend's neck. Comprenday?" A wave of dizziness curled her stomach. Sweat started beading on her skin.

He complied, though for a second he looked like he wanted to rush her. Two knives and a gun were silently kicked towards her and he righted himself. Lips pursed, he straightened with his hands still up. The one in the chair did the same, though he only had a handgun.

"Nathan, where is he?" The only possible exit was the window. She couldn't get by Scarface without him attacking her to get to the door.

"If you'll just let Reid go—" The big scarred one was still talking and the one in her hold had stopped sputtering.

"Do you have him? Did you kill him? Tell me where he is and just who the fuck you are, and I'll let him keep his neck as it is."

"My name is Jackson Savage." He jerked his head towards the quiet one on the other side of the room. "That there is Holden Savage." With a small gesture, he motioned to the one in her choke hold and grimaced. "And Reid... *Savage*. See the pattern here, Xena?"

"Savage?" Her hold loosened automatically at the name.

No.

No fucking way was that true.

Nathan had said he'd had brothers, and that they were soldiers. They'd magically tracked his ass down? Then found them again in the tiny house? And what? Whisked them off into the sunset? But there was no fucking way that anyone, not even Nathan Savage, was that lucky. No fucking way.

Caden had been through mind games before and came out the other end mostly unscathed. Just because he knew Nathan's surname didn't mean shit.

"Yes, ma'am," he grunted and tucked his head in, effectively angling the damaged side of his face away from her, like it had something to do with why she was freaking out.

What had he said about Jackson? She couldn't remember. All the names he'd spouted had blurred in her mind. Another bout of nausea had her stomach knotting and more sweat leaking out her pores. How could she test them?

"What's Nathan scared of?" She remembered the things he'd admitted about himself.

"Anything with more than four legs, the man's a pansy. Can't even squash a fuckin' bug without screaming his fool head off," the quiet one decided to chime in from all the way across the room. "His middle name is Albert. His favorite color is yellow. His eye color is blue. He weighs like, what, two hundred and something? He cries like a baby whenever he watches *The Lion King*. Want his social security number?"

They were both stone-faced and scowl-y and somehow those scowls were familiar. Caden could feel herself relenting. Indecision had her tightening her hold on Reid, who didn't make a sound.

Reid was the one with a squirrel and the PHD in doctoring, fuck, what was it called? Medical science... practice? Who fucking knew. She'd liked the stories Nathan had told her about him.

After a long moment of hesitation, Caden forced herself to let go of the only leverage she currently had and released him from her choke hold. She kept the needle in an upright and ready position. Reid righted himself, rubbed his neck, and took a step back towards her.

"Back off," Caden snarled and shoved the needle in his direction.

"You've got to sit down at least." His hands went up at her growl, and he took a step back. "I've got to reattach the IV and get some meds in your system. I didn't know what you were allergic to and Nathan didn't either—"

"Nathan..." Her arm was trembling now and her knees were quaking, but she was only a foot from the window. She couldn't make her voice cooperate. She didn't want to ask. Didn't want to know that she'd failed yet another person she was responsible for. Didn't want to know that he was lying dead in a ditch somewhere. Dead, the blue-white kind of dead that he couldn't come back from. "Is... is he... where is he?"

They all started talking at once. Well, Reid had never stopped; he'd just gotten louder and more indignant. Caden could feel exhaustion setting in. Adrenaline was wearing off.

"Goddamn soldiers, you are not invincible, you need time to heal." Reid just kept on ranting and eyeing her like she was going to kill over at any moment. "Sit down! Pick up the weapons if it makes you feel better. But please just sit down. You need stitches and we need to put that arm in a cast."

"Oh yeah, Reid—that's a good idea. Tell her to pick up a gun and shoot us all." The one Scarface had said was named Holden was scoffing and moving forward at the same time, like she wouldn't notice his giant ass getting closer.

"He's alive. He's in the other guest room." Jackson's voice was rough and gravelly and hit her like a fist in the gut.

"You're aggravating your busted ribs. I have to get some antibiotics in you. Please, just sit down."

"All right, shut up!" Caden raised her voice and jerked the needle in Holden's direction. "Take another step, Gigantor, and you'll fucking lose an eye."

He stopped in his tracks, hands up in surrender, and shot her a smile. "Can't blame me for tryin'."

"Where is he?" She steeled her voice and dug her nails into her palms until she could speak without her voice breaking and began again. "He's alive?"

"Jackson..." Holden spoke up again. He jerked his chin towards her, which obviously meant something to the other one.

"I see her. There ain't no need to go plunging out the window, ma'am." His tone was all kinds of annoyed. As if he hated the fact that he was telling her not to jump out the window. "We didn't go through all the trouble of keeping ya alive just to hurt ya. You are safe here."

"Where's here?" Caden halted her progress to the window and cursed herself for being so obvious.

"Reid, go and wake him up." He jerked his chin towards the blond who'd taken a seat on the bed, rubbing his neck.

"No, stay where you are," Caden growled at him and then turned her irritation back on Jackson. "Take me to him."

"You shouldn't be walking around in your condition. You should be sitting down and telling me what you're allergic to so I can start fixing you!" More indignant and loud now, Reid stomped his foot and motioned to the bed rather violently.

"All of you. Over by the door. Now." There was no reason they should listen to her. She no longer had any kind of leverage. They could rush her and get the needle out of her hand in less than thirty seconds, but they obeyed.

As soon as she was sure they were all out of lunging range, she stooped, keeping her eyes on the men, gripped the first weapon that hit her palm, and stood upright again.

It was one of Jackson's knives. Ugh.

She didn't want to do close-quarters combat again. Caden tucked the thing into the waistband of her sweats and stooped one more time. This time, she palmed a handgun.

"You don't need a weapon," Jackson growled, still angling the damaged side of his face away.

"Lead the way." Caden motioned for them to exit first and all but hobbled out behind them.

They were in a house. There was carpet under her bare feet; there were even vacuum cleaner tracks. Pictures on the walls like some kind of sitcom family. Which meant the baking bread she'd smelled earlier was real. Oh god, maybe they would let her eat some. The thought made her mouth water and her eyes go blurry with tears.

They stopped at the door on the left side and waited till she caught up.

"Inside." She had to swallow the excess saliva in her mouth before she could properly speak.

They obeyed again, all scowling, though for different reasons. Reid seemed to have no self-preservation instincts. His only concern was for her. Holden didn't like that she had a weapon and was telling him what to do. And it seemed Jackson was pissed that she hadn't jumped out the window.

The room was small and cozy but still had that sterile, hospital-clean smell. Closet on the right wall, two man-sized windows on the furthest wall, and a big bed pushed against the left wall.

And there he was. Bare chest heaving up and down. His eyes were open, a bit glazed, like he was drugged, and blinking up at her with that big stupid grin.

Shirtless and smiling and alive.

Wow, she really liked that combination.

"Caden!" he slurred and wobbled to his feet but kept on smiling. "You look so pretty!"

Caden watched through blurry eyes as he came right towards her. Delirious giggles bubbled out of her throat and echoed around the room. He was so ridiculous. He was alive. He was smiling at her.

"No, no Nathan, don't get up." Reid's voice sounded from somewhere behind her, but she couldn't give two shits about them now. "Just because you can't feel the pain right now doesn't mean that you're not doing damage to your leg. Dammit, Nathan! Listen to me. I'm a doctor! Don't just yank out your IV!"

The relief at seeing him alive and kicking made her go boneless and weak-kneed. But that was okay because

Nathan and his furnace of a body had caught her before she face-planted and was all but dragging her back towards the bed he'd just vacated.

"Don't lift her! Your shoulder is not magically going to re-stitch itself! Don't do the thing that I am specifically telling you not to do!"

"These your brothers, Nathan?" Caden didn't know what she was saying. She was too caught up in the fact that Nathan was alive and squashing her to his body like she was a missing limb.

"Yeah... Jackson," he slurred and blinked slowly, like a big cat. "Jackson, put it in my ass."

"What?" That got her attention. "He did what?"

Caden wiped the treacherous tears off her cheeks and looked over Nathan's shoulder towards his brothers. More had appeared now, and most of them were guffawing and outright laughing. She recognized one as the ass-hat she'd had to dislocate her arm for. Jackson was scowling.

"Tracker." Nathan put his face in her hair. "He put a tracker in my butt cheek. Don't cry, Caden... you're safe now."

Caden couldn't concentrate enough to follow that statement. They finally reached the bed and Nathan toppled them onto it. Earning an outraged shriek from Reid.

"Are. You. Hearing. The. Words. That. I. Am. Speaking?! Stop stressing your wounds, you idiots! I refuse to re-stitch anything! You can both just suffer!"

Caden could hardly breathe with Nathan's weight on top of her. But she didn't care. His heat was soaking into her. His heartbeat was thumping against her palm. He was alive. They were alive.

"You're safe." It was a slurred chant he kept whispering

into her hair. "You're safe." Nathan's muscles relaxed on top of her and almost immediately his breathing evened out.

Caden relaxed her tense muscles and allowed herself to melt into Nathan and the soft mattress under her. She could sleep. Sure, there was a shit-ton of things that needed doing, escape routes that had to be planned, and six brothers she didn't know if she could trust.

Trust.

Fuck. She was thinking of the word trust, like it meant something to her. Sure, it applied to Nathan, but that was different.

Caden couldn't believe how casually she was considering trusting them just because they were Nathan's brothers. What the fuck was wrong with her?

She'd deal with that later, though. She didn't have the energy enough to care either way. Besides, she was armed now. Should they prove untrustworthy, she would be able to defend herself. The adrenaline she was running on was depleted. Exhaustion and bone-deep relief had her now, and she allowed herself to be pulled under.

"Wait." An annoying tap on her cheek. "Wait, don't pass out yet." Reid. Caden grunted and opened her eyes. If she could've punched him, she would have, but her arms were trapped under Nathan's body. "Are you allergic to anything? Is there anything I should know before administering drugs?"

"No. Go away." Caden tried for a menacing growl, but she was too tired. She was out before she was even halfway to making her face do the thing that scared people.

17

NATHAN

Nathan didn't want to wake up. He was warm and safe and holding Caden. Not just holding, but *cuddling*. He'd even go so far as to say they were snuggling. Not one-sided half-assed snuggling, but the kind of snuggling that had two consenting adults and full-on participation. It was enough to pretend he didn't feel Reid poking him in the face and go back to sleep.

"Nathan, I can tell that you are awake. Stop pretending." If goddamn Reid and his goddamn social ineptitude woke her up, Nathan was going to kill him. "You were never very good at playing possum."

Did the man not see that he was cuddling Caden Quinn, thief extraordinaire and quintessential badass? Two pre-qualifiers he'd never known he'd had for potential life partners.

His brothers, the same ones who also loved human contact and feeling a warm body snuggled all nicely against them but pretended like they didn't need it, gave him hell about it. He was as human and needy and comfort-seeking as the next guy (the next guy being any one of his emotionally stunted brothers). He could not care less what those insecure jack-wagons thought. Nathan loved cuddling, and he didn't care who knew it. Be it animal or human, Nathan cuddled. He cuddled hard.

"Nathan." Voice impatient and bordering on annoyed, Reid poked him harder in the face. Nathan continued to pretend he didn't exist and reveled in the feel of Caden cuddled up to him.

For Caden, he knew it was different. From what he'd learned about her, she'd been conditioned not to ever want human contact. Contact meant getting hit. And being the badass that she was, pretended not to need it, much like his brothers. She did, however, enjoy it.

The way she was clinging to him like he was going to up and float away was a testament to that fact. Her legs were wrapped around his waist and her good arm was twined around his bicep. Her face was pushed into his chest. Even in sleep, when she was supposed to be relaxed, her fingers dug into his flesh like ten little anchors.

"Nathan." It was an annoyed huff, followed by a couple more pokes.

Nathan didn't want to wake up. He didn't want to stop snuggling, and dammit, didn't he deserve a nap after the shitastical week he'd had? The face poking got more insistent and hard. Why wasn't he allowed to sleep? Reid had already patched him up. There was no reason he should be waking up.

"What?" Nathan didn't open his eyes, wanting to keep the illusion of being asleep for a little bit longer.

"Nate." Another poke. "Nate."

Still not opening his eyes, Nathan shifted to swat at the infuriating finger. White hot searing pain ripped down his back and arm and reminded the former soldier that he was sporting two shiny new bullet holes. The drugs had worn off, and he was now officially awake. His empty stomach churned and rolled. Cold sweat broke out all over his skin and sent tiny shivers down his spine.

"Goddammit Reid! What the hell do you want?" It came out less angry and more pathetic than he was aiming for.

"I want you to get off of her," Reid snapped, all impatient, like Nathan should be able to read his mind.

Nathan tensed, instinctively going into battle mode and squaring his position on top of the sleeping woman. No goddamn way was he getting off of her. She was cuddling him. Holding him like he was important to her. He wasn't letting her go. They'd have to pry his dead goddamn body off of her.

"What? You gonna kick my ass for providing medical care?" He could practically hear Reid rolling his eyes.

Unfortunately, Nathan was evolved enough to realize that he couldn't drag her off to his cave and keep her all to himself, like the Neanderthal part of his brain was telling him to do. It was a nice scenario to play out in his head and maybe later when they were both fully recovered, but he had to be reasonable about things. She needed medical attention and she probably couldn't breathe too well with his entire body weight on top of her.

Still though, Nathan had to reassure himself that his brother wasn't telling him that he couldn't have her. He wasn't. Reid was just doing his job. It was almost embarrassing how long it took to convince himself to relax his guard. The man eventually got a grip enough to carefully extract himself from their tangled limbs.

"Careful, don't rip your stitches again. And if either of you take out your IVs again, I will keep you both in medical comas forever."

"Yeah, yeah." Nate perched on the edge of the bed and had to take a few breaths to steady himself.

He'd been shot before, a few times actually, so he was familiar with the burning sensation running up his leg and arm. Didn't mean he particularly liked the feeling, it was just familiar.

Tortured and starving was a new thing to him. He wasn't exactly hungry. He felt hollow and shaky and like he might die if he didn't eat, but the thought of food made his tongue sit heavy in his mouth and his stomach churn.

"Are you in pain?" Reid wasn't paying attention to him; his full focus was on the mercenary and the handheld... doctor things (were definitely not the right words but Nathan could only ask so much of his aching brain) in his hands.

"Yes, shit." A throb in his head made him lurch forward.

"Need more drugs?"

"I don't want to be all loopy again so soon." The vibration of his voice caused his head to throb harder.

"You won't. I'll give you something to numb the pain, but keep you alert."

"M'kay."

"So remind me, 'cause I'm kinda fuzzy on this, why exactly were you in Moscow again?" The voice was not Reids. It was Holden's. Pissy, snippy Holden. Mentally, the soldier groaned.

In waltzed Holden, looking all kinds of angry and impatient. The same way he'd looked when Nathan had jumped off the roof and broken his arm twice. Despite all outward indicators, it was his 'concerned' face. Nathan didn't want to deal with him or his many faces.

"Vacationing." Nate tried to keep the snap out of his voice, but it wasn't working. Holden, the darling, was immune to Nathan's bad moods. Well, he wasn't so much immune as he was just ignoring it. For the moment.

"You hate crowds, you hate Moscow in particular, and you don't ski. Did I miss any other tourist attraction that you could possibly pretend to have an interest in?" There was a very short pause, in which Holden pretended like he expected an answer. "Or were you really there because that's where Marskib's base of operations is and you're still keeping tabs on the son of a bitch?"

As usual, Holden cut right to the soft spot and went at it with both barrels. Nathan held in another groan. So maybe vacationing wasn't the only thing on his Moscow itinerary, but that didn't mean he'd gone looking for trouble. He'd just happened to be in Moscow and he'd just happened to frequent seedy pubs and he'd just happened to slip in a question or seven that just happened to revolve around Marskib and his organization.

"Nate, I know what it's like to fail a mission, but it was not your fault. And you can't go off on your own with no backup!"

"Holden." Guilt knifed his insides until he felt like he was going to puke. "Can we *not* right now?"

"Fine." Holden folded his arms across his chest and shifted his position against the wall.

Nathan ignored the guilty rage building in his gut and watched through the throb in his head as his brother glared at him.

Holden took after their mother in looks. He was shorter than Nathan by two inches. He had her bright blue eyes and her soft smile. Nathan took after their father, being the bigger and beefier of the two. But when Holden was angry, their father showed through his features, what with the scowl and the pinched lines of his face and the way his eyebrows pulled down in the middle. Nathan closed his eyes against the sight. He did not want to think about his scumbag father.

"Okay." It took all of thirty seconds for Holden to start in on him again. "So then, let's talk about the mercenary you brought home."

"Her name is Caden, and what about her?"

"She's a *mercenary*, Nathan." He made sure to annunciate every sound in the word like Nathan had never heard it before.

"Yeah, she is." Nathan shifted in his seat on the bed to crack an eye open at his brother. "What's your point?"

His hackles were in the upright position and a scowl was growing on his face. Nathan internally sighed and resigned himself to an argument because that's what Holden's scowls always meant.

"Well, I guess my point is that she is a mercenary. A woman who kills, maims, and steals for money, and you have her in the same house as Mom."

"Stop with that look." Nathan was growling and glaring and getting all kinds of offended.

"What look? I'm not doing any look!"

"Yes, you are! It's the 'I disapprove because I'm a jerk' look."

"Well, I disapprove and my face is gonna show it." Holden shook his head in seeming disbelief and Nathan wanted to deck him. "Why do you think this is a good idea?"

Nathan let out a sigh and ran a hand over his face. Holden, by nature, was suspicious and untrusting. It was most likely wreaking havoc on his protect-what's-mine mindset, but the man was going to have to deal with it.

"She is a good person." There was no way to convince Holden of anything he didn't see for himself, but he was going to try, anyway. The throb in his head was lessening, and the nauseous feeling in his gut was dissipating.

"A good person?" It wasn't really a question, more of Holden trying to process the thought.

"And you should be thanking her. This woman has saved my life. I don't know how many times. So don't look at her like that when she wakes up. I'll already have a hard enough time convincing her to stay without your face messin' it up."

"Stay? You want a killer and a thief to stay here? Here with Ellen and Bobby?" All incredulous, like Nathan had given Dracula an all-access pass.

"Yes goddammit, she's just as much of a killer as you or me. She's a good damn human being and a soldier before anything else, you ass. So if you can't keep your face polite, you need to leave."

Nathan watched as surprise and anger morphed his brother's features. There was a moment of fight in him, but his shoulders relaxed and he crossed his arms in grudging surrender.

"Fine, I'll keep my face judgment free, but I ain't leaving this woman alone. Ain't she the one that shot you? *Twice*?" Holden was suddenly remembering all of Nathan's bitching about this woman and Nathan was suddenly regretting all the complaining he'd done.

"Yes, she did. Good shots too, both of 'em." It came out more admiringly and less defensive than he was aiming for, but he was number one in the Caden Quinn Fan Club and would be the first to admit it.

"Are you serious—how?" Holden cut himself off and took position at the far side of the room, obviously deciding not to question his brother's insanity.

"She's the one that shot you in the ass?" Kade grinned, taking up the position Holden had vacated.

"Yep, and the one that kicked your ass." Nathan took the trouble to insert that little tidbit. The scowl and the accompanying growl on his brother's face was enough to make that trouble worth it.

"Yeah, what's it like to be on our level now, oh-demoted-one?" Holden snickered from his side of the room.

"First of all, what have I told you about quoting Mulan at me? If you don't love it, you don't get to quote it." He wasn't grinning now. "And secondly, the woman—she—you weren't there! I thought she was, I don't know... *not* a fighter. I was not prepared for her to break her own damn arm."

"Are we talking about when Kade got his ass handed to him?" Maddox appeared in the doorway, permanent wide smile on his face. "I watched that go down—I thought she was gonna kill him."

"You watched but did nothing to help?" Kade was now outraged and looking all accusatory at Maddox.

"I was piloting the chopper. What'd you want me to do, land it on top of her?" Maddox was still smiling and making a beeline for the window seat.

"I don't know, something other than giggling with D about it," Kade returned, only slightly less miffed sounding.

Nathan was feeling marginally better now that there were numbing drugs in his system. It was good to be back. It was good to hear his brothers bickering again. Damn, it was good to be alive.

"Hey, I giggle like a man. 'Sides Daisy was on the ground exploding shit; there was no giggling on her part."

"Actually, she did do some giggling when she blew the charges," Reid chimed in. "Crazy woman." That was muttered, but not low enough for Nathan to miss.

"Of course, she giggled—she giggles. That's D." Maddox was smirking again and turning his attention back to Kade. "But what we were actually discussing is how Kade Savage can no longer lord over us with his undefeated title of two years running. Caden knocked him off that particular high horse."

"She may have... caught me off guard, but I can still kick all your asses." Kade was shoving his finger around the room like he was going to take them all on at once.

"No—no fighting." Reid's voice was authoritative and stern all at once. "Not until those ribs have healed, at least."

Maddox let out a laugh at Kade's scowl, and Holden even cracked a smile.

"Wait, wait—" Reid's voice sounded again, this time concerned. "I'm Reid, remember?"

A small panicked sound came from behind him. Nathan wrenched himself around, forgetting about his injuries, but had to stop mid-wrench. The pain was somewhat numb, but he felt it now. White hot and tearing into his muscles. Caden was awake and panicking and he was sitting there uselessly. He had to reassure the mercenary before she went into defense mode and annihilated his brothers or hurt herself, but he was too slow.

A scuffle sounded behind him. A pained moan. A feminine grunt and then a body was flung off the bed behind him and landed with a thud on the floor at his feet.

He half expected it to be Reid. But Caden was the body moaning in pain before him. She glanced up at him, eyes wild and breathing heavy. She was battered six ways to Sunday, but she was alive. Alive, because she'd gotten them out. Even when they'd walked into a war zone and he'd been lying down, shot. She'd fought and fought and got them out.

Recognition sparked and the wild in her eyes dimmed a tad.

"Nathan." She smiled.

An honest to god smile and pushed to her feet. She took position beside his seated figure and subconsciously squared her stance, preparing for an attack.

"Caden, it's all right. You're safe here. They're my brothers." It was aggravating how slowly his body was moving. "We're safe."

"You gonna live?" She was examining his bullet holes and ignoring Reid's pointed huff.

"Yep. One bullet nicked an artery, but they both went clean through. Reid patched me up." How could he tell her he brought her home to meet his parents without her bolting?

"Will you sit?" Impatient and concerned, Reid hovered three steps away, looking like he had murder in mind. "How are you burning through the meds so quickly? You should still be out cold. And you've pulled out your damn IV again."

Caden sat.

Beside him.

Her knee touching his knee.

Her thigh touching his thigh.

18

CADEN

There was just silence.

Awkward, awkward silence.

All eyes were on her. Holden was glaring. Reid was muttering to himself, going over every battered inch of her. Nathan was grinning stupidly at her knees. The unknown was smiling widely at her.

It was unnerving as fuck. Inwardly, she was noting exits and using her peripherals to check for the lumps of her confiscated armory. They, the knife and gun she'd made them surrender, were still there. An arm's length away. Outwardly her face was fixed in a placid expression she saved special for interrogations.

Nathan wasn't helping the awkward silence at all. He kept grinning at her knees like they'd up and sprouted cancer-curing flowers. The silence stretched. The awkward intensified and Caden was two seconds from bolting. She wanted to swat the grinning idiot. He wasn't pumped full of morphine. His green eyes lacked that glazed-over drugged quality they'd had the day before (Was it just a day? Who the hell knew how long she'd been out?). So all that happy was just him being Nathan.

Weirdo.

Grinning, ridiculous, finely toned, idiot.

Holy Christ, she wanted him.

That thought shut down her whole brain for a good ten seconds. She'd known before that she wanted to kiss him, feel him up a bit, and maybe get in his pants. But this was a whole other level of want.

Reid's unceasing mutterings brought her back around. She had to focus on the current situation and not be plotting on how she was going to get in Savage's pants. It probably wouldn't be too hard. He seemed like the easy kind. It didn't hurt that he seemed to already have their next ten years mapped out.

Weirdo.

Unabashed, smiling, muscle-bound male whose pants she was going to get in.

"You alright there, Nate?" The unknown one spoke up and slapped Caden right back into defense mode. "You look like... you're high as a kite. You gonna pass out?"

"What—no." His head jerked up to swivel towards Reid, caution in his eyes. Like those words would trigger the 'only goddamn certified doctor in the room so they had better listen to him by god or there would be hell to pay' into some kind of rampage. "I am fine. The painkiller is kickin' in."

"You sure? 'Cause you look like you could use—" He shifted in his seat and glanced towards the leaner meaner version of Nathan with a small grin.

"I am fine, Maddox. Thanks for the moving and heartfelt concern." Nathan was glaring now, and the giant was smirking. "Now if you'd like to see yourself out—"

"What, so you two can make out while we're in there

slaving away over a hot stove?" This was a new voice that came from the door. Caden recognized the guy as the one she'd broken, her toes breaking his ribs. More men, big men, stood behind him trying to shove past into the room.

Alarm bells clanged in her mind. Her heart kicked into overdrive, and Caden positioned herself so that the weapons were within reach. And then immediately felt foolish for responding like they were the enemy. They were his family.

"*You* cook?" someone said; Caden lost track of who was speaking. There were too many threats to contend with. Too many giants filling the room.

"My right fuckin' ass cheek *you* cook."

Well, anyone that hit six foot and beyond made giant status in Caden's eyes. Why did anyone need to be that tall? What was the point? It had to be a southern breeding thing.

"You're safe here, Caden," Reid muttered in her ear. His thumb was on her pulse and his eyes were on her strategically placed good arm.

First, Caden schooled her expression and carefully moved her arm out of his reach. She didn't need anyone, especially someone she didn't know, reading her that easily. She'd learned a time too many that blind trust was something only idiots and victims gave. Reid didn't take offense. He only moved on to the next battered part of her with the same scary single-minded resolve he seemed to do everything with.

"I can cook. You just can't eat it."

Someone laughed. Probably the smiley one. The room was full now. All seven brothers were in attendance. One was scowling. Another was glaring. The smiley one was smiling. Another one, the one with the scarred-up face, was stoic and staring at her. Nathan was staring at her knees again.

"Not if you don't want to get food poisoning. Jesus, my stomach was fucked up for days."

Caden wanted to grip his collar and drag him out the open window with her. Everything in her was screaming to bolt. They were all too big, too threatening, and she was too weak. She couldn't fight off a cadaver in her current state, let alone six healthy, possibly hostile, combatants.

"Fuck you; Nate's the one who starts fires if he even walks into a kitchen. At least I'm not that level of incompetent."

They were his family, she reminded herself again. They weren't going to attack.

"That was one time. *Two* at most." Nathan was all indignant. He glanced sideways at her, his neck and ears pink. Christ, she wanted to rip off his clothes.

"No, actually, it was more like seven."

They were his family, not her family. Which meant only that they wouldn't attack him. She was free game.

"You still owe me a new microwave."

There was a groan. The scarred one kept looking at her. The olive-skinned one shifted closer. Someone else giggled.

"Aww, look at that. You're embarrassing the wee lamb."

At the very least, the one she'd beaten in Russia would want some kind of revenge. Nathan stiffened beside her and started throwing glares around the room. Caden watched his jaw tense and his eyebrows furrow.

"Then we definitely shouldn't mention the adult diapers."

Nathan turned a slightly brighter shade of pink and someone giggled. Finally, after an annoyingly thorough examination of her cuts, Reid quit his hovering and pushed through the throng of males to get to the other side of the bed where his tools were. Someone shifted closer again and the hair on her neck stood on end.

"Oh, thanks ass-wipes, but she already knows and loves me all the more for it." Nathan attempted to put an arm around her but quit mid-movement when he discovered his injured arm wouldn't cooperate.

"I do?" How very presumptuous of him. Not wrong, but still presumptuous. Someone laughed outright, and Nathan started smirking.

"Yes, you do. Remember the part in the cell when you said." He straightened his posture and, in the highest falsetto he could manage, started lying through his teeth. "Oh Nate, pissing your pants in public wasn't your fault—you heroic, lone wolf, bit of tasty man flesh. If anything, it makes you *more* attractive."

She couldn't keep herself from grinning when he coughed and eyed her like it would be madness to debate him on that solid bit of evidence he'd just pulled out of his ass. Someone was snorting. Someone else was chuckling.

"Oh yeah." Caden rolled her eyes and successfully restrained the ridiculous giggles trying to burst out of her. "I forgot."

"Nate, you're supposed to change your voice when you're doing an impression of someone else. Otherwise, we all get confused."

"Yeah, yeah." He turned to stare down his brothers. "Now, if you would all fuck off, that would be great."

"Nathan Albert Savage!" Someone was all pretend outrage and gasps. "Language! What would Mom say?"

Albert? Why did that little revelation make her want him even more? There was something wrong with her.

"Since Nate here seems to have forgotten his manners,

I'll help ya out." The scarred one was suddenly in front of her.

Oh yeah, there were other people. Other dangers still in the room. There were threats she had yet to contend with and here she was mooning all over that bit of tasty man flesh.

Automatically, Caden took the scarred one's measure. Face ingrained. Every little tidbit she could get memorized and analyzed.

Olive skin. Hazel eyes. Sharp features. The left side of his face and neck were scarred. Deep, long scars that roughened his skin. His voice was deep and too gravelly for it to have been natural. Had the bomb that went off in his face torn up his voice too? Damn. Jackson was how he'd introduced himself before. One or two inches shorter than Nathan. Led with his right foot. Knife in his right boot. Glock on his right hip. Right-handed.

"We didn't get properly introduced before. I'm Jackson. Nathan's older brother." He extended his hand.

Caden flinched on reflex and watched his arm hang in the space between them. She tried to analyze the type of hit that was coming and attempted to brace for it. But he just left it there in the space between them, like he wanted to get her opinion on the thing. Slowly, embarrassingly slowly, she realized that he was offering to shake her hand. Heat rushed to her face and someone cleared their throat.

"Oh." One arm was out of commission, the other one was positioned to grab a gun. They were his family. They were Nathan's family. Caden could trust Nathan. "Caden Quinn." She gave him her hand.

"Nice to meet you, Caden." He gripped her hand with both of his. "Thank you for bringing Nate back alive."

"Er..." He gave her hand back, unharmed, and nodded.

Off balance, the mercenary grappled to form some kind of reply. "I... it was a two-man effort, actually."

"Caden, I was conscious long enough to get shot. *You* did all the work." Nathan smiled at her, and it was Caden's turn to go pink.

"Maddox." The smiley one maneuvered around Jackson to shove his hand at her. This time Caden took the proffered hand and shook it like she did that kind of civilized thing all the time. "I'm the handsome devil Nathan's probably told you all about."

Maddox was brown-skinned, brown-eyed, brown-haired, and beautiful. Full lips, square jaw, wide eyes, broad-shouldered and tall. Tall as Nathan and beefier, with crinkles around his eyes and mouth like he did nothing but smile. He led with his right foot, but his gun holster was on his left hip—ambidextrous?

"Nice to meet you." Caden mentally channeled Julie Andrews. She could do this. She could be polite and all civilized-like.

"You ever been to Texas, Caden?" His palm was rough, and he was smiling, brown eyes bright and happy.

"Er... no." Was he smiling flirtatiously at her?

"Maybe I can show you around sometime." He grinned wider when Nathan sputtered.

"Over my dead goddamn body, you whore." Nathan pointedly unhooked their joined hands and shoved the opposing giant away. Maddox only threw his head back and laughed. "Trust me," this he directed at Caden but made sure his voice was loud enough for everyone to hear, "you don't want what everyone has had."

"Hey." Maddox retook his chair across the room. "I love love and love loves me."

"I'm Daxley." Another body took position in front of her.

"Thank you, really. Nathan gets into all kinds of trouble. Thank you for looking after him and bringing him home alive."

Daxley was shorter than Nathan by about four inches. His features were smaller and more pointed than the rest of the clan. Lean, built like a swimmer. Pretty green eyes, dark scruff, defined cheekbones, and brown hair that curled over his ears. Lefty. Two knives in his belt. Hand cannon on his left hip. He searched her face like he expected to find someone else. Odd.

"Nice to meet you, Daxley."

Her danger barometers were slowly decreasing. It was marginally safer somehow now that she had their names. The hair on her neck no longer stood on end. Which was something.

"You can call me Dax." He smiled warmly at her and released her hand and went to punch Nathan. "You had me worried, you son of a bitch."

Then the one she'd had every intention of killing at the compound stepped up and put his hand out.

"We didn't officially meet before—maybe you remember me?" He was smiling like they were already old friends. Black skin, bright blue eyes, square features. He was as tall as Nathan but lean with cords of muscles under his shirt. He was a lefty.

"Yeah." Caden cringed and took his hand. The side of his hand was rough. "Sorry about that."

"Nah, I would have done the same in your position. I'm Kade, by the way." He took his hand back, but settled his stance beside her. Like he was planning on staying right beside her for the rest of the day. "You're pretty skilled, Caden. Where'd you get your close-quarter combat training, if you don't mind me askin'?"

"Nope, no, there will be no bonding until she is stitched up and her arm is set! I let you all meet her, but now you all have to get out. Out!" Reid was suddenly in front of her, his hands up, and his voice firm. "Everyone out."

Slowly, the males moved to comply, but not before putting her through the torture of their gratitude once more. They all had to reiterate how much of a trouble magnet Nathan was and how much they appreciated her keeping him alive and bringing him home. Which was just so very awkward. What the hell was she supposed to say? Finally, they eventually all trickled out. She got two parting smiles, one nod, a smirk, and a particularly suspicious glare from Holden.

"Maddox's a big flirt, and Holden is just naturally suspicious of everyone. Don't let it get to you." Nathan glanced sideways at her again, a rueful smile on his lips. "They're all a bit... overwhelming all at once like that."

"Nah, they are nice."

"I'll be right back." Reid quit his muttering to glance up at the both of them and then glare. "Do not stress your wounds. Do not even move. You especially, Caden, I should have taken care of those cuts when you were sleeping. Nathan was on top of you, though, and he's a little hard to move."

"Can I shower first?" Caden didn't particularly like the thought of him, or anyone for that matter, stitching her up, but it had to be done. She'd like to be a semblance of clean when he did it.

Reid scowled at her and folded his arms across his chest, obviously not liking that request. He sighed after a moment and rubbed his face like she was a perpetual thorn in his side. Like they hadn't just met. He'd been her hostage, and he was treating her like they went way back. The casual acceptance and familiarity was almost alarming. Maybe it was a doctor thing.

"Fine, but it has to be quick and lukewarm, so you don't swell." He unfolded his arms and turned on his heel. "Stay there. I'll be right back."

Reid strode out and silence fell again. This time, however, it was a hell of a lot less awkward. Caden watched as Nathan carefully maneuvered himself so his back was resting against the headboard and his long legs stretched to the end of the bed. He was still smiling, but he was no longer staring at her knees.

"So..." She could do femme fatale. How hard could it be?

He glanced sideways at her when she didn't finish her sentence. His face was busted up, and all bruised and his lips were chapped and split in the middle. His beard was thick and there was still some blood caked in by his ears. He should not have been appealing to her.

No, she couldn't fuck him.

There were reasons, a whole list of reasons, why she should not do what she was most likely going to do, anyway. Caden tried to find her resolve. She had to not look at him and not think about those muscle-bound arms wrapped around her. Or those big, calloused hands touching her.

Fuck.

Reason number one: he had her real name. He had her dead sisters' names. Which hadn't mattered when she'd given them to him, but now that she was not in fact dead— she was fucked. And not in the way she wanted to be.

Reason number two: she was technically a thief, and he was a former G-man. He'd arrested her a grand total of two and a half times. Which she could forgive because the arrests never stuck, but he had intentionally and with malicious glee (the malicious part was only speculation but there had definitely been glee happening) ruined many heists.

Reason number three: he was smart. He made her laugh. She trusted him. He was pretty. He had all that muscle that she wanted—wait, shit. No. He owned a fanny pack. He'd worn socks with sandals in Liverpool. She'd nailed him in the stomach with her elbow once and he'd farted. His choice of ties never ceased to make her cringe. He knew every step of *All the Single Ladies*. The man had used his body to play chicken with a car. What kind of foolhardy dumbass did that kind of thing?

Okay. Valid points. Nathan's pants and all his other parts were off-limits.

"Wanna make out?" Fuck it all. She wanted him, she'd have him.

The mercenary formed a plan of action. She'd shower, get stitched, get casted, fuck Nathan, and then vacate the premises before she could do any more damage.

"Well..." He blinked, surprised, and smiled that megawatt smile at her. "Yeah." Like the answer was obvious.

Caden couldn't help but grin.

She liked him.

It was difficult not to with him smiling at her like that. Caden shifted, so she sat beside his undamaged shoulder. She hesitated for a moment, not because she didn't want to kiss him until he was blue in the face, but because she wanted to burn the moment into her brain. His lips were centimeters from hers, his eyes were on her lips, his hand was on the side of her neck. This was a moment she'd keep with her.

Caden fit her mouth to his. He let out a low groan. She soaked in the vibration and couldn't help but sigh when his hand traveled to her hair. He licked over her lips, pushing gently so she'd open her mouth to his advance. He pulled her, one-armed, into his lap and deepened the kiss.

He was being too soft. Too gentle with her, too loving. It scared her and kind of thrilled her all at once. The thief decided to ignore the gentleness with which he took her mouth and let herself go blind, deaf, and dumb to the world around her.

Nathan had her back.

She could trust him.

19

———————

NATHAN

"Stop that." Her breath was hot puffs of air against his lips. She pulled back a centimeter and was frowning at him all accusingly. Heat and lust and confusion had her bruised face flushed and her eyebrows furrowed.

"Stop what?"

"Kissing me like that." She huffed, annoyance overriding her lust for the moment.

"Like what?" Nathan knew exactly what he was doing and why she was annoyed.

She didn't want him kissing her like she mattered to him. He watched her waffle for the right words, annoyance furrowing her brows and casting shadows on her already bruised eye sockets. Her eyes narrowed and settled on his lips. Like she couldn't put all her attention on being ticked at him, like he distracted her. Good, he liked that.

"You know *what*. Stop."

"Fine." Nathan couldn't help the accompanying growl.

She wanted to pretend like this, them, was some inconsequential encounter they could forget about later. He didn't know at what point he'd made up his mind about having her, but damn it, why couldn't she just not be difficult?

Right. And world peace would descend and he and all his family and half the world's population would all be out of a job.

"What are you smirking at?"

If she knew his thoughts, he'd either receive a sucker punch to the gut or she'd laugh in his face and roll her eyes. Neither option sounded particularly fun.

"You're alive. I'm alive. We're not sporting toe tags or body bags and we're safe." Nathan watched her head tilt and then her dark eyes started to look concerned. Like she was afraid all the blood loss had crippled his brain.

"Yes... and?"

"Well, if memory serves, this is the part where you kiss me until I am blue in the face."

Lush lips pulled into a sweet smile and her eyes lit from within. Dark chocolate brown eyes were locked on his own. Had she always had such pretty eyes? Had they always been that color? Hadn't they been black? Under the mess of bruises, blood, and swollen lumps, she smiled a genuine, honest-to-god smile. Nathan swayed where he sat, once again rendered deaf, dumb, and speechless at the rare glimpse of her soul.

Sweet Jesus, he wanted more of that. All of that. He wanted to kiss her pretty lips and taste her mouth and feel her tongue against his. He wanted to bury himself inside her.

Her lips covered his. Her warm, soft mouth stopped any and all thoughts. Soft and sweet. He couldn't kiss her like that but she could him? What a hypocrite.

Her bruised eyes closed and her good hand settled on his chest. The warmth from her hand seeped into his chest and made a shudder rack his body. Christ, it was like he'd never experienced sex before.

He needed to control his shit before he embarrassed himself.

She didn't like soft and tender. Fine. Nathan could do hard and hot.

He bent his head and took control of the kiss. Her lips fit perfectly to his, supple and soft under the bruising heat of his mouth. She gripped his shirt like she needed something to keep her grounded and moaned. He caught it and pressed deeper, and Caden opened her mouth.

She tasted like Skittles and copper.

Nathan used his good arm to anchor her to his chest and then ran his hand over her side and cupped her ass, bringing her up to meet the hard bulge between his thighs. He braced for protest, but she only blinked her pretty eyelashes at him and gave a hungry moan. Her teeth found tendons on his neck and her fingers sunk into his hair again.

Another shudder went through him. More and more blood left his brain to surge to his dick. His head spun, even as he pulled her tighter against him. Caden let out another breathy moan and arched into him, the swells of her breasts pushing against his chest. It was at that moment Nathan's brain poured out his ears and all the remaining blood in his body rushed to his dick.

He bit her lip, and she gasped and moaned. The sound made his hips buck of their own accord, and Caden pressed closer to him.

Closer, he needed to get her closer.

Too many clothes.

Her fingernails raked down his chest and made him kiss her harder in response.

But then her lips turned cold and calloused. Why did

she smell like a dog? He felt her body jerk away, but her lips stayed—no, not lips. It was a hand.

Not at all as shocking as it should have been, Reid was scowling down at them. His cold, calloused goddamned hand all but muzzled Nathan's face in a death grip.

He was going to strangle Reid with his own stethoscope.

Heat dissipated and blood returned to his brain. Well, enough to string together a few different colorful curses and threats that had no outward effect on his goddamned brother. Probably because they were all muffled by the hand still covering his face.

"What the hell, Reid!" Finally, Nathan thought to remove his hand from Caden's backside and use it to pry the fingers off his face.

"No intercourse." It wasn't so much that Reid was woefully unadjusted, it was just that any and all social niceties went in one ear, were deemed trivial and tedious, and slid out the other ear.

"What the hell is your problem?" Sexual frustration was pumping through him in waves. Caden's frame trembled on top of him and Nathan couldn't bring himself to look at her just yet. If Reid scared her off, Nate was going to kill the bastard.

"No sex." This he said like he was scolding a couple of teenagers intent on getting knocked up. He casually wiped his hand off on his slacks and then put them on his hips, looking for all the world like they were the ones doing something insane.

"Are you insane?"

"What?" Reid blinked like he was confused as to why Nate was yelling at him and not the other way around.

"You can't go around shoving—this is not—read the room, shit." Nathan did not want to have to explain why a person did not go around shoving their hands into people's faces. Especially not in front of Caden. He wanted her to like his family, not run away screaming.

Caden's body jerked and Nate glanced up to see her biting her lip like she was trying to restrain laughter. Well, at least she wasn't looking like she was going to hightail it out the door.

"What's to read?" Reid got angry and defensive. His arms folded across his chest and he glared. "There ain't no writing on these walls."

"It's an expression. Look at what's going on around you, process that information, and then adjust."

"I did." Reid was scowling now and doing that thing with his face that made him look annoyed and exasperated and derisive all at once. "You two were too busy to hear me. So I read the room, deemed you both too horny to acknowledge my presence, processed that information, and then adjusted so your horny asses would pay attention."

"Clear your throat next time, damn." Nathan rubbed at his face and felt the flush of heat and arousal dissipate completely.

"I did!" He unfolded his arms and then started looking stern. "I already told you both, *multiple times,* do not stress your wounds! But do you listen to me? No! I only saved your lives and am responsible for your well-being—no need to listen to the only certified doctor in the room! No sex!" He paused in his rant to glare pointedly down at Caden until she slowly removed herself from Nathan's lap.

Ridiculous. Nathan sputtered and tried to form some kind of coherent protest at the absence of her heat.

"We aren't stressing our wounds," Caden spoke up, frowning.

"No fornicating—which was where you both were going

with that little spit-swapping session you were doing. Don't even try to deny it! I was here, remember? No sex! None whatsoever. Do you understand? Do you need a reminder that you have two bullet holes in you, Nathan? And Caden, you aren't even stitched up yet! And you're battered and broke seven ways from Sunday! We haven't even x-rayed your arm or checked your forearm stab wound for infections! Neither of you will be doing so much as batting an eyelash at each other until you are both better healed. Honestly, Caden, I expected better from you."

Caden deflated and looked completely flabbergasted. Like she couldn't comprehend how he came to that conclusion. Nathan didn't understand it either.

"*Her*? Why her? She's the stubbornest, most single-minded woman on the planet." Nathan watched as she tensed and quirked her eyebrows and got that look in her eye that said he was the special kind of stupid.

"Says the stubbornest male on the planet." Caden shot a glare at him and cocked her eyebrow like she was daring him to deny it.

"No sex!" Obviously, Reid felt like his message wasn't getting through. "None."

"You're not my mother, Reid. We are two grown adults capable of making adult-like decisions." He only felt slightly guilty for completely disregarding his trained professional of a brother's advice.

Cold, calculating silence fell. Reid glared for a long minute before he turned on his heel and marched right out the door. Which was weird. Reid didn't give up. He stood his ground until the other party either gave up or died.

"Wow." Caden's voice was teeming with amusement and warmth. "I've never been so unsubtly cock-blocked before."

She was grinning. Damn, he liked those smiles.

It took him longer than it should have to speak. But he was okay with losing his mind every time she smiled like that. Embarrassment stung his cheeks when he realized that a full minute had passed and he still was unable to speak.

Mentally, he rallied.

He needed to get his shit together. He was supposed to be seducing her into loving him and his crazy family. He was not going to do that by turning into a blundering idiot whenever she smiled.

He needed to go Bond.

James Bond.

Women loved that, right? He could do suave and sleek and smooth as a baby's bottom.

Her head cocked at him again and another tiny smirk pulled at her lips. Shit. Had she asked a question? Was he supposed to respond?

"Yeah..." What was the question?

Who the fuck was he kidding? James Bond was his antithesis. He'd have to hope and pray that what little charm he did possess worked on her.

"Sorry about Reid." Nathan did not have an excuse for his brother. "He's always been..." What was the right descriptor? "Reid."

Reid slunk back into the room. Triumph all but oozing from his smug face. Suspicion crawled up Nathan's spine, and he glared.

"Reid what—"

All bright colors and dimples and stern looks, his mother waltzed into the room.

The bottom dropped out of Nathan's stomach and he had to bite back the curse he wanted to hurl at his brother. He wanted to introduce her to his family in small doses. Not chuck her into the deep end without a floaty. His brothers had already swarmed her and now Reid was playing tattle-tale. Nathan was going to strangle him with his own stethoscope.

"Ma." It came out sounding like an excuse, but hell, it was a knee-jerk reaction to the scowl on her face. He could just feel the reprimand in the air around her.

Caden went rigid beside him. She tensed. Her muscles locked. Her jaw clenched, and she stared forward. She was going to bolt.

"Nathan Albert Savage—you listen to your brother. He knows what he's talking about." Her thick born-on-the-bayou accent rang with reprimand.

Already her focus slid off him and to the woman beside him. He wanted to reach over and touch her or hold her hand or move closer, but he felt that any sudden movements on his part and she'd be up and out the door before he could blink.

"Can't believe I had to get Ma." Reid was muttering again, but Nathan tuned him out. "I'm a doctor, for Christ's sake—I shouldn't have to tattle to your mommy to get you to listen to me."

His mother's dark face softened, and she broke into her all-consuming smile. Gold glinted in her teeth. Necklaces tinkled and bracelets jingled as she moved closer to the bed. She reached a hand out to touch Caden's shoulder and her smile gentled.

"My boys tell me I have you to thank for bringing Nate home alive." He watched her hand squeeze Caden's good shoulder, and she leaned closer. "Thank you. Thank the heavens you were there." Caden's face went white under her bruises and then pink, but she remained absolutely still. "Can I hug you, darlin', or are you too beat up?"

"Err... yes—no." Caden pulled out of his mother's reach

and shook her head. "Yeah, I'm—I've got blood all over—my back is—" She leaned further back as if his tiny mother had hidden weapons on her person and was planning to use them. "No. No hugs."

"All right, I understand." Not at all put off, his mother took a step back and outstretched her hand. "I'm Ellen Savage, these hellions' mother."

"I'm Av—Caden Quinn." She took his mother's hand and shook it. "Mercenary." Like she was reminding herself.

"Caden, thank you for bringing my son home." She grinned mischievously and leaned closer. "And for scaring the hell outta them all when you woke up. I hear you woulda handed all their asses to them if Nate hadn't been produced." She leaned back and beamed at the younger woman. "They need to be taken down a few pegs." She cackled, and Caden tensed.

"I'm sorry about that—I thought they were the enemy—I didn't—"

"Don't you go apologizin'. You have every right to protect yourself. It is their own fault for not explainin' things better." His mother jolted and glanced down at her watch. "Oh shit, if I don't get that bread outta the oven before it burns, Bobby'll never forgive me." She turned back to Caden and smiled again. "Gumbo and cornbread if ya'll are up for it tonight. Bobby is makin' it, so don't you two start complainin'." She turned on her heel and waltzed out, but not before shooting Nathan a look and ordering him to listen to his brother.

"Damn right, you should listen to me." Reid had never really quit his ranting. He'd just gathered more steam. "Tattle to your mother. Ridiculous. You can maybe have the broth but we're gonna take it slow with food. I don't want to be cleaning up vomit."

"Err..." Caden cleared her throat and unlocked her muscles. "Where's the shower?"

The only certified doctor in the room turned even more grumpy at the mention of a shower. But he was knocked out of his sullen stupor when the woman carefully stood and started messing with the lines on her wrist.

"No, don't you dare take them out." Reid reached over and blocked her hand. "You can take it with you. It has wheels."

"What—no, I'm good. Honestly. I don't feel dehydrated at all." Caden was using her earnest voice and Reid's face was pinching with irritation.

"That is a crock of shit and you know it. It won't kill you to take it with you. Don't make me get Ma back in here." He folded his arms across his chest and already looked smug. Like tattling to someone else's mother would work on Caden Quinn.

Nathan waited for Caden to scoff at his social leper of a brother and roll her eyes.

"Fine." She capitulated instantly. Eyes going wide and alert like she was waiting for Ellen to burst through the door at any moment. "Where's the bathroom?"

"Turn right out this door and it's the last door on the left in the hallway." Reid hovered over her as she struggled with the portable IV. "Lukewarm water, I mean it. I want to get you stitched and cleaned up, and I don't want to have to deal with swelling."

"Got it." Caden glanced back at him and Nathan was relieved to see the calm in her gaze. Maybe he was wrong about her bolting. A devilish smirk curled her lips. "Nathan, do you want—"

"No sex," Reid growled and glared for all he was worth.

Caden glared back and scowled harder. Which made Nathan grin like an idiot.

She wanted him as much as he wanted her.

Her shoulders slumped the tiniest bit, and she frowned and then turned towards the door.

"I put some towels and extra clothes in there for you. If you get dizzy or feel like you're going to faint, sit down. Don't overdo it, Caden."

"All right. All right." Caden nodded absently and frowned at Reid as she hobbled out the door. "I understand."

Nathan watched her exit with a stupid grin on his face. Reid had a certain effect on people. Socially inept he may be, but when he wasn't doing awkward things, he was making people feel like being where they were and who they were was the easiest thing in the world. For that, Nathan decided he wouldn't strangle him.

"You know she's leaving, right?" After a long moment of silence, Reid turned his attention back to him and Nathan frowned at the confidence in his brother's voice.

"Maybe." It was a strong possibility, but she'd most likely stay for a couple of weeks. Long enough to heal, at least.

"As soon as she gets what she wants... she's gone." His words were stated so matter-of-factly that Nathan didn't register what they actually were until they'd sunk in and put him on the defensive.

"Reid, there's nothing she wants from me." What the hell was he saying? Was he accusing her of something? Nathan growled and Reid rolled his eyes and looked ten shades of exasperated.

"Sex." Like it was the most obvious thing in the world.

"Well, maybe." He couldn't help but grin again. As soon

as they got a moment alone, Nathan planned to have her naked and going mad.

"No, not maybe." Reid shook his head and frowned like he was being purposefully stupid. "Sex is what she wants from you. She doesn't want to stay because she feels too vulnerable here. She's scared of us and of you. Give it up to her and she's out of here."

"She's not scared of me." No way in hell was Caden Quinn scared of *him*.

How many times had the woman charged at him without an ounce of fear? Women who were scared didn't seek out men just to beat the hell out of them. Okay, so she'd never actually sought him out, but she'd never run from him without standing her ground first.

"Not that kind of scared, you idiot. Gah, never mind."

20

CADEN

Still damp from her lukewarm shower, Caden followed the vacuum cleaner tracks down the hall and into the living room. She was breathing heavily and leaning most of her weight on the portable IV pole Reid had insisted she take with her. The shower had all but depleted her. It felt good to be clean.

Caden halted in the living room, struck by the sight. A recliner that looked well-reclined sat beside the puffy sofa that sat in front of a big TV. Framed pictures and portraits and drawings hung on the walls. Bookcases lined the far wall. Flowers and pretty curtains made everything look... surreal.

Fuck, everything had been so surreal since the moment she'd come to.

Sure, she'd seen living rooms before, but she couldn't shake the otherworldly feeling. It looked like every other living room she'd seen, but there was something about it that just screamed "We're not in Kansas anymore". She couldn't pick out the difference that made this particular living room feel so much different from all the other ones.

It was like she was stepping into a place of fiction that had come to life. Nathan had talked about his family, but she never counted on meeting them and being forced to acknowledge their existence as real living beings. They were real, his mother was real, and just as he'd described her. The place and people she'd built in her mind were real, and that was disorienting as fuck.

The place she'd called home for her formative years had a small living room that was the polar opposite of the one in front of her. Terror and guilt and rage had seared that place into her memory. She hadn't thought of it in a long, long time, but suddenly it was shining bright in her mind's eye.

Brown rough carpet that felt more like sandpaper than anything cloth-related, one lonesome recliner that smelt of beer and stale smoke, white walls gone grungy and stained from catching bottles that had been aimed for her head, and a TV that, when it wasn't sitting in the pawnshop, sat in the dust outlined square on the bedside table that acted as an entertainment center.

She'd been weak, pathetic Ava in that living room. She'd been dead for two minutes and thirty-seven seconds in that living room. Quinny had stayed dead in that living room.

Then there was the first foster home. Formal and foreign. The furniture was all angles and squares. The walls were white and bare. The second and last foster home had been less angular but more foreign. Ezra had liked it, but they'd left before the scuzz-bucket of a foster dad could do more than leer. The places they'd squatted and eventually rented weren't big enough to have living rooms. After that, it was all barracks, dorm rooms, safe houses, and hospital rooms.

This was a living room that housed a happy family. It was like stepping into a slightly messy national monument.

Caden blinked a couple of times, trying to shake the dream-like feeling.

The front door was hanging open. A black cat was sat in the middle of the doorway, blocking a sad-faced dog's entrance. A fly buzzed in and then back out again. Another cat, this one smaller and orange, pounced on the black cat's flicking tail. A deep belly laugh drifted in through the door, followed by some garbled words that Caden could only assume were curses. The sight of the open door reassured her a wee bit. She could leave whenever she wanted.

What exactly was stopping her from waltzing out that door and hopping on the nearest plane and getting the hell out of Dodge?

Nathan Savage and his ridiculous smiles were what.

It wouldn't hurt to stay just long enough to bed the man. (She had to think up a better moniker for the dirty deed.) Or maybe it would hurt. Maybe the family were all just lulling her into a false sense of security. Maybe they'd called the authorities already.

Probably not.

Maybe mostly not.

Regardless, the house and its people made her feel uneasy. Like if she didn't run at the first chance... something would go down and she would not come out the victor.

"You leavin'?"

Caden jolted into the crouched and ready position, ignoring the sharp pains coming from just about every-where on her, and located the threat. Her portable IV wobbled and squeaked at the sudden movement but stayed upright. Ellen stood in the kitchen, sawing away at a loaf of bread.

A flush of guilt colored her cheeks pink, but she forced herself to quell any outward reaction. If they started accusing her of stealing, she was out. She wasn't stealing or doing anything to incur any kind of reprimand. Still though, it was very hard to stop looking guilty.

"What—no. Maybe." Smooth. Caden was smooth as silk.

There was a grimace on the woman's face as she dragged the knife through the bread. Crumbs and bigger crumbs fell onto the counter and made Caden cringe. Ellen was butchering the beautiful, delicious-smelling bread.

"Don't look so shocked." Ellen paused in her destruction of the bread to grin and quirk an eyebrow at her. "You were eyeing the door like you were two seconds from running."

"I wasn't gonna *run*." Was she so transparent? That made for a grand total of two complete strangers who had the magical ability to read her like a book. She didn't like it.

"Well, have some of this bread before you go. You have to be starving." Finally, Ellen got a piece cut and waved it at her before refocusing on the loaf. "Bobby made it special for you and Nate."

The fresh bread smell was mouth-watering and alluring. The seasoned mercenary decided to stay where she was. It was ridiculous, she knew, but it was innate. The ridiculous innate part of her did not approach armed unknowns. Caden had long since learned an ounce of prevention was worth a pound of not getting stuck with a bread knife and bleeding out all over the nice, clean floor.

"He made it for me?" Shit, was that her voice? That pathetic croak?

"He figured ya'll would be hungry for some home cookin' now that you're home." Ellen got another piece cut with minimal damage and then made quick work of the rest. "God damn, let's pretend this doesn't look like a tornado hit and enjoy it, anyway." Ellen smiled, gold glinting and necklace tinkling, and tossed the bread knife in the sink behind her.

Unarmed, the woman posed less of a threat and there was all that bread made special for her. Ellen smiled at her again and held out a hunk of mutilated bread. Caden was in the kitchen somehow. Cold tile was under her feet and she couldn't remember telling her feet to move.

"The man can cook, let me tell ya. He takes the house down with his snores, but the man can cook."

Suspicion crawled up the Hitter's spine. Caden was almost eighty percent certain that this woman was not some devil in disguise. Seventy-three-ish percent sure that the bread Ellen was offering was not poisoned. That this woman was as genuine as anyone could be. And about ninety-five percent positive that she was being a paranoid idiot, but still she couldn't make herself take the proffered bread.

It wasn't as if she'd never been the recipient of human kindness. She knew what good people were, but this whole experience was throwing all her carefully honed spidey senses off. Why would this woman give anything to her? Caden was a thief and a killer and a mercenary, and many other unsavory things that good people didn't abide.

Sure, Ellen thought that Caden was solely responsible for the return of her son, but she'd already thanked her for that. Good people were confusing and annoying, and Caden wanted to be done with them.

Goddamn, did she want a piece of that bread, though.

There was a pause in movement where the woman stopped to study her. Amber eyes were warm and understanding. Guilt pounded down on her shoulders once more under the woman's scrutiny. Caden attempted to use her IV pole to maneuver herself into a more upright position, but gave up. It was not worth the effort. Ellen was asking Caden to trust her on blind faith.

Fat fucking chance.

"Butter?" She was already smothering her slice, and Caden's mouth flooded even as she controlled a flinch back at the sudden appearance of another knife in the woman's hand.

"Yes." Caden had to swallow twice before she could get a word out and then try to remember what manners were and if she'd ever learned any. "Please."

Ellen handed over the knife without batting an eyelash and took a big bite out of her piece. Relief just about overwhelmed her, and it was all she could do to quell the trembling in her arms to work the damn knife.

"Hot damn, my man can bake!" Ellen took another bite of the bread and gave a satisfied grin.

"Ma." Holden appeared in the room behind his mother and glared accusingly at her. Caden, suddenly feeling ten shades of guilty, dropped the knife and took a small step away from his mother before she caught herself enough to glare back.

"Holden can cook too, though he pretends like he can't." Ellen whirled on the much larger being and patted his scowling face. His features softened only when he glanced down at his mother.

"You know I prefer your cooking, Ma." He smirked impishly as his mother scoffed and swatted at his chest.

"Oh, stop lyin'." Ellen rolled her eyes and whirled back around to hand him a piece of bread. "Is Jackson still here?"

His attention refocused on her, and his eyes narrowed. Caden took a hungry bite out of her bread and glared right back. It slid down her throat like a slug and settled in her gut like a brick.

"No, him and Dax are going back to HQ." He paused to annihilate his piece in two bites. "They'll be back for supper tomorrow."

"Will you go find your father for me? And tell Kade that if that dog keeps chasing my ducks, I'm taking it to Penelope's."

"Penelope can't take another animal. You should see the barn. It's ridiculous how many animals she's got in there."

"I'm not keeping a duck killer. Tell Kade that. And let your dad know that the bread is done."

Holden frowned at his mother and then sent a pointed glare towards Caden. It took him a long minute to obey, but he eventually gave a curt nod and disappeared down the hallway. Caden went back to eating her bread and ignored the queasy feeling building in her gut. Ellen turned to the fridge that was suffocated in magnets and pictures and fished a pitcher of tea out.

"He doesn't want me alone with you." Lacking any kind of subtlety, Caden just laid it all out there. The woman had to be aware of the suspicion practically rolling in waves off her son. Caden watched for a reaction, but all the thief got in response was a flippant nod that did not look at all as alarmed as it should have been.

"Holden's always been... overprotective of the people he allows himself to love. Don't worry, Caden, he'll warm up to you eventually." Ellen reached over and patted her hand like it was the most natural thing in the world to reach out and touch someone.

"No, that's not—he doesn't want me around you because I'm a mercenary." Why did the people in this family treat her like she was part of the family?

"Oh, I know. Nate's told me all about you."

Shame and guilt knifed at her gut again. It was

becoming more difficult to stay upright. Caden adjusted her sweaty hold on the IV pole and watched the woman's face for the disapproval and disgust she knew was there. Had to be there. Ellen was a good, respectable woman.

"A thief." Maybe she had to spell it out. "I shot Nathan twice back when he was... chasing me."

"I remember." Ellen glanced up from the pitcher and grinned like she'd heard a good joke. "His brothers still give him hell about getting shot in the ass."

"I stole stuff—*steal* stuff. Art mostly." But that wasn't the worst of her sins. Stealing stuff from dead guys wasn't a sin. Not the way Caden saw it. If museums had no qualms about pilfering ancient items, then it just stood to reason that she wasn't committing any huge no-no's either. "I've killed people."

Ellen's head jerked up, but instead of the fear and disgust, Caden expected to see in the older woman's eyes all she saw was warm concern. Which only served to agitate and confuse her further.

After a moment of pensive silence, Ellen reached for her hand again, careful not to jostle all the little tubes sticking out of it. Her hands were damp from the condensation on the pitcher and calloused.

"Caden, you're talking like you owe me an explanation—like you're guilty of something. You did what you had to do. You don't owe me or anyone else an explanation."

No. No, that was wrong. This whole conversation was wrong. Never had she been met with such utter acceptance and empathy. Caden didn't know what to do with it. How to respond. She deserved absolutely zero empathy or acceptance. She'd killed people, for Christ's sake.

Okay.

She wasn't brain dead. She could formulate a response.

So. Retreat? It only took a moment to come to terms with her own cowardice.

Retreat.

"I've got—Reid... he's waiting. For me. To stitch. Gotta set my breaks." Words had never really been her forte. "Yeah, for— because... and thanks for the bread."

She clutched what was left of her piece and hightailed it as fast as her battered body could move back to the relative safety of the other room. Ellen didn't say anything. Only nodded and watched her retreat.

So, she was a coward. That wasn't the worst thing in the world, right? Caden carefully pushed the odd conversation to the back of her mind and focused on dragging her body back to Nathan.

"What took you so long?" Reid met her in the hallway with an impatient frown. "Did you faint? How are you feeling?"

"I didn't faint. I'm fine." She was all but gasping for breath by the time she got back into the room and seated on the bed. Nate was nowhere in sight, and Reid was already rummaging around on his table.

"Where'd Nathan go?"

"To use the other shower." He turned back around with a tray that held an assortment of hypodermic needles and wipes.

"Whoa, what the hell's that?" She already knew what it was. There was no way in hell that she was going to voluntarily be put out again. "No, no sleeping. I do not want to be out again.

Reid's eyes narrowed and his lip twitched like he was holding back a snarl. He set the tray down and grabbed at his nose in a sign of agitation.

"Caden." It was a burdened sigh. He shook his head

and then glanced up like he was praying for patience and then glared back down at her. "You have a fever. You have been stabbed. You have twenty-one cuts that require stitching on your legs alone. I have not counted the ones on your arms or the gashes on your back, where I am assuming they used a weed whacker or some other twisted shit."

He paused for breath and what Caden was assuming (judging by his adopted brother's penchant for the theatrics) dramatic effect. He took another noticeable, deep breath and continued his tirade.

"You have two broken and four fractured ribs. You have internal goddamn bleeding. You have three broken fingers, two broken toes, and one dislocated elbow and shoulder. For the love of all that is holy, just please trust me to know how to fix you."

"Reid," Why was it that this man treated her like he'd always known her? Like they were old friends, and she was being her usual frustrating self and he was just trying to be the good doctor? "I understand. I can feel most of it. Trust me, I know what's going on."

"Yeah, I'm aware that you can feel the pain of your injuries. Well aware." Another issue that was making his jaw clench. She almost felt bad. He had a set of ice-blue eyes that somehow pierced and did the puppy dog thing at the same time. It was hard to ignore.

"I can deal with the pain. I really can. I do not want to be drugged or unconscious." She ignored his angry huff and continued. "You can stitch me up and set my breaks. I won't fight you. I promise."

"This is not something I want to debate with you on. It would be inhumane of me to operate on a patient who is not drugged or unconscious."

"You wouldn't be operating. It's not like you're gonna cut me open."

He huffed again, and this time paced away, a dark scowl growing on his handsome face. He whirled again and stood in front of her, triumph alight in his eyes.

"What if we have Nathan in here the whole time?"

Instantly, Caden's hackles rose. It wasn't like he was trying to insult her. He was trying to do the opposite. But the fact that he thought she needed someone to hold her hand was insulting as all hell. Nathan's presence would make her feel better, but she wasn't going to admit that. Out loud. With note-taking witnesses. Weakness was not something she liked to have broadcast.

"He just got in the shower. Why do you need him?" Holden sidled into the room, eyes sharpening at the mention of Nathan.

"Nothing. I don't need him." Caden tried to sound less defensive. Where had all her finely honed nonchalance gone? "Fine, all right, you can put me out. But only for like... an hour."

Reid was already up and injecting something into her IV line. Unease gripped her gut and clawed at her perfectly calm exterior. She did not know these assholes. Why the hell was she letting herself be goaded into doing what they said?

"Look," Holden stepped closer, all scowls and awkward-ness, "I never thanked you for what you did for Nathan." He rubbed the back of his neck and Caden was sharing in the awkward that was coming off him in waves. "You saved his life. You could have just left him behind, but you didn't... so thanks for keeping my brother alive." Holden was starting to go fuzzy. She was starting to feel lighter.

Slightly fuzzy herself. Warm too. The cool sheet under

her hands felt nice. Better than cement. The absence of rat sounds was almost comforting.

"Nobody could let Nathan die." Was that slurry voice hers? "He's rainbows... and sunshine... I'm not Voldemort—I don't kill unicorns."

"No, you're not Voldemort." Holden's fuzzy face was beside hers and helping her lie back.

She was in a bed. A bed with springs and pillowcases and shit. Nathan was alive. She had bread, actual home-made bread, in her stomach and Harry Potter was such a good series.

Unidentified drunken emotions swelled in her chest. She could feel them turn liquid and fill her eyes as the world became even warmer and fuzzier. How was she supposed to explain her stupid random crying? Goddamn drugs, making her crazy.

"Neville was such a badass." Her explanation wasn't coming out right, and she knew she sounded like an idiot. But then it didn't matter because everything blurred completely and went black.

21

CHARLES

Charles Marskib was completely and utterly enraged.

So very enraged that the baseball bat in his hands would have pulverized Kyott's skull if he'd been standing in front of him. As it was, his office took the beating because Kyott and his unexploded head were safely on a different continent.

He'd not been so thoroughly pissed in a very long time.

Counting was doing nothing to calm his temper.

Deep breathing did not calm him.

No, no. He was fine. He was thinking again. He could focus now on something other than destroying his once lovely office.

"Sir?" Rage erupted once again at the sound of his employee's timid voice.

No. He was fine. He was under control. He took classes for this shit. He was in control of his anger. Talk it out. He could talk it out. Charles knew the steps.

"I am not happy, Kyott." Fucking understatement of the year. "Not fucking happy."

Charles Marskib had spent a good amount of money on merchandise that his incompetent employees had let run off. A 'good amount' of money was a slight under-exaggeration.

"Yes, sir." Kyott's voice was a whine made even more grating coming through the speaker of his phone.

He'd spent an obscene amount of money. An *obsessive* amount of money.

Obsessive was the right word for that and all things Caden Quinn. Absolutely manic obsessive about the bitch he'd bought and paid for that had just up and walked out of his secure compound.

If nothing else, Charles Marskib was self-aware. Aware of his faults, his weaknesses, and just exactly how fucked up he was over one tiny woman. The knowledge that she was out there somewhere having escaped him ate away at his sanity. He'd finally recaptured her. She'd been his for all over seventy-two hours.

"Do you know why I am not happy, Kyott?" He had to think hard about each word to focus enough to speak instead of growl.

"Yes, sir." He kept saying sir like the word would somehow keep him alive. "Caden Quinn escaped."

By all rights, the woman should not have even been a blip on his radar. She was nothing. She was a fucking mercenary. Compared to her, he was a goddamned king.

Inconsequential. She was in-fucking-consequential.

So why was the mercenary front and center in his mind every free moment? Why was he obsessing over one little mercenary?

"Explain to me again how you let her walk right out the door?"

He knew the answer to that, though. It was because she

didn't break. No matter how imaginative or depraved or just fucking cruel he'd gotten in the three weeks they'd shared together in those dungeons, she hadn't broken. Hadn't even cracked. Only a special kind of person stood up to that kind of horror. A special kind of person that he wanted to have. To keep.

"She had help, sir. She wasn't alone." There was a panicked, almost angry pause in which the man did nothing but mush his words and stumble his way through a half-assed explanation. "There was a whole goddamned private army. We weren't expecting her to have help."

She'd escaped. Unbroken. And had then eluded him for years. When she'd been put up to bid, it was like his prayers had been answered.

"The help you provided her."

He could kill them. He could slaughter every single one of the idiots that had let his woman escape. But dead was dead. The dead didn't learn from their mistakes. Still, he had to count backward from twenty just to get his breathing level again.

"Err..." The sound of the man's hesitant halting speech put Marskib back on the fence: to kill or not to kill. "I—I didn't give her any help." Then he added, "Sir."

"Do not waste my time, Kyott. You used my men and my compound to capture and detain an ex-government agent." The same agent that had been on his ass for the last two years.

Charles was in complete control of his rage now. Now he could focus on alternatives and punishments and Caden Quinn.

"I... I thought... I—he was in Moscow. He was right there without any—"

"Tell me, Ralph. Did I ring you up and say, 'hey, you

know what would be the ultimate birthday present? You know what would make my life complete? Nathan fucking Savage.' Did I give you explicit instructions to capture and torture the man?"

"No, sir, you didn't. But I thought—"

"How about," a migraine was throbbing to life in his temples, "you tell me what I did instruct you to do."

"You, uh... You said to keep her. To not let her escape. That'd you be here in seven days."

"Perfect. Yes. I said that. I gave you the money, the manpower, and the goddamn hidden away compound. And you let her escape."

"I'm sorry, sir." A pathetic, useless apology and another gulping pause decided it. Kyott would live until the very moment his use ran out. "I'll get her back."

"Oh, you'll get her back?" He'd spent countless hours and thousands of dollars trying to do that very thing. And then he'd only captured her because she'd been for sale. "So where is she, Ralph?"

"She escaped, sir."

"I didn't ask what she did. I asked where she is." Charles righted the chair he'd chucked in his rage and carefully sat. "You seem to know where to find her. So, please, enlighten me."

"I... I'll find her."

"Okay, so now explain to me why I should allow you to continue breathing."

There was a sharp inhale and Kyott started sputtering. Charles didn't usually make threats. Actions speaking louder than words and all that. But he felt like maybe this was a special case. Kyott was proving to be especially stupid. Maybe he'd need it spelled out for him.

"You have not only put my business in danger by

detaining and torturing and failing to kill a US government agent, but you've also failed to do the one job I assigned you. So tell me Kyott, why is it that you are still alive?"

"I'll find her." Kyott's voice was cold now that he'd masked his terror. "I will."

"How are you going to do that?" The computer was now trashed. The screen was busted, and the keyboard was in pieces around the room. He'd have to wait to do anything until he got home.

"I've got information on her. Information we didn't have before." His voice didn't betray a tremor. "I'll find her."

Charles knew that Kyott was lying in an attempt to save his own skin. There was no information on Caden Quinn. No little bits of evidence that pointed in any discernible direction—he knew this for a fact. He'd hired plenty of private detectives to find out that exact fact. Kyott knew that. Kyott was also aware that dangling Caden Quinn's possible whereabouts in front of him was the only thing that was going to save his life. The enraging part of it was that it was going to work.

"Bring her to me and you'll live." Fucking woman. Just like his temper, she was a weakness a man like him could not afford to have.

Charles disconnected the call and counted to ten before he allowed his temper to destroy the phone.

Kyott would most likely run and hide, but a small stupid part of him was holding out that the man really did have new information. Kyott had had her for three days. Maybe she'd let something slip. Maybe she'd left a trail.

It was stupid to hope, he knew, but hope he did. It had already been three days, and the idiot had only just reported. Had she left a trail, which was unlikely, then it was already cold. The woman was a wraith who only surfaced to do quick jobs before she disappeared again. Another ghost was what he needed to catch her.

And he obviously needed to handle the Nathan Savage situation. The thought gave him pause. Savage was supposedly retired. Would he escape with Quinn and hand her over to the powers that be? He'd been told that Caden Quinn had been in bad shape when she'd walked out of his compound. Did she have a chance of escaping that giant pain in the ass?

Forming a mental checklist, Charles picked up his phone again and decided on a course of action. He'd hire someone to torture and kill his disappointing employee after he came back empty-handed.

He also needed to deal with Nathan Savage. Savage was retired, but he was well-liked and connected. If handled improperly, he was going to have a shit-storm of trouble.

As for Caden Quinn, it was only a matter of time. She'd eventually be his again.

22

CADEN

"And checkmate." The voice was deep and male and... only slightly familiar. No inner alarms rang. But that was probably only due to drugs clogging up her brain.

Her mind felt slurry. Like only part of her was present and the rest of her was floating somewhere just above and just slightly out of reach. Caden couldn't decide if she liked the feeling. It didn't hurt. In fact, she didn't hurt at all, which was odd because she knew she was supposed to be hurting. There was a muffled dull throb radiating from somewhere she couldn't pinpoint. *That* was pain. She knew it, but it was too blurry to feel.

She was fucking drugged. Again.

The usual rush of fear-induced adrenaline didn't slam through her at the thought, though. She was cognisant enough to remember where she was and who she was with.

The brothers. The ridiculous number of brothers.

One of them, Caden couldn't recall his name, needed to get punched. His name just wasn't coming to her. Annoying and exasperating, however, were descriptors that popped up pretty quick. It should have been frustrating how slowly little bits of information leaked into her brain, but she was too drugged to feel it. Probably morphine.

"There is no checkmate in chessckers. There is only Twinkie and not Twinkie."

Why she wasn't panicking at the distinct sound of males surrounding her was almost cause for panic. But she didn't. There was no reason to panic because she was warm, so very warm, and that meant she was safe. Although she wasn't sure why it meant that. And she knew it was stupid to think she was safe when she was drugged and there were male voices around her. But the warmth she was feeling was accompanied by a familiar weight. She knew that her drugged mind tried to grapple for the name that belonged to the weight but it wasn't coming to her. Now she was getting frustrated.

"No, my dear poor sweet, naïve brother, the rules state that upon a half-eaten Twinkie, which *you* ate, checkmate can be invoked if said invoker has both the Butterfinger and the half of the Oreo with the frosting on it. And I've got both."

She could smell him. She knew him. She liked him. What the hell was his name? Fucking morphine. Goddamn Reid. He smelled clean and her drugged nose could detect no trace of blood or cordite. He smelled like Nate, that was almost his name, smelled when he wasn't three days into a captive torture situation. Like laundry detergent, tater-tots, and ketchup. The thief couldn't help but grin stupidly as she sniffed at the warm weight, all but smothering her.

Nate. Nate. Nate. There were more letters to it. More sounds as well.

"True, but I've got the gummy bear riding the cinnamon

bear, which makes all half-eaten Twinkie-invoked check-mates null and void."

"Since when did your cinnamon bear get knighted?"

Caden gave up trying to get her brain to work. Whatever Reid, that exasperating, annoying one, had her on would wear eventually, and she'd be back to full bacon.

Holy shit, she wanted bacon.

And cinnamon rolls.

And twice-baked potatoes.

"Well, Holden, Carl was knighted after he took your fortress of Skittles. I can understand why you would have repressed that particularly painful memory of my owning your ass."

But more than bacon and maybe even more than twice-baked potatoes. She wanted to sleep. Actually sleep. Not be half awake listening for trouble. She wanted not to be drugged and holed up in a dark corner of the world some-where no one could find her and just sleep for days.

"Fine then, no checkmate, but I do believe that I can move here... and do... oh man, well, that just tastes like victory." There was an outraged gasp and some distinct chewing.

These people seemed nice enough, and they had the *Him* that Caden wanted to keep. They were brothers. And wasn't family supposed to be loyal?

But they weren't hers and she couldn't let down her guard. Because of that all-important thing that she didn't have anymore. What was the thing? It was a word... a T word... but it was mostly an idea... and it was supposed to be an integral part of relationships. Toothpaste?

Sweet Jesus, did she need some of that. Maybe Nate would share his toothbrush.

"How dare you eat Carl! He had a wife and three kids to

feed you vindictive asshole and you know cinnamon bears are my favorite!"

"Carl should have decided against a knighthood and gone for the wizard badge if he didn't want to get ate."

"You let him roll onto her again?" That voice was more familiar and somewhere in the slurry that was her mind, she got the distinct impression that he was the one that needed a good punch. Her limbs were not in working order, though. Everything was too slow—too delayed. They weren't listening to her commands. "You two have one job! *Monkeys* could do it!"

"Every time we pull him off, he just rolls back over on her."

"Besides Cade—" Alarm rang faintly in her mind. That was her. Caden was her. She didn't want their focus. Focus was bad. "Gets all kill-y and foul-mouthed when he's not on her."

"Kill-y? How the hell can she be kill-y when she's got morphine pumping through her?"

"She's not out. When Nate's not smothering her, she thinks we're the enemy and tries to fight us."

"Or curse us. And boy, howdy, I can tell that they would be doozies if she wasn't so high and slurring her words."

"Not out!? How is this woman burning through my drugs so quickly? She is tiny and thin and she's got barely any sustenance in her—I don't. She should not be awake still!"

Reid came closer. She could hear him mumbling to himself and she willed her arms to move, to punch out at him. God dammit, she didn't want to be drugged again.

But then the slurry in her mind became worse and the rest of her floated off and the world started to go black. But that was okay because Nathan was moonlighting as her human blanket again, and Caden trusted him to have her back.

"LISTEN TO ME, YOU…" Caden had been waiting for Reid to show his lying face for the past hour. She was still groggy and somehow her voice refused to do the menacing thing she scared so many people with. "You *punk.*"

Reid stopped mid-step to look at her, eyebrows scrunched, and looking for all the world like she'd just called him a scum-sucking rat bastard. She wanted to pull out the big guns and call him something worse, but, for whatever reason, it was difficult to insult Nathan's brother.

"*Punk*?" Reid was outraged. Good, Caden hadn't thought it would offend him, but apparently, it worked. "*Punk*?!" His tone implied that it was the vilest insult that had ever been thrown at him and he was flabbergasted as to why he was being treated so horribly.

"Yeah, *punk!* I agreed to let you drug me for an hour— *two* tops. I've been out of it for four fucking years!"

"It's been three days, *max.*" His eyebrows smoothed out, and he rolled his eyes. Like she was being dramatic, and he was the only reasonable person in the room.

"*Three* days! Reid!" Caden would have hauled herself upright, out of bed, and right into his stupid annoyed face, but the drugs in her system were making it hard to focus, let alone move. "I can't believe—you fucking—I said two hours —you… *punk!*"

Maybe it was the drugs that were softening her anger towards the asshole, but she couldn't make herself say anything worse. And Caden knew so much worse.

"No, you're the *punk!*" Reid shoved a finger at her like

he'd just delivered a knockout hit and he expected her to pass out from the shock of the insult.

A delirious giggle bubbled up in the back of her throat, but she didn't let it escape. This was *serious,* dammit. She was pissed off.

"You had so much damage done to your person that it would have been inhumane. Do you know how many hours I spent on stitching up your back alone?!"

"I could take it."

"Caden. You. Are. *Not.* Invincible." Reid, hands on his hips, spoke so slowly that, had she been able, Caden would have reached up and punched him right in the kisser. "All you goddamned soldiers thinkin' you're the toughest sons-abitches in town—you're not! You're human! With nerve endings and fucking trauma enough already without me adding to it!"

"I told you I can handle it!" What was not getting through? Caden wanted to strangle the man.

"Well, *I* can't." He said it with so much authority that Caden fell quiet. "Don't even be moving around just yet. You know how much time I put into your stitches alone?"

"You are insufferable. Do you know that?"

"*I'm* the insufferable one? *Me*?"

"Yes, *you.*" This man was easy to offend. Noted.

"Well, this *insufferable* person is going to take out your IV. I hope that's not too *insufferable* for you."

"Are you two done fighting?" Kade waltzed into the room with a stack of stuff in his arms.

"We're not fighting." Caden folded her arms across her chest and glared. "One of us is being reasonable and one of us is being *insufferable.*"

"Yes, they are," Reid stated as he pulled the tape and IV off her arm.

"Sure sounds like you're fighting." Kade set his stack down on the side table and plopped himself in a chair next to her bed.

"What's all this?" Caden ignored him and motioned to the pile of crap on her bedside.

"Good ol' competition." Kade threw his arms wide and grinned. "Since Reid says we're not up for combat yet, we'll just have to settle for board games and the like until we can actually spar."

"Why are we competing?"

"So I can reclaim my title as the biggest badass in the family."

"I took that title?" Caden liked the sound of that, though she wasn't sure when and how she'd taken the title from him.

"Yeah, remember when you fucked up your own arm to get the drop on me? You beat me, therefore you're the biggest badass in the family. But not for long. I'm pretty good at board games."

"I've never played a board game in my life."

"Great, then I'll wallop you and reclaim the title."

"It doesn't really count though because I beat your ass in sparring and this is not sparring. So I'm technically the champ until we can fight again."

"Yeah, but that's what the board games are for. Seeing who's the most badass until then."

"You're on then."

By the time Maddox found them, they had exhausted all the board games and card games twice over. Caden had won all but three of the board games and Kade had walloped her at cards. They'd moved on to small physical challenges that Reid couldn't object to, like who could do the Vulcan salute (Caden) or who could twist their tongue all the way around

(Also Caden). Caden was in the lead, with Kade right behind her.

"Okay, okay." Maddox entered the room rather abruptly. "Did you figure out who the biggest badass is yet, or what?"

"I am," Caden said with no small amount of satisfaction. Kade scowled at her, but couldn't refute that fact.

"Whatever. We're doing video games next time."

"Okay, get out. It's my turn." Maddox shooed Kade out of the room.

"Your turn for what?"

"Hangin' out."

"With *me*?"

"No, with the bedside table. Of course, with you."

"Oh." Caden was shocked, but tried to be all kinds of nonchalant about it. "Okay. What's all that?" Caden motioned to the baskets in his hands.

"We're having a spa day. These heathens only let me do a spa day with them every once in a blue moon."

23

CADEN

aden couldn't sleep.

Mostly because every time she closed her eyes, she saw her baby sister getting murdered. Which was just *great*.

It had been two weeks since she'd woken up in the Savage household.

Two weeks of home-cooked meals, board games, family dinners, shopping trips, video games, movie marathons, spa days, and just general fucking around.

Every time she even thought about leaving the all-consuming camaraderie and the Savage family as a whole, they sucked her back in. That and Reid gave her a disapproving doctor *look* every time she even glanced at an exit.

Caden turned over again and punched her pillow until it laid better under her head.

The Savages themselves were all ridiculous and stupidly lovable. Ellen and Bobby treated her like she was their long-lost daughter and acted as though they couldn't fathom life without her. While their boys treated her as part of the family. As if she'd been there from the start.

It was disconcerting and intoxicating.

It had been a long time since she'd been a part of a family.

Giving up on sleeping in her own bed, Caden stood, grabbed her pillow, and made her way down the hall.

"Nate." She pushed the door open and whispered into the darkness. "Nate."

"Caden?" His voice was groggy, like he'd just startled from deep sleep.

Caden wasted no time. She lifted the covers and crawled into the bed beside him. His arms wrapped around her and pulled her flush against him.

He was warm, so fucking warm. And solid. Caden felt her muscles relax in his hold.

"Why can't you sleep?" His voice was in her ear and alert now.

"I see my dad when I close my eyes lately." Caden had no intention of telling him what was really on her mind, but something about being held in the dark by his warm solid arms made her tell the truth.

"That can't be pleasant."

The dark pressed in around her, but she was warm and Nathan's chest was pushed up against her back. His arms were wrapped around her middle. She was safe here. Safe and protected and so fucking warm.

"She was six when he killed her. Just a baby." The words came out unbidden.

"Quinn?"

"Yeah, Quinny. She was... she was my baby. So brave. She didn't fear him at all. It was my fault she wasn't scared of him. I kept him away from her since the day her mama left her on our doorstep."

"What happened?"

Caden opened her mouth to tell him, but then closed it again. This was the darkest part of her soul. The worst thing she'd ever done. And she was just going to say it out loud?

"He'd lost his job again, and he'd been taking it out on me all week. And then something... snapped. He was beating the hell out of me and I just knew he was going to kill me—he wasn't going to stop."

He squeezed her to him, and Caden felt compelled to go on.

"Quinn, she came out of the spot I hid her in. Started hitting him and trying to get him off of me. She was tiny. Of course, she bounced right off of him. She went and got a pot and that got his attention."

The little shit never stayed where Caden put her. She always popped out of the closet or from behind the sofa like she had no fear whatsoever of their father. And that was Caden's fault too.

"He stopped wailing on me and took it from her. And then he—he hit her with it. And kept hitting her. I didn't get him off of her in time. And then it was too late."

Tears tracked down her face. Even after all this time, it still hurt like it had just happened.

"Then he turned on me and... he just fucking killed me. Choked the life right out of me. Ezra had run to the neighbors when he started in on me and had them call the cops. The paramedics resuscitated me at the scene, but Quinn was... gone."

Caden silently cried in the darkness as he pulled her even closer. It had been the worst day of her life tied with the day that Ezra died. It had been her fault. She hadn't gotten up quick enough. Hadn't gotten him off of her. Had failed as the big sister she was supposed to be to protect her baby sister.

"I'm sorry, Caden." Nate nuzzled into her neck and squeezed her tight. "I wish I could take it all away."

Eventually, the tears stopped and the ache that burned in her chest whenever she thought of that night eased a bit. With his arms wrapped around her and his front pressed to her back, it was easy to forget that it was all her fault.

"Nate."

"Caden?"

"Tell me why you were in Russia. Holden seems to think you weren't there for a vacation." She'd heard Holden question Nathan constantly about it and had grown curious herself.

"I was there to track down Charles Marskib." He sighed and her hair fluttered against her neck. "The last case I worked was centered around Marskib and his operation. He was doing all kinds of evil shit. So it was an interagency task force."

Usually just the mention of Charles Marskib had her clutching her favorite weapon and finding a place to hide. But she was warm and Nathan was holding her. She was safe.

"I was partnered with a couple of people. Good people. Except Sisco. He was a turncoat. But we didn't figure that out until it was too late. Marskib setup a trap and we walked into it blind because of the information Sisco brought us. A lot of people died."

Caden twisted in his arms so she was facing him. In the light coming in through the window, she could see the silhouette of his form. It was her turn to hug him.

"Good people dead all because of one man's greed. There was a guy that I really connected with on the team. Agent Adam Fletcher. He was the father of two, with one on the way. I had dinner with his family the night before the bust was supposed to happen. He died right in front of me."

She wrapped her arms around him as best she could and snuggled into him. Caden had never *snuggled* in her life, so it was her best approximation of a 'snuggle'.

"I retired after that. Took two years off to deal with it—I'd left Special Ops because of all the death and loss and I just thought... there wouldn't be any working for the government. I was wrong. I went after Marskib. Didn't really have a plan. But then Kyott got to me first and tossed me in with you."

Where would she be if Nate hadn't been tossed in that broom closet of a cell with her? Probably dead. Or still being tortured.

"Thank god he did." Nate's lips brushed her forehead and warmth bloomed on the spot and tingled down her spine and into her limbs.

Caden felt a surge of belonging at his words. Like she was where she was supposed to be—in this house, in his bed, in his arms.

"Yeah, thank god he did."

24

NATHAN

Nathan paced the small kitchen area, trying not to panic. It had been almost three weeks since he'd brought Caden to his childhood home. Three weeks was a long time in Caden's world. It was a miracle that he'd somehow gotten her to stay as long as she had, but he knew that time was running out.

She would move on soon if he didn't do something. He'd had his brothers entertain her when he couldn't. He'd had his parents talk to her and work their magic. But he was afraid that it all wasn't going to be enough to make her stay.

"Grab me the cartoon of eggs, will ya?" Bobby stood at the central counter and motioned towards the fridge that Nathan kept passing in his pacing.

"How do I make her love me?" Nathan took out the carton of eggs and waved them around while he talked.

"You can't trick her into loving you, if that's what you mean." Bobby scowled up at Nate as he grabbed the eggs. "You are gonna crack these if you keep handling them like that."

"That's not what I mean." Nate sighed and leaned against the opposite counter. "I mean... how do I get her to stay? She's gonna run, I know it."

"Maybe you should let her if that's what she's going to do." Bobby cracked a few eggs into a big mixing bowl as he spoke.

"You know, your fatherly wisdom isn't very helpful right now." Maybe he should have gone to his mother instead.

"Then don't listen to me."

"But you're the only one that I know with a good and lasting relationship."

Bobby grunted, completely focused on the baking instead of Nate and his problems. Which was annoying, but not unexpected.

"How'd you get Mom?" Nathan reframed his questioning.

"I didn't pick her out of a lineup or anything." He whisked the eggs with a fork. "I asked her out three times before she said yes to me."

"Yeah, but how did you make her fall in love with you so well that she'd stayed with you for—what's it like, thirty years now?"

"Thirty-four years, actually."

"Well?" Exasperated now, Nathan started pacing again. To the oven, past the fridge and to the kitchen table.

"Well, what?"

"Well, how'd you do it?"

"I don't know, son. That's like asking why's the sky blue —this is something you should be asking your mother."

"Okay then, how'd she get you?"

"She said yes."

"Ugh!" Nathan stopped pacing to point an accusatory finger at his adopted father. "You're so unhelpful!"

"Look." Bobby finally put down his fork and looked up. "If you love her, *tell* her."

"But she's... *complicated.*" The word didn't even begin to explain Caden Quinn.

"Do you love her?"

"Yes." Obviously.

"Then it doesn't matter. You'll figure it out." Which was vague as hell and not at all instructional like he wanted. He knew in his rational brain that there weren't step-by-step instructions for making someone fall in love, but, damn it, there should be.

"So your advice is: tell her I love her and then let her run."

"No. My advice is to tell her that you love her and then, if she runs, go after her."

"Okay, finally. Some advice." Nate threw his hands up in the air while his father shook his head.

"My second piece of advice is: go ask your mother." He jerked his thumb towards the front door.

"Fine, fine. I'll leave you alone." Nathan backed away with his hands up.

He had advice now, but not the kind he wanted.

Nathan sighed and made his way towards her room. Kade was most likely in there trying to out badass her.

What he needed was a plan. If he didn't do things just right, she would run before he even had a chance to tell her he loved her. Hell, she would probably run when he said the words.

He had to romance her. Seduce her into staying with him. Which wouldn't be too hard, right? The question was, how did he go about doing that?

It couldn't just be sex. That wasn't enough.

Caden wasn't the type that was into grand gestures and

flashy declarations. He had to make her feel it deep down. Had to show her that he could be the stability, the love, and the home she needed.

He just needed to come up with a plan.

25

CADEN

"Why are we here?" Caden stood on the threshold of an Italian restaurant with Nate in front of her, grinning.

"I'm taking you on a date."

"Nathan, I don't need to be wooed to have sex with you —I'm there."

"Who says *I* don't need to be wooed?"

Caden raised an eyebrow at him, a playful smirk tugging at her lips. "Oh, is that so? You need to be wooed now?" she teased as she watched him with a mixture of amusement and curiosity.

Nate's grin widened, and he shrugged, looking as if he had a secret he was dying to share. "Absolutely. I mean, what if I want to be romanced? You ever think about that?" His eyes sparkled with mischief, and Caden felt a flutter in her chest at the sight. How Nate could be this open and unguarded was a mystery to her. She envied him.

"Fine," she said, stepping closer to him, her tone challenging. "But if we're doing this, we're doing it my way." She glanced around the restaurant, noting the colorful décor and the lively atmosphere. "And that means shots. Lots of them."

Nate chuckled, clearly pleased with her response. "I wouldn't have it any other way."

They stepped inside, and Caden immediately felt the air conditioning blast her in the face. It was a nice contrast to the heat of the day outside. The place was cute, with strings of lights hanging overhead and the sound of music filling the air. Nate led her to a small table in the corner, away from the bustling crowd.

As they sat down, Caden couldn't help but feel a sense of anticipation. She hadn't expected this—hadn't expected to feel... excited about a date with Nathan. But here she was, looking across the table at him.

"Alright," Caden said, leaning back in her chair, her eyes never leaving his. "How would you like to be wooed?"

Nate leaned forward, his grin now a full-blown smile. "Give me your best attempt and we'll see what happens."

"*Attempt*? You make it sound like I'm not a femme fatale or something." Caden tried to look hurt by his words, but her lips refused to do anything other than smile.

"You're definitely fatal, but I don't know about the femme part. You've beat my ass one too many times for that particular descriptor to be accurate."

"Rude!" Caden put a shocked expression on her face and smacked his arm. "And here I was going to bring out the big guns and go all simpering female on your ass."

"God no—I don't think you could do that even if you tried, Quinn."

"You don't like simpering females, huh?" Caden sat forward, walked her fingers up his arm, and fluttered her eyelashes up at him all girly like. "So what do you like?"

"You."

Caden felt heat race up her neck and settle in her cheeks. What the fuck was wrong with her? Blushing? *Actually* blushing as a grown ass woman?

"Shut up, Savage." She swatted him again and tried to regain her composure. "I'm supposed to be wooing *you*, remember?"

He held his hands up in surrender and smirked at her.

"What's the matter, Quinn? You can dish it out, but you can't take it?"

"Oh, I can take it."

"I don't think you can. You're too... brutish." He smirked as he said it and Caden knew he was trying to get a rise out of her, but she couldn't help but respond to that particular insult.

"Brutish!?" How dare he. She was just the same as every other woman. "I am refined and sensitive—thank you very much."

"Prove it."

"How am I supposed to prove it?"

"Dance with me."

"You're on."

He smirked again, and Caden realized she'd just talked herself into a trap. But she couldn't back out now. Not when her dignity was on the line.

"You better be wearing your steel-toed boots because I've never done this before."

"I'm honored to be your first."

Again with the blushing. She didn't even know why she was blushing, just that she was and it wouldn't stop. Caden decided to ignore it and let herself be pulled to the dance floor. A few other couples swung around the floor, but not enough to put Nathan off of his mission, unfortunately.

"It's easy enough." Nate pulled her close and put her

hands on his shoulders. His hands clasped her waist, she could feel the heat of his hands through the thin fabric of her shirt. Despite the cool air, she was feeling flushed. "All you have to do is follow my lead."

They moved slowly across the dance floor despite the tempo of the music being played. After a few minutes of barely breathing and trying to control the color in her cheeks, she pulled away from his hold and arched an eyebrow at him.

"Have you been properly wooed yet?"

Nate gave her a slow smile, the kind that sent a thrill through her despite herself.

"Caden, I'm sensing some impatience—are you just trying to get into my pants?"

"Well hallelujah! You finally caught on."

26

NATHAN

"You realize we didn't even order drinks—they probably hate us for just up and leaving."

"It's okay, I left a tip." He held open the door for her as she rounded the truck, his fingers aching to tuck under her jaw and angle her head towards him.

"Oh, good." She grinned up at him, and Nathan felt his brain turn to mush—how could she be so intoxicating just smiling? What right did Caden have to look so damned stunning just going through life?

Nathan watched as she took the small step separating them, reached up, gripped his shirt with her right hand, and jerked down. Her other hand came up and gripped the back of his neck.

He knew he was a goner right then because her smell filtered into his nose. Cinnamon and vanilla. It was all he could do just to keep his face clear of everything going on inside his head.

She pulled until his mouth was level with hers, and then she kissed him. Suddenly, it was nothing but the feel of her.

The feel of her breath on his face, her warm body pressed to his.

Teeth nipped at his bottom lip until he opened his mouth for her. All the thoughts poured out of his ears and blood surged to his dick. Getting her into his truck now forgotten, he reacted instinctively.

Nathan kissed her back with all the pent up frustration she'd been causing him for the past couple of weeks.

Her mouth was on his.

Her tongue was tangling with his.

Her soft, warm body was pressed against his.

Finally, they came up for air, and slowly Nathan returned to himself. His hands were on her ass, pressing her against his truck. All his blood was in his dick and his brain was going too slow.

His knees were mush. Nathan didn't think he get out of the truck to save his life.

Her chest heaved up and down and she watched him with heated eyes. Her lips were full and swollen. Her eyes were on his mouth and her tongue darted out to lick her lips.

She wanted to kiss him again. He wanted to ravish her lips. But first, he needed to get them somewhere no one's going to slap a court order on them for getting naked.

And the parking lot was definitely not the right place for that.

Exercising all the control he could muster, Nathan picked Caden up and deposited her into the truck. He took a moment to fasten her seatbelt, and that nearness almost broke his control.

Her chest was still heaving up and down and her pupils were blown wide. It took every bit of self control not to kiss her again but instead gently shut the door and walked calmly to driver's side.

It was a short, tense trip to his home. Half his attention was all he could afford to spend on the road. The other half was on Caden who was staring straight ahead like if she looked at him, she'd lose control.

"Nice house," Caden whispered when Nathan pulled up onto his driveway. It was a nice house, but he didn't give two fucks about it in that moment.

"Thanks," Nathan grunted, getting out of the car and hurrying over to her door.

He scooped her out of the car, and just as quickly hauled her tight against him until every part of him was touching every part of her. Her long legs wrapped around his hips and her arms snaked around his neck, all while she kissed him.

Nathan carried her blindly towards his home until they crashed through the front door. The door banged against the wall and bounced back at them. Nate sidestepped the thing just in time not to be battered by his own front door.

Caden untangled herself from him and pulled his shirt up and over his head. At the same time, he gripped the bottom of her t-shirt and ripped it up and off of her in one smooth motion.

His mouth landed on hers again, not tentative, not gentle, but hungry and demanding. He stroked a hand down her back to her ass, lifted her up and pulled her snug against his erection.

Caden belonged here, in his home, his arms, heating up his skin. Wherever and whenever, he would never tire of her.

She knotted her fingers in his hair and Nathan licked her neck and drew his teeth against the delicate skin, satisfaction burning his veins when she canted her head back to give him access to her soft skin.

She tasted so incredibly good that Nate didn't realize he'd headed for the bedroom until he rammed into the door with his back. He turned them so she was plastered against the door and dropped to his knees in front of her as he slowly kissed down her torso.

"Nate—"

He unbuttoned her jeans and pulled them down her hips to reveal her tiny cotton panties. It was so unexpectedly cute that Nate couldn't help but grin. It only made sense; she didn't have much of a chance to shop outside of excursions with Kade and himself.

"What?" she asked smiling too.

"Nothing—just can't believe we're finally alone."

Couldn't believe he could actually now explore her the way he'd dreamt of for so very long.

Couldn't believe she was in his home, panting and needy for him.

Nathan's breath hitched as he knelt there, his forehead resting against her stomach for a moment, absorbing the reality of the moment. Every fiber of his body buzzed with anticipation, the months of tension now boiling over.

Keeping one hand on her hip, he moved the other down her spine until he cupped her ass. He delved down, his fingertips playing between her legs and over her sex.

He just wanted to taste her, eat her out and leave her unable to move.

"Nate." Her voice was a guttural sound that drove him right to the edge of crazy.

He sucked on one finger, then stroked it over her pink folds. Caden hissed out a moan and it was all the encouragement he needed to increase the tempo.

Nathan bent his head, kissing her thighs while he teased her with all he could be doing with his tongue, his lips, his fingers.

He slid in one finger and she moaned and arched her back in response. At the same time, he licked a hot stripe through her thin cotton panties. Intertwining his fingers with the waistband, he slid them down her legs.

Now completely exposed to him, Caden's fingers dug into his scalp as his fingers dipped in and out of her. She was warm and tight around him.

This woman would be the death of him. Nathan held her still as he tasted her skin with his tongue, his fingers stroking deeper, being coated by her wetness.

His tongue darted out fast, sucking at her clit. Caden's eyes fluttered closed like she'd been waiting for just that moment. Her legs shook beside his head as she wheezed out a ragged moan.

"Fuck me." Her voice was all breathy, and Nathan repeated the sweep of his tongue just to hear her gasp again. "Nate!"

"I've been dying to taste you." He hissed the words, sucking on her clit as his free hand gripped her ass.

Nathan wanted to inhale her, breathe her in, revel in Caden writhing against his bedroom door. He'd dreamed this moment, fantasized about it, but the reality of it still shocked him.

Caden's little moans were all the encouragement he needed; soft little sighs that tightened his stomach and made his blood roar faster to his aching cock.

Her fingers tightened in his hair, rocking his head back to look at her. Her lips were swollen as she darted her tongue over them. "Nathan?"

"Caden?" Nathan wanted to explore her body, to run his

nose down every ridge of her skin, and to discover as he did what places made her moan, what places made her scream.

It took all his control to keep his fingers pumping in and out of her wet body as her eyes swept over him. She bit down on her bottom lip before she glared at him.

"Stop fucking teasing me," Caden growled, her words sparking heat and a smirk from Nathan.

"Yes, ma'am." Nathan bent his head, licking a red hot path down her stomach to her navel where he bit her softly.

He placed a soft kiss an inch above her clit. Caden whimpered as his hot breath fanned out against her most sensitive spots. His tongue swept out against her clit and a feral groan escaped his throat at how delicious she tasted.

Nathan locked his lips on her clit, rolling his tongue over her again and again until she jerked away from him, panting in short bursts. He dragged his tongue all the way up to her entrance before sweeping it back up and clamping down.

Caden moaned and thrashed and pulled on his hair. Nathan locked his lips around her and licked it all up, biting down softly, enough to send pleasure scattering along her body but not enough to truly hurt.

Nathan felt his body tightening with need, lust rippling through his veins to his cock. He didn't waste anymore time teasing her. His mouth on her pussy, he slid his finger inside her. Caden's hips bucked against his hand, sweat sliding down her thighs and slipping his hold for a second. He gripped her harder, curling to hit that sweet spot.

Her body reacted by arching, pushing her pussy further on his finger. He added a second finger, curling both up.

Fuck. She was perfect. "You're fucking perfect, Caden."

She responded with an unintelligible gabble of words he couldn't decipher if he tried. He leaned up to watch her face as he pumped his fingers in and out of her. She was flushed and needy and wanting more. Begging for more if the tightly pleading look on her face was any indication.

He fucked her with his fingers faster, stroked her with his tongue, his teeth sliding every so often over her clit.

Caden's ass curved towards his fingers. Nathan watched as she threw her head back and let out a long, guttural moan. Brows scrunched tight, eyes clamped shut, legs clenched around his arm, and her head thrown back—he had never seen anything so perfect.

Satisfaction burned in Nathan's body, and he smoothed his tongue over her slit again, licking slowly, taking languid strokes over her clit as she relaxed against the door, going limp as her orgasm softened.

"Fuck me, that was amazing." Caden's voice was smoky as he got off his knees and stood to his full height, placing gentle, playful kisses as he went. He curled his hand under her jaw and tipped her head up.

"I'm glad to be at your service, ma'am."

Her giggle was all the reward he could have asked for.

27

CADEN

"Caden." The rough sound of his voice sent a delicious shiver down her spine. "Caden."

"Nate." It was a whisper of a sound. His blue eyes were pinned on her as he moved up her torso, kissing and licking as he went.

He held himself rigid against her. He was warm and solid and everything Caden wanted. She could feel the hard length of him pressing against her midsection. A growl ripped out of his throat at the contact, and he wrapped his hands around her hips and yanked her closer, drawing a soft gasp from her. Grinding and panting, the big man groaned and Caden moaned too. The friction was just as delicious as it was frustrating.

"Pants off." Heart in her throat, Caden tugged at the offending things.

In two swift motions, he ripped off his pants and there he stood. Gloriously fucking naked.

There wasn't an ounce of fat on him. His cock was already rigid with want; it was long and thick, bigger than she'd expected. Dark, veiny skin was tipped with dark red, the head beading with pre-cum.

His hands returned to her waist. His grip was bruising in intensity. Caden loved it. She pulled him in for another kiss. Caden rolled her hips, letting his cock slide against her pussy and lower abdomen. The big man holding her groaned, shuddering slightly.

"Caden." Again he said her name when he pulled away. Like he wasn't capable of anything else. This time Caden could feel the vibration of the word pressed against his body like she was. It was a rumble of a sound and sent shivers down her spine and curling her toes.

"Nathan. What are you—"

He gripped her waist and pulled her up his body like she weighed nothing. His hot, throbbing cock dragged down her stomach until it was positioned at her entrance. Caden gasped in shock—really, he was just going to fuck her standing against the door?

"There's a bed, you heathen." Caden laughed as he shook his head like he was clearing his thoughts. She wrapped her legs around his torso. He gripped her waist and pulled her up his body once again like she weighed nothing. She loved it when he manhandled her like that. It made her feel delicate and protected in his hold.

"You're right." He gripped her hips and hiked her further up his torso then headed to the bed. He deposited her on the bed and turned to his beside drawer where he pulled out a box of condoms and dug around for one.

Caden watched him roll the condom on. She'd completely forgotten about condoms and the need for them. If he hadn't remembered—Caden didn't want to think about the consequences.

He turned back to her and leaned forward, pressing his palms on the sheets with his eyes boring holes in her face. Caden let out a gasp as she felt the head of his cock at her entrance, not pushing in, just teasing.

"Tell me you want this, Caden."

"I want you," Caden breathed without hesitation. "I want this."

Without preamble, he pushed the broad head of his cock into her.

"Nathan!" Caden couldn't help but throw her head back against the bed and breathe deep. Her body resisted, but he didn't relent. He just kept up the pressure and finally, he eased through. "Fuck."

The intrusion wasn't difficult; it was just shocking. She was so wet it helped ease him inside. Her nails dug into the skin of his shoulders as he pressed into her inch by inch, his own breaths coming in soft gasps with each inch was buried into her.

She looked up at his face and watched as his lips parted and a look of pain crossed his features as he slowly pushed into her. Another growl ripped out of his throat.

The pleasure of being filled and stretched was exquisite.

"So fucking tight." It was a growl of frustration as his cock sank deeper and deeper.

"Jesus fucking Christ." Caden moaned as he just kept pushing into her. Was there no end to his cock? How was she going to survive him?

Finally, after what seemed to be like an eternity of a mixture of pleasure and pain, he was seated to the hilt, and Caden could only gasp at the feeling of being so incredibly full. Panting, Caden gripped him harder and tried to get her bearings. His hands were tight around her hips panting along with her.

"Caden?" This time it sounded like a question instead of just a growl.

"Fuck me." It was more an utterance of the words than it was a command, but Nathan took it as such.

He gripped her hips anew and pushed her until his cock was just barely inside of her and then slammed her down on him.

Caden saw stars.

A tugging ache started to build in her belly.

He lifted her again and slammed her down on his length. Again and again, he lifted her only to slam her down on top of him. Each time stars appeared in her vision and it was all Caden could do just to hold on to him. His cock hit a spot inside of her that made her cry out.

Again, he slammed into her, and with every thrust, the tugging tingling sparking feeling got more and more over-powering. Gasping and trying to keep her hold on the big man, Caden panted and moaned like some kind of porn star.

Fucking hell. Caden had never been fucked like it before. It was brutal and so fucking hot.

Caden dug her nails into his shoulders as he relentlessly pounded into her. Over and over and over. The tingling built and built until it finally pushed her over the edge. An orgasm arced through her and through it all he kept pounding into her. Each time, stars appeared in her vision and all Caden could do was to just squeeze the sheets tightly as he fucked her stupid.

Her vaginal muscles clamped down on his driving cock as Caden came. Her eyes rolled back into their sockets, her toes curled till they hurt, her lower back arched so much that it was lifted off the bed.

After her orgasm and shivering uncontrollably from the

intensity of it, Caden tried to get her breathing under control. Her lungs burned like she'd just run a marathon. Her heart pounded in her chest like it wanted to break free, and she felt an electric wave coursing through her whole body.

Eventually, the aftershocks died away, but he didn't stop. He just kept pistoning into her, moaning her name, and spreading her legs wider.

All of that was too much for Caden, so much that that the tingle started up again and her toes curled.

"Nathan." Caden didn't know what she was saying, only that she needed to say something. "Nathan. I can't—"

"Caden." It was like he was only capable of her name.

His grip on her hips tightened as he brought her down on his cock again and again. Every muscle in her body shook as he just kept pounding into her, hitting the spot inside her pussy just right. The friction sent zapping pulses up her spine and dancing along her nerve endings. His movements became more frantic. He only pulled her partially off his cock before slamming into place again.

He moved faster and faster until he made an agonized sound deep in his throat.

"Fuck." Caden couldn't breathe. Caden couldn't think past the cock pounding into her. She was going to come again—which was mind-boggling. She'd never come multiple times before.

Her hands clutched at Nathan uselessly as a climax roared through her. Wave after wave of pleasure rolled through her as her mind went empty of all thought. Blackness crept into the edges of her vision as he just kept fucking her and fucking her through it all, chasing his own orgasm.

He groaned as he slammed into her again and again.

Caden could feel his muscles tighten as he buried himself deep inside her and kept coming.

"Caden." He panted against her skin when he finally stopped fucking her.

Head empty, breath coming in hard sharp pants, Caden sagged in his arms.

28

CADEN

After about twenty minutes of cuddling and giggling, Nathan took her in the bed again. Afterward, they found themselves in the shower, where the warm water cascaded over them, their passion reigniting amidst the steam and slick skin. It was slower, intimate and tender, the closeness between them palpable in every touch. Once they were both spent, they'd dried and climbed back into bed.

Wrapped in his arms, their bodies intertwined, Caden let the warmth of their shared space lull her into a peaceful, contented silence. That was quickly blasted apart by Savage making jokes.

"I love you."

He had to be joking.

Caden glanced up at his smiling face and felt a keen sense of relief. He was joking.

"Yeah, okay." She laughed along with him.

"I'm being serious." Now he was frowning and looking at her like she was the one being ridiculous.

"Well, stop being serious."

"Caden." He stopped playing with her hair and glanced down at her with a scowl on his face. "I love you."

"No, you don't. And besides, it's not about that, Nate." Why was he ruining this? Why couldn't he let well enough alone? Caden sat up in bed and glared at the man.

"Yes, I do. What's it about then?"

Caden stood and found her pants in the pile of clothes they had torn off each other and shimmed into them. Her shirt was next—she couldn't find her bra.

"Can we just drop it, please?" Caden turned to him and tried not to scowl. His face was a mask of confusion. "We were having such a nice time." Why did he have to ruin it?

"No, I can't drop it. What's it about? Just sex for you?"

"It's not that." Caden jerked a hand through her hair and tried to find patience.

"Then what is it?" Where was her goddamn bra?

"It's *me* okay? It's me! You *can't* love me!" The words were out there and she couldn't take them back. God damn Nate and his persistence.

"Why the hell not?"

"Because I'm no good, Nate! Okay? I'm not fucking good enough for you!" And there it was. They could have gone on in blissful ignorance if he hadn't brought his feelings into it.

"What?" Nate looked dumbstruck. "What do you mean?"

Frustration overrode everything else. Why couldn't he just leave it alone? Why did he have to go and say that he loved her? He couldn't love her, not really. He was too good. Too fucking pure for this world.

"You know what—I'm just gonna leave." It was for the best. She would leave and he could forget about her.

"What? No!"

"Yes, I'm leaving. Don't follow me." Caden stepped into her shoes and grabbed her phone. She had nothing else except for a bra that she could not find.

"Caden, let's talk about this." Nathan scrambled out of bed and tore through the pile of clothes on the ground.

"There's nothing to talk about." She was already at the front door.

Nate was still trying to pull up his pants when she shut the door. As soon as the door was closed behind her, Caden ran for all she was worth, which admittedly wasn't much, but still she ran.

She ran until her heart ached and she was gasping for air. The air was hot even for how early in the morning it was. She was dripping with sweat. It took her a long minute, but when she finally registered her surroundings, she found that she was in the middle of a neighborhood.

She didn't recognize anything—not that she had been paying much attention when they drove to Nathan's house.

Caden plopped on the transit bus bench and took a moment to gather herself, but she was too raw and scattered to do much gathering. So instead, for the first time since her sister had died, she let herself cry. Ugly, guttural sobs that tore at her chest.

Caden sat on the bus bench, her body trembling as she sobbed. Each cry was like a dam breaking, the pressure of everything she had tried to ignore finally rushing out. Her chest heaved, and she pressed her palms against her eyes, trying to contain the flood, but it was useless.

This wasn't supposed to happen. None of it.

Nathan wasn't supposed to care. He wasn't supposed to love her. He was supposed to be a fun distraction, something easy. They weren't meant to get tangled up in feelings. Not like this.

Caden felt the weight of her sister's death, the crushing guilt, the pain she had buried for so long. She had spent years convincing herself that she didn't deserve anything good—that she didn't deserve to be loved. And now, here was Nate, telling her he did. It didn't make sense.

Why couldn't he just let it go?

She knew she wasn't someone to be loved. She'd only destroy him, the way she destroyed everything else. Nate was kind and sweet, and he deserved better than her mess. He deserved someone whole, someone who hadn't been broken by life. Not someone who ran at the first sign of something real.

Caden drew in a ragged breath, trying to calm the storm raging inside her, but the tears kept falling. The loss of her sister, the guilt, the shame—it was all too much. She wasn't crying just because of Nate. She was crying because she hadn't allowed herself to feel anything for so long. It all came crashing down now.

Her phone buzzed in her hand, and for a second, she didn't want to look. But she knew it was Nathan. He wouldn't just let her go. She wiped her face, smearing the tears, and glanced down at the screen.

Nate: *Where are you? We need to talk about this. Please don't leave before we talk.*

A fresh wave of emotion hit her.

Why? Why couldn't he just walk away like everyone else had?

She put her phone back into her back pocket, feeling torn between wanting to run farther and wanting to go back. She didn't deserve his love, but the thought of him giving up on her twisted something deep in her chest.

For now, though, all she could do was sit there, surrounded by the unfamiliar streets, alone with her thoughts and the ache in her heart. She leaned her head back, staring up at the sky, and let the tears fall.

29

———————

BRIAR

Fate wasn't a thing Briar Hawthorne could escape. No matter where she went, what she did, or who she talked to it was fate. She'd tried to dodge it when she was young but matter what she did fate always found a way to get her where it wanted her.

She had eventually learned to just go with the flow. It was easier that way.

Which was why she found herself wandering aimlessly through an airport trying to find the person fate was pulling her towards. She was studying faces and trying to pump herself up for another reading when it happened.

Usually she was so careful about touching people, but she was in an airport and there were just so many people to worry about that she couldn't keep track of them all.

So when she bumped shoulders and lived through a torture session, she was shocked and horrified. It immediately made her cry. She'd never endured torture before. But this person had recently undergone *torture*.

Briar stood stock still as the rest of this woman's life whirled in her mind.

Caden Quinn. Mercenary. Sometimes a thief. Ezra: dead. Quinn: dead. Her fault. Nathan Savage: a shining beacon in the darkness that was Caden's life. Death, murder, suicide, guilt—so much guilt.

Briar cried harder.

This was the person fate was pulling her towards.

Caden Quinn and her fucked up life.

"Excuse me." Tears still streaming down her face, Briar went after Caden. "Excuse me!" Too loud, people turned around to eye her and the commotion she was making. The amount of times she'd been embarrassed because of her goddamned gift was staggering. She was used to it now.

Finally, Caden turned around.

"Hi, Caden?"

The woman was shorter than her and pale. Unstyled dark hair fell to her shoulders and darker eyes looked startled at her name being spoken. Her face was sharp and angular. Her dark brows were pulled down in consternation.

"My name is Briar Hawthorne. Nice to meet you." She didn't offer her hand but nodded and smiled.

"Do I know you?"

"No."

"Then how do you know my name?"

Now, this was always the part she hated. No one ever believed her, and she sounded ridiculous. Besides the fact that there wasn't a name close enough to do justice to what she could do. So she always just settled on psychic.

"I'm psychic." Which never went over well.

"And I'm a duck." The woman rolled her eyes and turned on her heel to leave.

"Wait!" Briar caught her elbow and was assaulted with even more of Caden's miserable life. "Wait, please. Can I talk to you for a second?" Briar ignored the tears streaming down her face and tried not to look entirely pathetic.

"Why? There's a whole airport full of *other* people for you to harass." She gestured around her and huffed out an annoyed breath.

"There's something important *you* need to hear."

Caden glanced at her phone and then around at all the people coming and going and finally sighed. "Fine. What is it I need to know?"

"Do you mind if we sit down?" Briar pointed to a bench several feet away and waited for Caden to head there before she started walking.

"Okay, we're sat. What do you have to say to me?" Impatient, the woman glanced at her phone again and then at the passing people.

Briar wasn't sure where to start. What could she say that Caden would believe? Probably nothing.

"What would make you believe me?"

"You tell me." She scoffed. "You're the psychic."

"Okay, just listen then." How was she supposed to put this in a way that this woman would believe? "You have had a very hard life."

"Who hasn't?" Caden nodded and looked around like she was losing interest in their conversation quickly.

"It wasn't your fault. None of it was."

"Hmm," was her only response.

Okay, so that approach wasn't working. Time to change it up.

"Your sisters Ezra and Quinn." That got her attention. Her demeanor shifted abruptly, a dark, threatening presence replacing her previously calm exterior. Briar threw her hands up. "Wait! Wait! Don't become Scary-Caden."

That seemed to deflate her a tiny bit. But she continued to look menacing.

"You have thirty seconds to explain how you know those names."

"I already told you—I'm psychic."

"Yeah, right."

"It's true."

"Fine, if you're psychic, how many fingers am I holding up?" Caden put a hand behind her back and arched an eyebrow at her.

"Can I touch you?"

"Sure."

Briar gingerly touched her shoulder and was assailed with living the life of Caden Quinn once more. She had to dig through everything to find the fingers.

"You're flipping me off." How nice of her. "So one."

"Wow." Caden looked truly impressed. "Great guess."

"It *wasn't* a guess." Briar was getting annoyed now. "I'm fucking psychic."

"Fine, you're psychic." Caden rolled her eyes again and shrugged. "What is it you want to tell me?"

"Hear me out, okay? Don't interrupt."

"Fine."

"Quinn being murdered by your piece of shit father wasn't your fault. Ezra dying from breast cancer wasn't your fault. Your team being set up and then killed wasn't your fault."

With each sentence, the smaller woman's face became paler until she was as white as porcelain.

"You walking away from Nathan and the potential happiness that he represents *is* your fault."

Caden's mouth opened and closed a few times before

she just shut it completely. Color slowly came back to her face. Finally, she opened her mouth.

"You don't know what you are talking about."

"Don't I?" Feeling snarky, Briar made a face and said, "I am psychic, remember?"

"No, you don't." Caden shook her head. "Because if I had just been—"

"Whatever you're going to say is stupid and self-pitying." Briar held up her hand to stop what she knew was going to be a lot of guilt and self-blame. "You were a kid, a sister, and a teammate. You are not God. Get over yourself."

Perhaps she'd been too abrupt? Usually, Briar was much more gentle. Caden had driven her to the point of snapping, and now she regretted not keeping her cool.

"Look..." Briar rubbed the back of her neck. "I'm sorry not to be more gentle with this. But if nothing else, do it for Ezzy and Quinn. They'd want you to be happy."

Caden looked too pale again and her eyes were distant, but at least she seemed to be contemplating what Briar had told her.

"I hope you'll choose happiness, Caden."

Briar straightened and walked away. She had done what she could for Caden. She had tried. And maybe that would be enough to nudge Caden toward the light.

30

CADEN

Well, that was... unexpected. Caden's mind whirled as she sat on the bench that Briar Hawthorne, psychic extraordinaire, had just vacated. She had a lot to contend with after their conversation.

First, that psychics were a thing. Like a real actual thing. Briar was one of them. Caden knew this to be true because no one knew of her baby sisters. Not their names, not that they once existed—nothing.

No one besides Nate. And Nathan wouldn't have told anyone. She believed that so much that she was certain that psychics were a real thing.

Which was just crazy.

But facts were facts.

Psychics were real.

Second, and the most mind blowing of all, that she deserved happiness.

It was a problem she hadn't been aware of before the psychic. But it made enough sense. Why was she running away from Nate? She wasn't good enough for him. She'd just trash his life as she had so many others. Which basically all boiled down to her believing that she didn't deserve happiness.

Obviously, it was something that she had to think about. Her not believing that she deserved happiness... probably had to do something with her childhood. Wasn't that the case with all mental health problems?

Which made complete sense considering the shit hole that was her youth. Was she set up for failure just because of some unresolved stuff from her childhood?

Fuck that.

She wouldn't give her father that much power over her.

Could she forgive herself for her sisters' deaths?

Ezra's death really hadn't been her fault. It didn't mean that she didn't feel guilty as hell about it, though. Caden could hardly claim that she had control over breast cancer. So why did she harbor so much guilt?

No, what she actually felt guilty about was being away on jobs so much instead of spending time with her baby sister. Caden regretted it so much. It was an ache in her chest every time she thought about Ezzy. But it wasn't like she could go back in time and fix it. Her job had kept them fed and clothed. It wasn't like she could have said no to Uncle Sam. She'd have been court-martialed.

All she could do was come to terms with the fact that she'd prioritized her job over her sister.

Quinn's death *was* her fault. Quinn had been so young, so good. If she'd only got her sisters out of that monster's house sooner, then Quinn would still be alive. Why had the psychic said it wasn't her fault?

Quinn was dead.

And it was her fault.

If she'd only hidden them better. If Quinn had only

listened to her to stay hidden. If only she'd tried harder to get him off her. If only her father wasn't such a fucking monster.

Which was maybe what the psychic had meant when she said it wasn't Caden's fault. Why let her father off the hook? He was the monster in the story. He was the fucker who'd murdered his own child.

Caden had been just a kid herself. Kid Caden hadn't known leaving was an option.

Maybe it *wasn't* her fault. Maybe she was carrying around the guilt because she knew her father wasn't.

Caden reeled in shock at this revelation.

Maybe it wasn't her fault.

Which meant what?

That she wasn't as bad of a person as she thought she was. That *maybe* she deserved happiness. That *maybe* she was a person Nathan could want.

It took her a long minute to realize her phone was ringing and even longer to find the capacity to pick it up.

"Hello?" Who even had her number? She'd gotten the phone maybe three or four days ago.

"Caden." Jackson's no-nonsense tone was on the other end.

"Jackson," still reeling from her revelation, she could only sputter, "how'd you get this number?"

"What do you mean? I've had this number since day one."

"I mean, how'd you get it? My phone has been locked since day one."

"Like it was hard guessing your password. You're obsessed with him. I guessed *Nate* in two tries."

"Shut up." Caden was blushing hard. "What do you want?"

"Nate has been taken."

"What?" Ice ran through her veins. "What are you talking about—I literally just left. What do you mean, he was *taken*?"

"We think he was going after you when he was intercepted and taken. His tracker is on its way to Mexico."

"Well, shit."

"Are you coming back or is this it—no more Caden in our lives?"

"Yeah, I'm coming back."

"Good." His voice was clipped. "We're bugging out in a few hours. Be at HQ before then."

31

CADEN

Mexico was hot, dry, and, so far, aggravating.

Caden hadn't taken orders in a long time and hadn't been on a team even longer. Taking orders was not something she was used to doing anymore. So when Jackson told her she was on the distraction team instead of the extraction team, she got annoyed.

"I'd rather be on the extraction team." She knew this wasn't how teams worked or how orders worked, but she had to try.

"Too bad you're on distraction duty." Jackson wasn't paying much attention to her but to the layout of the building in the maps before him.

"Distraction duty is too far from the action." She wanted to get Nate.

"You'll be a liability—you're too close to it." He finally looked up from the maps and scowled at her.

"You are all literally his brothers. How are you not too close to it too?" How was she a liability when they were his brothers? It didn't make sense.

"That's why you, me, and Holden are on distraction duty and *not* extraction. Maddox is heading up the extraction team. We'll get Nate, but in order to do that we need you on the distraction team and I don't want any more shit about it."

"Fine." Caden folded her arms and sat back, not at all pleased with how things were shaking out.

"You get to play with explosives on the distraction team," Maddox offered from his position across from Jackson.

Caden's interest piqued momentarily, despite her frustration. "Explosives, huh?"

"Fuck yeah," Maddox said with a broad smile.

"So what's the plan?" Kade spoke up from his spot across from Caden.

Jackson shifted his attention back to the maps, tracing a route with his finger. "We're hitting two points simultaneously. Extraction team goes in from the east, where security is thinner. Distraction team will hit the west side, drawing as much attention as possible. Explosives, smoke, loud noises —whatever we can use to create chaos."

Holden leaned back, cracking his knuckles. "Got it. How long do we have?"

"Twenty minutes from the time we breach to get Nate and get out," Jackson said, scowling at everyone present. "No mistakes. No deviations."

THE DRY GRASS crunched beneath her feet as they advanced on the east side. Holden was on her six and Jackson was in front of her. Her pack was heavy with explosives. The blue light of the very early morning put everything in shadow and gave her a sense of ease that they wouldn't be easily spotted.

Setting up the explosives took a hot minute, but she was on schedule. Setting up the timer was the tricky part. They had to be synchronized if this was going to work.

She glanced up at Jackson, who was busy securing the charges to the gate, his face set in a determined expression. Holden was still at her six, keeping watch for any signs of movement from the compound. The tension in the air was palpable.

With a deep breath, she began setting the timers, her fingers working quickly yet carefully. As she finished setting the first timer, she double-checked it, then moved to the next one.

"How are we looking?" Jackson whispered, his voice barely audible.

"Almost there," she replied, adjusting the final timer. "Just need to sync them all up."

Holden glanced back, his eyes narrowed with concern. "Dawn's coming, and we can't afford to get caught in the open."

Caden nodded, her hands steady despite the adrenaline surging through her. She synced the last timer and stepped back, giving a quick thumbs-up to Jackson. He nodded in return and gestured for them to retreat.

A little niggling thought in the back of her mind, Caden had the sudden urge to look under the building. She squatted where she stood and carefully shined her flashlight under the building.

"Caden, what are you doing?" Jackson's voice was quiet and angry.

Explosives upon explosives were attached to the foundation of the building.

Adrenaline spiked in her blood and she was on her feet before she realized she was moving. The blast range was going to be much bigger—they wouldn't have enough time to get far enough away.

"Run!" Caden hissed, waving her arms as she ran. Jackson stared at her blankly, but Holden ran without a second thought. "Run!" How much clearer could she be? What the hell was his problem with just staring at her?

Finally, he moved, but not fast enough.

"Jackson, run! Goddamn it!" Caden yelled this time. The dry grass crunched beneath her feet and she was running with abandon now. She checked her watch. Five seconds to get to safety.

Five.

They weren't out of the blast radius. If she got Nathan's brothers killed, she could never face him again. Shit, she should have checked it before putting up the charges.

Four.

She cleared a bush and then a rock, but tripped when a hole in the ground caught her ankle. Holden picked her up and put her back on her feet, and they were off again.

Three.

Jackson was a good ten feet behind them. He wasn't going to make it in time. The blast would hit him. Hell, they *all* weren't going to make it in time. The blast was going to hit them all.

Two.

Her lungs burned and her side ached, but she kept up her speed, jumping over saplings and shrubbery. Holden was right behind her, gun holstered at his side, and running for all he was worth.

One.

The charges went off.

They weren't far enough away.

It took a second, but the blast caught up with her. It was like getting hammered in the back with a battering ram. It pushed the air out of her lungs, lit a trail of pain all over, and knocked her off her feet.

32

NATHAN

Nathan had been caught and tortured too many times in the past month.

It was getting tiresome.

He'd been on his way to convince Caden to stay with him when he was run off the road, pulled out of his truck, and tossed in the back of a black van. They'd then proceeded to beat the living hell out of him until he'd passed out.

The worst part of it all was that he'd missed his chance with Caden. She could be literally anywhere now. She'd probably gotten on that plane and hadn't looked back. He'd have to start from scratch in finding her again.

Fucking Kyott.

Nate was going to kill him.

And just what the hell did Kyott want with *him*? He was retired. Any information he did know was outdated and useless.

He'd been getting beat on for the past hour with no questions asked. If they wanted to torture someone, any old

Tom, Dick, or Harry would do. Why track him down and go through the trouble of kidnapping him again?

Which made him think that this all had something to do with Caden Quinn. She was the only thing he had information on. Unless, of course, he was there for some random reason he couldn't possibly fathom. She was the only thing that made sense.

Another hit to the face and Nathan was seeing stars. The goon delivering the beating had himself a powerful right hook.

Nathan spat blood onto the floor, his vision blurring as another punch sent his head snapping back. The metallic taste of blood lingered in his mouth, mixing with the bitterness of frustration.

As the goon pulled back for another swing, Nathan braced himself, biting down on the urge to groan. His mind raced, trying to make sense of the situation. Maybe Kyott had gotten wind that Caden Quinn had been staying with him? Maybe this was another one of those bought to be tortured things. Not him, but Caden.

The next punch didn't come. Instead, there was a pause. Nathan blinked through the blood and sweat, his eyes locking on the figure standing just behind the goon. He recognized that smug silhouette anywhere.

"Marskib," Nathan rasped, his voice hoarse but laced with venom. That mother fucker. "Finally decided to join the party, huh?"

Charles Marskib stepped forward, his hands clasped behind his back, a cold smile tugging at the corners of his lips. Kyott and the goon took a step back and stood in the shadows of the room. Nathan couldn't decide if he was satisfied or not with this turn of events. He'd been in Moscow to track Marskib's movements, but all that had changed when he'd gotten captured.

"Savage. You've always had a talent for being in the wrong place at the wrong time. But this? This is different—you're exactly where I want you to be this time."

"What do you want, Charles?" Nathan's jaw tightened.

"I want Caden Quinn."

"I don't have her." Nathan shrugged his shoulders. His heart pounded in his chest, his mind scrambling to piece together the puzzle. Why did Charles Marskib want Caden Quinn?

"But you know where she is." He crouched down, leaning so close Nathan could smell his aftershave. "What did you do with her once you escaped my compound?"

"That was *your* compound?"

"Yes, it was unfortunately run by idiots." He tsked and shook his head ruefully. "Had I been running it, you would have never escaped."

"I heard that Caden Quinn escaped you." Nathan couldn't help but remind him. Just to nettle him.

"That was a fluke, and I assure you, it won't happen again."

"Ah." The pieces were coming together in his mind. "You want Caden Quinn so you can take up where you left off. Torturing her."

"Is that so much to ask?"

"I think so." Nathan nodded his head and watched the man sigh dejectedly and stand.

The goon came out of the shadows, wielding a cattle prod and a self-satisfied smirk. Charles sighed again and stood to face Nathan. "If you don't tell me what I want to know, Jacoby here is going to stab you with a cattle prod until you are cooked from the inside out."

Great. Electrocution. Nathan took a deep breath in through his nose and tried to remember his SERE training. The cattle prod came down on his arm and pain shot through him. Electric hands gripped every muscle in his body and squeezed until he was in a tight ball of electric pain.

"Okay, okay." As soon as he gained control of his voice again, he spoke. "What if I told you I took her home to meet my parents?" Nathan smirked as Marskib rolled his eyes and motioned for the goon to electrocute him again.

"You're not funny, Savage." He got close again and gripped Nathan's hair in a fist to bring his head back up. "Where is she?"

"No, seriously," Nathan stated again, knowing that there was no way in hell that they would believe the truth. "I took her home and had her meet my mama—"

Another shock with the cattle prod.

"Where is she?"

"Why do you want her, of all people?" Nathan's breathing was ragged and his muscles spasmed erratically.

"That woman is mine."

"I didn't get real *taken* vibes from her." Nate cocked an eyebrow. Was this guy for real?

"Caden Quinn is *mine*," Marksib growled, grabbed the prod out of his goon's hands and struck him with it. As Nathan burned and burned under the electric onslaught, the man went on. "She thinks she can escape me, doesn't she? That after all the time we've spent together, she's somehow free? But I know better. Deep down, she understands. I've carved myself into her mind, into her very soul. Every scream, every tear she shed in my dungeon was a symphony, and every scar a reminder that she belongs to me."

"Oh, so you're like a *psycho* psycho."

"Savage," he sighed and handed the prod back to his goon, "this can either get easier for you or harder. I can continue to play nice with the cattle prod and you tell me what I want to know, or I can get more creative and start with your teeth."

Nathan heaved a resigned sigh and opened his mouth to retort, but the building rocked under his feet, and at the same time, gunfire opened up.

"Fuck!" Marskib turned on Kyott and yelled, "I thought you checked him for tracking devices!"

"We did!"

"Then why are we being attacked?"

"I don't know, sir!"

"Get my chopper here," Marskib commanded as they left the room.

It was a few minutes of gunfire and yelling as Nate waited patiently for his brothers to get to him. Eventually, Nathan watched as the Savage Security team flowed into the room. They swept the area and Nate was cut from the chair.

"Can you walk, Nate?" Kade helped him out of the chair.

Nathan staggered to his feet, muscles still twitching from the cattle prod's brutal assault, but the adrenaline now coursing through his veins kept him upright.

"Yeah." Nate took the proffered bullet-proof vest. His feet were bare, but he would just have to deal with it. "They're headed to the roof."

The chaos outside was deafening—the sound of gunfire and shouts reverberating through the walls, making it clear that the rescue operation wasn't clean. The Savage Security team moved with military precision, sweeping through the room and covering all angles as they secured the space.

"Let's go, Nate," Kade muttered, his eyes scanning the door, already anticipating what was next.

Nate grimaced as he slipped on the vest, the rough material chafing against his bruised skin. He nodded at Kade, though the pain still lingered. "You got an extra pair of shoes in your kit, by chance?" His feet were already throbbing from the cold, hard ground, but he knew this wasn't the time to complain.

"Nope." Kade smirked grimly. "You want me to carry you?" he teased.

"You're hilarious." Nate's eyes narrowed as he heard the distinct sound of helicopter blades whirring from the roof above. "Marskib's making a run for it. You got a chopper on standby?"

"We'll catch him before he gets that far." Kade signaled the team, and they moved toward the exit. "Let's make this quick."

Nate limped behind them, pushing through the pain and the dizziness still clouding his mind from the electrocution. He wasn't about to let Charles Marskib slip through his fingers—not after the taunts about Caden. The thought of her, and what this madman had done to her, fueled his determination to see this through.

As they hit the stairwell, Nate's heart raced faster. "He's obsessed with her," he muttered to himself as they ascended the steps. "He's not gonna stop, no matter how many times she escapes."

"Obsessed with who?" Dax tilted his head and swept the staircase with his automatic.

"Caden. He's obsessed with Caden."

"Then let's make sure this is the last time," Maddox replied, his tone dark with purpose.

They burst onto the rooftop, the wind whipping against

their faces. There, standing near the helicopter pad, was Marskib—his cold, smug expression faltering as he saw Nathan emerge from the stairwell. The chopper in the air hadn't landed yet.

"We can either do this the hard way or the easy way, Charles." Nathan recited the man's earlier words and smirked when the other man looked enraged. "You can surrender your arms and come quietly or you can—"

"Fuck that!" The man raised his handgun and aimed it directly at Nathan's chest. Before he could get a shot off, one of the Savage Security team took him out with a quick shot to the torso. Kyott and the goon dropped their weapons and put their hands up in surrender.

It didn't take long for Charles Marskib to die.

Nathan watched as Marskib collapsed, a look of disbelief frozen on his face. The shot had been swift, surgical, and final. Nate didn't feel the satisfaction he thought he would—not yet. Marskib's obsession with Caden still echoed in his mind, the way he spoke of her as if she were some twisted possession.

Kade knelt down, checking Marskib's pulse out of protocol, but shook his head once. "He's gone."

"I've got to find Caden."

"Find? She's here." Maddox secured Kyott while Kade secured the goon.

"What do you mean?"

"Who do you think blew up the building?"

33

CADEN

Rolling. She just kept fucking rolling. She couldn't find purchase—she couldn't find a grip. But all kinds of things were finding all the soft bits on her.

Rock met shoulder. Tree bounced off her back. Dirt in the face. Another rock to the gut. Sapling right in the midsection.

All Caden could do in defense of the onslaught was curl into herself and try to protect her head as she rolled and rolled.

Fuck.

Reid was not going to be happy about this—if she had to go on bed rest again, she'd go fucking crazy. Every movement—every lurching roll down the goddamn mountain sprouted a new bruise or dent or fracture—fuck, she couldn't tell what body part was taking a hit; everywhere hurt all at once. She'd be lucky if she didn't bash her skull in on one of those lovely boulders that were doing absolutely nothing to break her fall.

There was a drop—no, a fucking cliff. The sudden

thought rang in her head and sent a lightning bolt of fear down her spine. Cold sweat broke out all over her. Blood surged in her head and her heart said fuck this and tried to beat its way out of her chest. There was a cliff somewhere down there—to the *there* she was rolling and tumbling towards. She was going to roll right off the damn thing if she didn't find a way to stop.

Curled into herself as she was, it was relatively easy to reach the knife in her boot but less easy to keep a grip on it without gutting herself.

Caden plunged it into the ground. It didn't stick.

A rock slamming into her prone stomach winded the thief and sent her head reeling for too long. Too fucking long—it was taking too fucking long to stop.

She could see the drop-off.

She could see the fucking drop. Where the mountain ended. Where there was nothing but air.

It was ten feet away. She could do this. She could fucking do this because if she didn't, Nathan was gonna find a pancake wearing her clothes at the bottom. Positive thinking —she could do this.

She wasn't going to go over.

Positive thinking would work.

Weeds came up as she grappled for a grip. Plant, rocks, dirt, a whole fucking sapling—weren't those supposed to have roots?

Fucking nature.

Five feet away.

She was not going to go over.

Her knife snagged a rock but then dislodged it right into her face. Pain splintered in her face, but she didn't have time to register the damage.

Four feet away.

She was not going to go over.

She gripped a handful of low hanging tree branch but it broke off in her palm and she kept rolling.

Three feet away.

She was not going to go over.

A rock found her kidney. Dirt, loose fucking dirt, went through her fingers like fucking sand.

Two feet away.

She was not going to go over.

Her knife found purchase—it wedged between two huge boulders and stuck. And fucking held.

Caden came to a bone jarring halt.

She didn't go over.

Her whole body was dangling over the ledge, but she did not go fucking over.

Tears blurred her vision. Her whole body was shaking—from terror or the beating her whole body just took, it didn't matter. Her bloody sweaty hands shook, but she was not letting go of her goddamn knife. Holy fuck—maybe positive thinking was an actual thing and not just something Maddox pulled out of his ass. Huh.

Holden was coming in fast after her. He was tumbling end over end. His body was limp, his limbs flailing—Caden couldn't help but cringe—he'd have lots and lots of broken bones if he wasn't already dead.

"Holden!" Three feet away and not even grabbing for a hold. "Cliff!"

He bounced off the boulders, keeping her knife wedged and was flung over her, head first, over the edge.

Caden was ready for him, though. She shot her arm out as he was airborne and gripped his belt. She fit her whole hand under the strap and braced for the jerk of his weight.

Then prayed with every fiber of her being that the knife and his buckle held.

They held.

Pain—so much fucking pain. Her palms were nothing but sweat and blood and bruises. Her muscles pulled and strained and her recently healed arm was burning. Mentally, she pushed it back and concentrated on breathing.

She could do this.

"Holden!" It was a pained groan that came out of her throat. "Wake." Inhale. "Up." Exhale. "Dead weight." Inhale. "Is killing." Exhale. "Me!"

"Busy bees..." His voice was slurred and slow. "Darwin's like... so... purple... I like it?" His limbs were still limp, but at least he wasn't dead. Maybe brain damaged for life, but not dead. "Penelope... she likes cashews... eww."

"Can't hold much longer. Fucking get it together!" Her muscles were screaming. Blood was running down her face and hands and back and throbbing in her head.

"Caden?" Suddenly he was alert. Caden could feel his weight shift and his muscles tense. "What the fuck!?"

And then came Jackson. Cursing and rolling and tumbling and umphing all the way down.

"Cliff!" It was more of a howl than anything else. "Cliff!"

"Fuck!" His body started wrenching around as he tried to find a hold. But it was too late. He bounced off the same boulder his brother did and shot past her. Caden couldn't help him—all her arms were taken. Fuck fuck. He was going to die because of her.

Holden caught his boot.

The extra weight felt like it pulled her apart. Her shoulder popped out of its socket and Caden was seeing little dots.

"Mother fucking—"

White hot pain was ripping up and down her muscles. Her arm, the one holding Holden and Jackson and the same one that'd been dislocated last time, popped out of its socket. Her fingers went numb, but she gripped his belt with everything she had. She wasn't breathing now, just hollering out the hurt.

"Was that your arm?" Holden's voice sounded from somewhere below.

"Hold on, Caden!" Jackson bellowed as he swung his weight towards the cliff. "Just a little bit longer!"

The movement sent fresh shockwaves of pain through her. Her blood-soaked hand was making her grip on the knife precarious. She was slipping.

"Can't—slipping." She was fucking slipping. Her palm was no longer in contact with the hilt. Her fingers were the only things gripping now.

"One more second."

Jackson swung again; this time he body slammed the rock face and shoved his knives into crevices at the same time.

"Fuck!" Her fingers lost the hilt, and Caden experienced a moment of complete and utter terror.

Her heart stopped.

She didn't—couldn't breathe.

Everything came into sharper focus. The sky was bright blue, birds were chirping, there was a beetle crawling over a mound of dirt right in front of her face. She could hear Holden breathing, deep and fast. Jackson was grunting and wedging his knives deeper into the mountain side. The pain in her arm was overwhelming. And she was going to fall to her death.

And then she dropped.

And dropped.

And was yanked to a halt.

She was still clutching Holden's belt. Her arm was still in an incredible amount of pain, but she'd endure because Jackson's knives were holding. They were dangling off the rock face, but they weren't falling.

They weren't fucking falling.

But they were moving. Down. Slowly.

"Son of a—" It was Jackson growling.

Slowly suddenly became faster as the knives dragged down the mountain side under their combined weight. And then they were airborne and dropping like rocks.

Caden released her grip on Holden's belt and watched as his ass followed her down.

She didn't want the last thing she'd ever see to be Holden's ass outlined by nothing but blue sky. She wanted to see Nathan's ass. She wanted to see that stupid, ridiculous grin. She didn't want to die.

But she kept falling. Kept dropping like a stone. Down. Down.

Then something big slapped all the breath right out of her. Again and again.

Trees. She was hitting branches. Still dropping, but the branches were slowing her descent.

A ridiculous giggle erupted from her throat when she got oxygen back.

Someone, Holden, was laughing too.

Caden tried to find a branch to grip with her good hand, but she was getting bounced around too much. She was getting pummeled by branches and bouncing off trunks and getting slapped around by the more flexible branches.

Finally, she caught and held a branch with her good arm. But her weight was too much. It snapped off in her palm. She fought for a grip again, but she couldn't get a good hold.

But that didn't matter anymore because her back landed on the ground. The wind was once again knocked out of her. Something snapped—several somethings.

Something heavy thudded down beside her, but she didn't catch a glimpse of it because she was rolling again.

Fuck—she couldn't catch a break.

But then a warm hand caught and held her.

"No more rolling." Holden had her. His face was tight and bloodied, but he was smiling down at her, and Caden couldn't help but smile back.

"Anybody dead or seeing bright lights?" Jackson's pain-filled voice filtered in through the roar in her ears. "Don't go into the light. Reid will just bring you back and put your asses on bed rest for the rest of your lives."

"Oh fuck, not bed rest." Holden's voice was an agonized growl. "Don't go into the light, Caden—Reid'll kill you."

"Alive." Caden finally found her voice. "I'm alive. No bright lights. Only a terrible burning—what's that, Satan? You want me to go with you?"

Holden cracked up beside her for all of three seconds before the light sound turned into a pained moan and he quit laughing.

"You are so fuckin' hilarious." Jackson was somewhere north of her head and not sounding at all amused, just marginally shocked.

After a few minutes of deep breathing and pain management, Caden forced her body to obey her commands. With her good arm, she rolled over and pushed her aching body into a sitting position. She took stock of her surroundings and the men scattered around her.

Jackson was sprawled face up in the bushes a good six

feet away. His chest was heaving up and down and his face looked flushed. Holden was on his back right beside her, skin pale, breathing irregular, and face pinched in pain.

"Holden!" It came out louder than she intended. His eyes popped open, and it took him a second too long to track her face.

"What?" He shifted slightly and his face paled even more. "Can't you see I'm takin' a nap?"

"No napping." Caden shoved to her feet and swayed but stayed upright. "You were out cold rolling down the mountain—you probably broke a lot of shit."

"Definitely broke some shit," he agreed; his voice was a pained snarl of humor. "Looks like we won't be able to knock Kade off his high horse any time soon."

"What do ya mean *we*—speak for yourself, cripple." Caden needed to keep him awake and talking. "I just gotta shove this arm back in and shake it off."

"Pfft." Saliva and blood flew out of his mouth at the noise, and Caden only panicked a little. "Yeah, okay. Reid will most definitely go for that."

She wanted to say something along the lines of Reid not being her boss and she could do whatever the hell she wanted, but, as much as she didn't like to admit it, it was true. He would demand she stay in bed and not strain herself, and Caden would comply.

"You two are in-fucking-sane." Jackson wasn't moving from his sprawled position, but his voice was deep and strong. "Fucking laughing? Laughing? As we fall to our deaths? You're both just gonna fuckin' giggle as we free fall. Fuckin' nuts."

"What? You didn't find it funny?" Pain and sarcasm was all but dripping from Holden's tone. "You didn't think, 'huh, I'm free falling off a fucking cliff roadrunner style'?"

"No, crazies—I did not. I thought, oh shit—oh shit—we're gonna die and the last thing I'm gonna hear is their stupid giggles."

"Oh, come on." Caden finally found the SAT phone Jackson carried three feet from the man's sprawled form. It was crushed and useless. "You didn't think for even a second that it was even slightly funny? I mean, we were free-falling off a fucking cliff and trees were slapping us left and right. It was ridiculous and cartoony."

"When we get home, everyone is gettin' psych evals. You two especially. And Reid thinks Daisy needs therapy. Got fuckin' Thelma and Louise over here."

"Of the three of us, Jackiepoo, you are the one in the most need of a therapy session."

"Yeah, I already had my come to Jesus moment this week," Caden said.

"Does that mean you're staying or going?" Holden asked.

"I'm stayin'."

"Good," Holden said, his voice a pained moan.

They lapsed into silence. Jackson shifted in the bushes he was all but buried in. Caden took a seat beside Holden and watched him breathe. His chest moved up and down, but the breaths were labored and fast, like he'd just run a marathon. That couldn't be good.

What she needed to do was figure out how to contact the boys without a SAT phone. She couldn't get two grown men out of the woods all on her own. She needed help.

But she was just so tired.

If she just took a quick nap, she could be useful again. Caden laid down where she was and put a careful hand on Holden's forearm, right where his pulse was.

Minutes passed. Or maybe hours. She wasn't sure; she wasn't counting.

"A CLIFF?!" Reid's outraged howl jolted Caden out of her light doze and back into a painful reality.

"They're alive!" It was a familiar bellow.

Multiple feet started to pound the ground and Caden was suddenly staring up at familiar nose hairs. Nathan's face was tight with worry lines carved into his handsome face and made him look ten years older. His hands hovered over her like he wasn't sure where to touch.

Automatically, she sat up straight and checked on Holden. He was pale and still. His chest was heaving up and down, so he was still breathing. His pulse jumped under her fingers.

"You jumped off a *cliff*?!" Reid was still shrill and his tone was outraged. It would have been funny if Holden wasn't in the state he was in.

"It's not like we did it on purpose." Jackson's drawl was dry.

"Yeah, we tried very hard not to go over the cliff," Caden put in, visually searching Nathan for any injuries.

"Where are you hurt? What do you need? Caden, talk to me." His voice cracked and his hands moved up and down ten inches from her like he was starting to panic.

"I'm not too bad. It's Holden who needs the most medical attention."

"Bah," Holden groaned and waved a hand like his injuries were negligible. "I'm good."

"Shut up, you were out cold rolling down the mountain! Who even knows what's all wrong with you," Caden snapped at him as Nathan's hands continued to roam all over her, looking for injuries. "Nate, I'm fine. It's Holden who needs attention."

"Get the stretcher." Reid's voice was calmer now that he was hovering over Holden, his hands moving all over him. "Jackson, can you walk?" This he directed at the man still sprawled in the bushes.

"I think I broke my leg on the way down the mountain—give me a hand, Dax." Dax and Maddox hovered over Jackson's sprawled form. They were grinning in relief.

"Don't move," Reid commanded. "Let me splint it first."

"Yes, sir." Jackson settled back into the bushes with a salute.

"Caden, can you walk out of here?"

"Nothing wrong with my legs, just my arm. It came out of its socket again."

"So explain to me how you ended up at the bottom of a cliff?" Reid's voice was calm and reasonable, like he was discussing the weather.

"I don't know—Caden said to run, so we ran. And here we are." Jackson was scowling again. Caden could hear it in his tone.

No way was she taking the blame for this.

"First of fucking all, I didn't push us down the mountain. The blast did. Second of all, how come all your plans didn't account for them rigging up their foundation with explosives?"

"Is that what it was?" Holden chimed in.

"And I saved your life—*twice*!"

"Twice?"

"Yeah, or did you not remember the part where we were dangling over the side of the cliff?"

"Yeah, yeah. You're a hero." Jackson sighed a put-upon sigh. Caden decided to ignore him.

34

CADEN

Caden sat in the cargo bay of a military transport aircraft opposite of Nathan. His brothers were strapped in as well. Everyone was too quiet, and they were avoiding eye contact like they could get a disease just by looking at her.

"So... Marskib, he's obsessed with you," Nate yelled over the sound of the engines.

"Marskib was behind your kidnapping?" That explained a lot. Why they had gone after Nate again.

"Yes. He made a whole speech about you and how you belong to him—you two have history, I take it?"

"Yeah. Uh, he tortured me for a while and I eventually escaped. Guess he's still mad about it. He said I belong to him?"

"Yup."

"Creepy ass weirdo."

"He was indeed."

"*Was*? Is he dead?"

"Yeah, he got shot."

"Okay. Good." That was one nightmare taken care of.

Silence settled. Caden fidgeted in her seat, knowing she should probably say something. Nate opened his mouth and then closed it again. It didn't help that his brothers were there, watching every move they made. Money exchanged hands and Caden glared at the duo, Kade and Maddox.

"Caden—"

"Wait, Nate. Don't." Caden had to yell in order for her voice to carry over the sound of the plane's engines.

He looked crestfallen. Clearly, he thought she was going to reject him again.

"I've got something to say." Caden decided to ignore their audience and turned to face Nate.

"Okay." Nate's voice was unsure, but he sat up straighter.

"I'm not good at this. Not good at talking or sharing... *feelings.*" The word ripped out of her like she'd never said it before.

Which was the understatement of the year. Caden shoved a hand through her hair and tried to put the words she wanted to say in the right order. Her brain was a jumbled mess.

"I thought you shouldn't—*couldn't* love me because... because I didn't deserve you. I thought I didn't deserve happiness or love because of the things I have done."

"Caden, I'm a mercenary too."

"That was part of it, but mostly I thought I didn't deserve anything good because I let my father murder my baby sister."

"That wasn't your fault!" The outrage in his tone made her feel warm and misty eyed. Which was ridiculous because she wasn't going to cry, damn it.

"You're right." It took her a long moment to collect herself enough not to burst into tears. "It *wasn't* my fault. It wasn't my fault when Ezzy died either—none of it was."

She'd said it in her head a million times, but there was something about saying it to Nate that made it real. She believed it. He believed it. Again, tears threatened to spill, but she held them back.

"Nathan, I deserve love. I deserve happiness."

"Well, *yeah.*" Like it was the most logical thing in the world. Like it hadn't taken her thirty years to understand herself. "If it's with someone else—"

"No, there's no one else. There's only you. I want to be happy with you. I love you. I want to spend the rest of my life happy and in love with you."

Caden could feel the weight of her words hanging in the air, like she had just released something she'd been carrying for years. It was strange, the way her chest loosened as the confession settled between them. She glanced at Nate, expecting to see shock or disbelief, but instead, his eyes softened with something far more terrifying: hope.

Her heart pounded in her chest, the sound almost deafening in the silence that followed. She could still feel Kade and Maddox's eyes on her, the two of them probably bursting with smugness at the unfolding scene. She didn't care anymore. She had finally said what needed to be said.

Nate's expression flickered, a smile tugging at the corner of his mouth, but he seemed too cautious to fully let it show. He leaned forward just slightly, his eyes locked on hers like he was afraid she might vanish if he moved too fast. "You mean that?" His voice was quiet, like he wasn't entirely sure this moment was real.

Caden nodded, her throat tightening again as she tried to find the strength to continue. She had spent so long running from herself, from her past, from anything that might make her feel vulnerable.

"I love you," she said again, and this time the words

came easier. More solid. "I don't want to keep pretending that I don't. I don't want to keep fighting something that feels this right."

For a moment, Nate just stared at her, like he was processing, his gaze flicking over her face as if searching for any sign of hesitation. Then, slowly, his expression broke into that wide, easy grin that had always made her stomach flip.

"You sure you're not just saying this because of the high stakes adrenaline-heavy situation we just got out of?" he teased, though there was a tremor in his voice, like he was holding back emotion.

Caden rolled her eyes, but she couldn't stop the small laugh that bubbled up from her chest. "No, Nate. I'm saying this because I'm done being afraid. Done running. I want you. I want us."

He stood then, crossing the airplane in two steps before pulling her up from her seat. His arms wrapped around her, strong and warm, grounding her in the moment. She could feel his heart hammering against his chest, matching the rhythm of her own.

"Damn right you deserve happiness," he murmured, pressing his forehead against hers. "And I'm going to make damn sure you have it, Caden. With me."

Caden leaned into him and Nathan nudged her head up with fingers under her chin. As he leaned forward, she licked her lips and launched herself at him. She would have jumped on him but his injuries held her back.

Her mouth landed on his, open and hot. Immediately, she tasted the metallic sharpness of blood on his tongue as she took his mouth without reserve. She couldn't help but make a sound of hunger and deepen the kiss before realization came back to her that they had an audience and she reluctantly pulled away.

His brothers were whooping and whistling and hollering their fool heads off. Caden rolled her eyes at their combined ridiculousness and grinned up at Nate, who was staring down at her with something like wonder in his eyes.

"You really love me?" Nate whispered, his voice barely audible over the roar of the engines.

"Yeah, I really do," she replied, her fingers tightening in the fabric of his shirt. "I love you, Nathan Savage."

"Good," he whispered back, his lips brushing against her forehead. "Because I fucking love you."

And for the first time, Caden believed it.

PLEASE LEAVE A REVIEW OF SAVAGE ESCAPE ON AMAZON, IT ALLOWS ME TO KEEP WRITING BOOKS.

JOIN MY NEWSLETTER FOR UPDATES!

ABOUT THE AUTHOR

Hela Richards is five feet and nine inches* of pure unadulterated bad jokes and has a penchant for writing. She's got four cats, a tenuous will to live, and a passion for writing that will hopefully get her paid well enough to keep doing it.

*She'd have been 3/4's an inch taller without the little splash of scoliosis curling her spine about 17 degrees. So the five foot nine inches is up for debate.